PLAYING with

Temptation

ERIKA WILDE

TEMPTATION HAS NEVER BEEN SO HOT . . .

When Raina Beck is given an invitation to The Players Club, all she wants is a night of decadence with a gorgeous, sexy stranger. The seductive, mysterious man she meets fulfills her deepest desires and most erotic fantasies, giving her a night she'll never forget. But forgetting *him* isn't quite so easy.

Logan Cruz prefers his women submissive and compliant in the bedroom… everything the independent Raina is not. Yet from the first moment he lays eyes on her, he's determined to make Raina his. Despite her resistance.

When Logan is assigned to protect Raina from a stalker, everything between them changes. Sex becomes more than just physical, and emotions run deep. Falling in love was never on Raina's agenda, but can she let go of the past and surrender the one thing he wants the most… her heart?

Chapter One

RAINA BECK FINISHED helping a customer select a bottle of warming massage oil, then headed over to the lingerie section of her store, Sugar and Spice, a sensual, upscale adult boutique that catered to the residents of San Diego. She paused at the rack of new arrivals, where her good friend, Jillian Noble, was perusing the gorgeous items.

"Find anything you like?" Raina asked as the other woman contemplated a leopard-print bustier before putting it back on the stand.

Jillian smiled at her as she shuffled through a few more pieces. "The problem is, there's too much to like, which is a good thing. I'm looking for something a little different than everything I already have..." Her words trailed off, and her eyes lit up as she lifted a hanger displaying a sexy red ensemble that consisted of a demi bra, a short flirty skirt that was only a few inches of fabric that would barely cover her bottom, and a matching lace thong, along with a garter belt and thigh-high stockings.

"I think this is it," Jillian announced with a succinct nod of her head.

"If Dean comes home to find you wearing that outfit, I think all bets are off," Raina teased her friend.

"That's what I'm counting on, and I think he'll really like the short little skirt, too." She handed the hanger to Raina. "I'll take it, along with one of those feather ticklers you have on display, the one with the soft ostrich feathers."

"You got it." Raina smiled, knowing Jillian, a good customer, appreciated the more sexually adventurous items Sugar and Spice provided to those who wanted to kink up their sex lives. Selecting a tickler with deep red feathers to match the outfit, she met her friend up at the front counter.

As she rang up Jillian's purchases, she asked, "How are you enjoying working with Stephanie?"

"I absolutely love it. I couldn't be happier," Jillian said, her expression reflecting her newfound joy. "I'm helping her design those fantasy suites at the hotel, and tomorrow I have a consultation with a woman who wants to redecorate her bedroom in a sexier version theme of The Secret Garden theme."

"Sounds like a fun project." Raina swiped Jillian's

credit card to process the sale. The two of them had become close friends over the past months, and because she knew Jillian's husband had been so opposed to his wife taking a job, Raina couldn't help but wonder how that was going. "Is everything still good with Dean and you working for Stephanie?"

"He's getting used to it and adjusting. I make sure I always make time for just the two of us, and it keeps him happy."

"Men really are such basic creatures," Raina said with a laugh. "Keep them plied with food and sex and they're happy, content, and satisfied."

Jillian lifted a curious brow. "Speaking of men and sex…when are *you* going to indulge a little?"

Raina shrugged as she wrapped her ensemble in pink tissue and tucked it into a bag. "I think all the good guys are taken. And then there's the men who find out I own a sex toy boutique and decide I'm fair game for outrageous, kinky sex, because, you know, I have access to all sorts of depraved items."

She rolled her eyes to make light of her comment, but the truth ran much deeper and stirred up other painful memories that reminded her of why she kept her heart and emotions under lock and key—the pain of such complete and utter rejection was something that had left her guarded and very cautious when it came to a man's interest in her.

Admittedly, she *did* enjoy hot, adventurous sex. After all, she'd opened Sugar and Spice as a way to help women empower themselves sexually, to get in touch with their desires and be confident enough to enjoy every aspect of sex. But she also knew it took an equally strong, self-assured man to accept her line of business, to not feel threatened or embarrassed by the fact that she owned a boutique that catered to enhancing sexual pleasure.

Unfortunately, over the years, she'd learned that she wasn't the best judge of character when it came to a man's motives and his reasons for dating her, which also made it extremely difficult to decipher what was *real*, or if she was nothing more than someone's dirty little secret that he used until the excitement wore off.

Too many painful experiences had taught her that because of what she did for a living, men were more than willing to fuck her like a porn star in private, but they drew the line at taking her out in public or bringing her home to meet the family, which made her feel cheap and dirty—as if her own father's fire and brimstone prediction about her being a whore had come true. Men didn't date *a woman like her* with long term in mind, and it had become much easier for Raina to keep her emotional distance rather than face criticism and the sting of rejection all over again.

She'd been burned a few times, and she wasn't allowing any man to get close enough to do it again. Now, sex was all about physical pleasure, nothing more, and she'd recently decided that if anyone was going to do the *using*, it was going to be *her* for a change. Unfortunately, an opportunity hadn't presented itself, but if the right guy came along, she certainly wasn't opposed to enjoying a no-strings-attached one-night stand.

"Maybe you need hot *anonymous* sex," Jillian suggested with a naughty twinkle in her eye, as if she'd had a direct link to Raina's thoughts.

"It's been a long dry spell and the idea is definitely tempting," Raina replied, a humorous note lacing the truth of her words. Vibrators and sex toys did the job as far as getting her off, but they couldn't replace the feel or pleasure of a strong, powerful, virile man thrusting deep inside of her or skimming his hands along her curves, his hot mouth seducing hers.

Yes, she definitely missed that, and the provocative thought made her feel a bit flushed.

Jillian bit her bottom lip for a second before reaching into her purse and pulling out a white envelope. "You've done a lot for me, and I want to do something for you for a change. Take this, and indulge yourself." She pushed the envelope across the counter to Raina.

Raina picked it up and read the word *Welcome* embossed in black across the front. "What is this?" she asked, confused and curious at the same time.

"An invitation to The Players Club."

Raina's eyes widened in surprise, and her heart fluttered in her chest with undeniable excitement. She knew exactly what The Players Club was—a private, members-only sex club that catered to an elite and prominent clientele in order to maintain its exclusivity. A personal recommendation was required to even visit the club, and since Dean and Jillian had recently become members, they now had the privilege of extending an invitation to a guest.

And Jillian had chosen *her.*

"Oh, wow," Raina breathed as she brushed her thumb over the embossed lettering on the envelope, still in shock. "Really?"

"Yes, *really,*" Jillian mimicked playfully. "You deserve a sexy night all to yourself, and I can guarantee that *any* fantasy you have can be fulfilled at The Players Club."

Raina had plenty of private, naughty fantasies stored away in the deepest recesses of her mind, none of which she'd ever shared because those scenarios were just too wicked and forbidden to reveal to any of the guys she'd dated up to this point, all of whom had big egos and had been self-centered lovers. Yes, she owned a boutique that sold all sorts of kinky items to enhance sex play, but it took a strong, confident man who didn't feel threatened by her expertise to give her what she desired, who knew what she needed without asking and made that pleasure his sole focus.

Finding that kind of compelling man at The Players Club in one night was improbable but certainly more possible than in her daily life, and she wasn't about to refuse Jillian's gift. She'd been given the equivalent of Willy Wonka's golden ticket, but instead of gorging on chocolate, she planned to indulge in as many orgasms as she could.

Chapter Two

Two weeks later…

R AINA WASN'T SURE what to expect once she
arrived at The Players Club, but as she stared up
at the huge, sprawling, three-story mansion that had
been built on the side of the mountain and overlooked
the city of Fallbrook below, she was certainly impressed by the gorgeous, majestic-looking house. At
night, the place was illuminated by low-profile lighting,
and the Mediterranean architectural style was warm
and inviting. From the outside, there was absolutely
nothing to indicate that this place was actually a club
that catered to those who preferred taking a walk on
the wilder side of sex.

Excitement and anticipation swirled inside of her
as a young valet took the keys to her car, slid into her
vehicle, and drove away. Holding just her invitation in
her hand, she inhaled a deep, fortifying breath and

climbed the stairs that led to a luxurious open court-yard, where a few couples were standing around, conversing and enjoying the cool summer evening before heading inside for more illicit indoor activities. One of the men in the group glanced at Raina as she headed toward the entrance, and their gazes met since she'd been casually looking his way, too.

As a woman who owned a sex shop, she'd learned to look people directly in the eye, without shame, embarrassment, or judgment. It also showed confidence, and that skill came in handy now. The man staring back at her was nice-looking enough, and though she wasn't attracted to him in any way, she gave him an amicable smile, the kind she'd offer a customer in her store to break the ice and let them know she was friendly and approachable.

A lascivious grin curved his mouth as he gave her a very thorough and blatant once-over, his gaze raking down the little black dress that hugged her curves and ended mid-thigh. His appraisal kept going, traveling all the way down her long legs to the rhinestone-studded strappy stilettos on her feet and back up again to the thick, blonde hair she'd left down in soft, tumbling waves around her shoulders.

His gaze, when it returned to hers, was heated and undeniably interested. Unfortunately, he didn't do a thing for her libido and didn't even register as a tiny blip on her sexual radar. It was then that Raina decided that if she was going to have any kind of physical contact with a guy tonight, she wanted off-the-charts combustible chemistry to accompany it. The kind of instantaneous lust that made her hot and wet with just a glance. The kind of excitement that made her entire body sizzle with electricity before he even touched her.

Not just anyone would do. Yes, she was setting her standards extremely high, but she'd rather go home to her battery-operated boyfriend than settle for a mediocre encounter that left her wanting more, anyway. Tonight was all about going for the gusto, taking risks, and reaping the kind of pleasure she'd denied herself for much too long.

"I don't think I've ever seen her here before," the man who'd been ogling her mused to the other couple with him, loud enough for Raina to hear as she walked past. "And you know how I enjoy breaking in the newbies."

The woman snorted inelegantly. "Contrary to what you might believe, not every woman enjoys being bound, gagged, and flogged."

"I've been known to change a woman's mind," he drawled arrogantly. "And just for the record, I use the softest, most supple leather available on the market. Women love the way it feels on their skin. I've yet to have anyone complain."

The man clearly had a giant-sized ego, and if he'd intended to excite her with his knowledge of whips and floggers, she wasn't at all impressed, considering she sold those items in her store. Truthfully, she wouldn't mind a man who gave a bit of calculated pain with her pleasure, but there was a level of trust that needed to be established first, and she'd never allow a stranger that kind of privilege.

With that in mind, she was grateful that The Players Club abided by the safe, sane, and consensual rules, which had been stated in the guest contract she'd signed, including a two-drink maximum and zero-tolerance policy on drug use of any sort to ensure decisions were made without any undue influence.

The standard safe word to stop any sort of sex play was *red*, and if it was ever ignored, the person who didn't heed the warning was immediately expelled and banned from the club. Jillian had assured her that there were attendants throughout the place to maintain all aspects of a guest's safety, and then there was also the confidential background security check and health screening everyone had to pass before their first visit. The discreet guidelines were set in place to maintain and preserve the integrity of the club, and they took those rules very seriously.

Raina continued toward the entrance, and just as she reached the giant-sized double front doors to the mansion, they opened, and a young woman greeted Raina with a smile. Once she was inside the gorgeous and elegant lobby, Raina handed the young woman her invitation.

The hostess introduced herself as Lise, and once she'd checked Raina's name on the approved list, she proceeded to give her the first-timer's spiel about *what* was located *where*. From the viewing rooms upstairs to the open playrooms and themed fantasy boudoirs to the dungeon and the Thursday evening *Rave* party down on the lower level of the mansion, and everything else in between.

"You can start in the Player's Lounge, where you can mingle, which is right that way," Lise indicated with a wave of her hand. "Or you can go ahead and explore the mansion, stop where you want, and indulge as you wish."

Raina wasn't one for small talk and pickup lines, not in a situation like this. Whatever happened, with whomever it happened with, she wanted it to develop naturally, so she opted for the latter. "I think I'd like to explore and see what my options are."

"Go right ahead," Lise said, then turned toward another couple who'd just entered the club, leaving Raina on her own.

Just as she stepped into the main entry hall, a neatly dressed waiter arrived with a tray of champagne flutes. "Would you like something to drink?"

Champagne sounded lovely, and she accepted one of the glasses. "Yes, thank you."

She took a sip of the sweetened sparkling wine as she contemplated the split staircase that led toward two separate wings of the house, along with the directional signs informing patrons that the public viewing rooms were to the right, and the private rooms were to the left. Another wide stairway led down to the area below designated "The Dungeon," where tonight's Rave party was also being held.

She headed up to the public viewing rooms first, taking in the plethora of sexual activities going on all around her, fascinated by everyone's lack of inhibition. Couples were openly having sex while others watched, and some even joined in on the fun. There were public spankings and orgies going on, and different themed rooms offered to fulfill fantasies that involved all sorts of kinky scenarios. She viewed some interesting fetishes, including watching as a dominatrix made a tied-up man drop to his knees and lick her leather, spike-heeled boots while she whipped him with a crop.

Men and women walked by her, some even touching her bare arm or back—a light caress that expressed interest without aggression. Even though her senses were saturated with all things sex-related, no one in particular appealed to her enough to accept their silent offers, though she did find all the various scenes and sights highly arousing.

Maybe she was more of a voyeur than an exhibitionist, she mused as she finished her champagne and set the empty glass on a table before deciding to see what the dungeon was all about. She took the stairs to the lowest level of the mansion, and it did, indeed, feel very much like a dungeon down below, with wall sconces providing a muted red illumination. Shackles and chains hung from the walls and ceilings, and the darkened chamber was also equipped with a few St. Andrew's crosses, along with all sorts of benches, cages, stocks, and swings.

Currently in progress were bondage scenes, slavery, and resistance play, and each scene drew a crowd of onlookers, while dungeon monitors stood nearby, supervising scenes to make sure everything remained safe and consensual. A man in leather chaps used a rope on another well-built man, tying his wrists and arms together behind him in the most intricate way, almost like an art form, before grabbing a handful of the bound man's hair and forcing the guy to suck him off.

Riveted by the erotic sight of two such masculine men together, Raina felt a flush of heat suffuse her entire body. The act was primal and raw and wholly sexual, and holy shit, the man's dominance over his partner was so freakin' hot it left her breathless.

Between the glass of champagne and the scene she'd just witnessed, her body was buzzing. Her sex throbbed, and her nipples peaked and scraped against the lace of her bra. It was like watching live porn, the scent and sounds echoing off the chamber's walls adding to the titillating and X-rated atmosphere.

She moved on to another less-crowded performance, showcasing a gentleman in a tailored suit bringing his "secretary" to heel. The woman was bent over a large desk, her arms bound, a ball gag in her mouth, and the man was smacking her ass with a wide leather paddle. Her skin was a bright stinging shade of pink, but with every swat of the paddle, she moaned and thrashed in the throes of pleasure, clearly loving the punishment.

"Like what you see?"

The low, masculine voice so close to her ear startled Raina. She turned her head and met the steady brown gaze of the man she'd seen out in the courtyard. She couldn't help but wonder how long he'd been following her throughout the club, watching her…and didn't care for the unsettling sensation in her stomach—even though he hadn't done anything to pose any kind of threat to her.

"Umm, I'm just…browsing," she said as noncommittally as she could manage, even as she realized how silly that sounded in a *sex club*.

He tipped his head, his interest in her unmistakable. "Maybe I could persuade you to participate in a scene of our own?" he suggested.

She shook her head and gave him a placating smile. "No, thank you."

He raised an arrogant, dark blond brow. "I can give you a whole lot of pleasure to offset the pain," he persisted and stroked a hand down her bare back.

She sucked in a breath, not appreciating that he'd taken such an intimate liberty when she'd made it very clear she wasn't attracted to him or his offer. Looking him straight in the eye, she said the word *red* very firmly and loudly enough for a nearby dungeon monitor to hear.

The too-cocky man immediately obeyed the safe word and stopped touching her. With an irritable scowl on his face, his raised his hands, and the supervisor stepped away again, satisfied that he'd complied.

His jaw clenched indignantly. "Jesus, that was a bit extreme."

"I just wanted to make it very clear that I have no desire to be gagged, bound, and flogged," she said evenly. "By you or anyone else here."

"You really should try it. You might like it," he said and smirked. "In fact, I'd bet money I could make you come better and harder than you ever have."

Oh, puleeze. She just barely refrained from rolling her eyes. Obviously, she'd bruised his fragile ego, and he felt the need to compensate. "Gamble your money elsewhere," she said very sweetly. "I'm really not interested; therefore *you* making me *come*, in any capacity, isn't going to happen."

His gaze narrowed ever so slightly at her wisecrack, but he'd pushed and he'd deserved the verbal smackdown. Unwilling to engage with him further, she walked away and headed down an adjoining corridor, following the sound of electronic techno music until she reached the opposite end of the mansion, where the Thursday night Rave party was being held. The huge, open area was designed to look like an underground warehouse, with laser light shows, erotic images projected onto the bare walls, and smoke machines adding to the sultry, sex-infused mood.

She glanced behind her, and satisfied that Mr. Bound and Gag wasn't anywhere to be seen, she moved into the fray of people. A lot of the men were shirtless, the women scantily clothed, making her feel overly covered in her dress and heels, even though she had plenty of skin showing. Most everyone was dancing like bohemians, without modesty or propriety. This was where the epitome of dirty dancing was defined, with men and women grinding and writhing against one another, unbridled in their passion and

17

pursuit of pleasure.

A few men and women reached out to touch her, to draw her into the ribald revelry, but she managed to evade getting swept into the gyrating, groping mass of people. Because she didn't want to get caught up in one of the many orgies going on, she veered off toward a stage, where half a dozen adult-size, gold-gilded bird cages were displayed and overlooked the rest of the room. A few of them were occupied, mostly with couples dancing and humping and groping one another. Feeling like she'd be the safest in one of those barred enclosures by herself, Raina made her way to the stage, then up the five small steps to enter one of the vacant gilded cages. She latched the lock from the inside, just to make sure she had no surprise visitors.

She took a moment to look around, to take in her view from her perch above everything and everyone. Besides the enormous dance floor, there was also a large lounge area with private chairs and couches for those who wanted more creature comforts, and right below the stage was a bar serving guests their two-drink minimum and bottles of water.

Feeling secure in her own little coop, it was easy to let the pulsing beat of the music infuse her body, inviting her to let go of her own inhibitions. She loved to dance, and she grabbed on to the stripper-like pole in the center of the cage and did a little dirty dancing of her own. She'd taken pole-dancing classes with her girlfriends, and it was incredibly liberating and freeing to wrap her calf around the pole, arch her back, and execute a graceful, sensual twirl that made her feel confident and incredibly sexy.

Closing her eyes, she let the provocative sway of her body sync with the rhythmic tempo of the music. After a few more erotic moves, including a few shimmies, gyrations, and a hair toss for good measure, she opened her eyes and glanced down, realizing that she'd drawn a small but avid crowd at the base of the stage—which so had not been her intent.

But out of all those men staring up at her, it was the stunningly gorgeous one sitting at the bar below who'd clearly been watching her performance who set her heart beating hard and fast in her chest. Even with the distance separating them, even through the haze and flashing lights, his intense, hungry gaze captured her attention and made her skin prickle in awareness. A frisson of lust shot through her veins, and her sex clenched with a desire so strong she could feel the slick heat and moisture gathering between her thighs.

Completely enthralled by the undeniable chemistry vibrating between them, she let her lashes fall half-mast and gave him a sultry, come-hither smile as she continued to dance around the pole, moving her body slowly, sinuously, temptingly. He never looked away, never turned his head to acknowledge the woman who'd come up beside him and was doing her best to try and distract him with the surgically enhanced breasts nearly spilling out of her top.

Raina couldn't tear her gaze away from him, either. She licked her bottom lip, suddenly knowing without a doubt that *he* was the one she wanted tonight.

As if he'd read her mind, he pushed away from the bar and started through the crowd, his stride purposeful and predatory as he made his way to the stage—and she felt very much like a bird in a gilded cage being stalked by a lithe, untamed panther. But instead of any sort of fear, her pulse raced with a heady anticipation, and the excitement building inside her made her feel wild and reckless.

He reached the raised platform and climbed the stairs that led to her cage, then stopped right in front of the door that led inside. She leaned back against the steel pole, taking him in—and oh, Lord, there was a whole lot of man to admire.

His hair was a dark shade of brown, cut short but tousled just enough to make her fingers itch to run through those soft-looking strands. Even wearing a black silk shirt and black pants, there was no denying the width of his shoulders and just how well built the rest of his body was beneath his clothes. In a flash of strobe light, she could see the hard, unmistakable ridge of his cock outlined against the front of his pants.

Her mouth went dry, her stomach muscles clenched in need, and she raised her gaze all the way back up to the bad-boy glint in those bright green eyes. Standing just a few feet away, he was tall and commanding, sexually confident, and a prime example of the word *fuckable*.

Her knees went weak at the decadent thought.

He didn't force his way into the cage. Didn't try to reach in and flip the lock himself. Clearly a man used to getting his way, he only had to ask for what he wanted, and he didn't hesitate to let his desires be known.

Let me in.

She read the words that formed on his full, sensual lips, knowing that the moment she obeyed his request and allowed him inside the cage with her—*and she knew she would*—all bets were off, and this man would claim her, here and now.

Oh, yes, please.

Stepping up to the locked door, she opened it for him, inviting him inside. He was so tall he had to duck through the entryway, and once he straightened to his full height again, he immediately backed her up against the side of the cage, aligning the hard length of his body firmly against hers, pinning her there in the most delicious, delightful way.

His gaze bored into hers, flashing with carnal lust. His scent—spicy aftershave and male pheromones—intoxicated her. Everything about him generated so much heat she felt like she was burning up from the inside out. Wanting to touch him, desperate to feel all that raw power he exuded, she placed her hands on his chest, the soft material of his shirt contradicting the rock-hard muscles flexing beneath the fabric.

Against her palm, she felt his chest rumble, right before he grabbed both of her wrists and lifted her arms above her head. He curled her fingers around the metal bars to grip them tight, making it very clear without speaking a word that he was a man who liked to be in control.

Normally, *she* was the one in control sexually and liked having the upper hand, so there was no chance of letting down her guard with a man and allowing him to have that much power over her mind and body. But tonight was all about stealing as much pleasure as she could with a man she'd never see again. And if he preferred to be in charge, she wasn't about to complain, because there was something incredibly thrilling about this man's very dominant nature in a place like The Players Club, where indulging in the forbidden and erotic was expected.

The techno music matched the frantic beat of her

pulse as he pressed a knee between her legs and used his feet to push her own wide apart and keep them spread. His hips gyrated against hers in a slow, tantalizing, grinding dance that made her ache for a more intimate touch and deeper penetration. His sinful gaze watched her every response, tracking the rapid rise and fall of her breasts beneath her dress and the way she shamelessly arched her back for a closer, tighter fit.

Intensity radiated from him, and a faint hint of satisfaction touched his mouth, giving her a glimpse of something darker and far more wicked. Lifting a hand, he slid it into her hair and fisted his fingers in the long blonde strands so she felt the slight stinging tug against her scalp, then pulled her head back so that her face was tipped up to his.

Her lips parted on a gasp, and he took advantage and kissed her, his lips hard and unrelenting as they captured hers. He licked his way into her mouth, gradually deepening the stroke of his tongue against hers, completely consuming her with his kiss. His free hand touched her thigh, his fingers brazenly caressing their way beneath the hem of her dress and up the inside of her leg, until he reached the silky barrier covering her mound.

She groaned into his ravaging mouth and clutched the bars above her head as he boldly pressed two fingers against her throbbing sex, rubbed along those swollen nether lips, and unerringly found her aching clit beneath the scrap of lingerie. She was drenched with arousal, her panties soaked with the need for release as he continued to stroke her like a man who knew his way around a woman's body. He could have teased her, could have easily kept her on that sharp edge of ecstasy, but instead, he pushed her right over that steep crest so that she was free-falling into a stunning, explosive climax that left her panting against his lips and her legs shaking.

The blissful orgasm should have satisfied her but instead made her crave more. Made her frantic to feel this sexy, dominant man filling her, hard and deep.

He leaned in close, brushing his lips against the shell of her ear. "Now I'm going to fuck you," he rasped, the gruff, guttural tone of his voice making her shiver.

The whispered promise was her undoing. *"Yes,"* she replied. *Anywhere, and any way he wanted.*

She expected him to take her right there in the cage, up against the metal bars, and she would have been fine with that. But instead, he grabbed her hand and led her out of the pen, down the stage, and toward the far end of the room, where there were couches and chairs and other more comfortable pieces of furniture in different alcoves. He chose a vacant corner with a big, over-stuffed chair and pulled a curtain around their little area.

The drapery was white, thin, and sheer, giving them only the barest illusion of privacy. Anyone who wanted to watch them could. Raina realized she'd gone from voyeur to exhibitionist, and with this man, she was beyond caring. She didn't know anyone here, would never return or see this man again, and she was at a *sex* club, for heaven's sake. It was all a part of the experience, and she wanted to fulfill this erotic fantasy.

When she turned back around to face him, the sizzling burn in his eyes was nearly her undoing. Every line of his body was rigid and taut, as if he was waiting for her to make the next move, to make sure that this was what she wanted. She hadn't expected that kind of courtesy from him, either, but a part of her appreciated the gesture.

No guts, no glory, no pleasure. Let's do this. She was meeting with her girlfriends in the morning, and she'd promised them the juicy details. No way was she going to disappoint them with anything but a spectacular encounter with a sex god of a man.

Splaying her hands on his chest, she pushed him back, until his strong legs hit the seat and he had nowhere else to go but to sit down. He plopped into the chair, an amused smile on his lips—though she got the distinct impression that he was just humoring her for the moment and her having any kind of upper hand was only a temporary reprieve. Spreading his legs wide, he sat forward and grasped her hips, drawing her in between his thighs before slipping both of his big, warm hands beneath the hem of her dress.

Grasping the waistband of her panties, he pulled them down her legs. She braced her hands on his shoulders as he helped her step out of the lacy underwear, then he stuffed the scrap of fabric into his pocket. He quickly unbuttoned his pants, freeing the thick length of his erection, giving her a few seconds to admire his gorgeous cock as he grabbed one of the foil packets in the crystal bowl on a table beside the chair, ripped it open with his teeth, and quickly put the condom on.

He hooked his fingers behind her knees, guiding her forward onto the chair so that she was straddling his lap and the engorged head of his erection slid along her wet cleft and tucked tight against her opening. Hands clutching her hips beneath the bunched up material of her dress, he lifted his gaze to hers, his eyes speaking a language her body instinctively understood.

I'm going to sink inside you so hard and deep you won't ever forget I was here.

She believed him. Her head fell back, and her breath caught in her lungs as he brought her down on his shaft in one smooth, firm thrust that filled her to the brink of pain. It had been a long time since she'd been with a man, and none of the penis-shaped vibrators in her nightstand drawer even came close to the shocking size and width of his cock.

That delicious burn quickly gave way to a greater pleasure as her body adjusted to accommodate him as he drove into her, again and again, the steady pump of his hips matching the rhythmic beat of the music pulsing around them. She fisted her hands in his shirt, so very tempted to rip open the buttons to look and touch, to lick and taste his smooth, taut skin. To revel in everything about this assertive, fascinating man so that the memories of this evening with him would be branded in her mind forever.

Giving in to the urge, her fingers fumbled with the top button to unfasten his shirt, but he let go of her hips and caught her wrists in his hands. Just like in the cage, he pulled her hands away and secured her arms behind her back, his long, strong fingers manacling her as effectively as a pair of handcuffs would. The position forced her shoulders back, caused her spine to arch and the swollen breasts confined beneath her dress to ache to be freed.

This alpha man was definitely all about dominance, and she was shocked to realize just how much being restrained by him turned her on…as well as the fact that they were being watched by others in the club through the sheer, gauzy curtain. They were both still decently covered, but there was no mistaking the joining of their bodies or what they were doing, and a part of her wished that they were naked so she could feel the heat of his chest against her hardened nipples, his muscled stomach flexing against her belly, her quivering thighs sliding against his hair-roughened ones.

The strobe lights flashed, accentuating his masculine features, the smoky hue of his eyes, the clench of his jaw as he continued to piston her up and down on his cock, fucking her long and hard and so damned good. He possessed and claimed, their coupling hot and raw and primitive.

Somehow, he managed to wrap the fingers of one of his hands around both of her small wrists, keeping her arms pinned, while his free hand dipped down between her spread legs. He grazed her burgeoning clit with his fingers, ripping a shuddering moan from her. He played her expertly, the unyielding pressure of his thumb stroking that bundle of nerves pitching her closer and closer to a combustible orgasm.

Through hooded lashes, he watched her ride him, watched as the explosion brewing inside of her gathered, threatening to send her up in flames. Watched as she completely unraveled and came apart for him with a soft cry of ecstasy. Her internal muscles gripped his cock, clenched him tight, giving her a small sense of power as he surged his hips upward, ramming home, his erratic thrusts signaling his own climax.

His head fell back, his irises deepening to a darker shade of green. She read the words *oh, fuck* that formed on his lips as his big body stiffened as he came, and his hips bucked hard against hers, leaving every inch of her flesh tender and sensitive and undeniably marked.

Boneless and utterly sated, she collapsed against his chest, her face buried against his warm, fragrant neck as she tried to get her bearings back on track. He finally released her hands, and she groaned as she brought her arms back around, trying to ease the delicious ache in her shoulders from having them restrained for too long. He skimmed a flattened palm up her spine, his touch light and gentle, a direct, startling contrast to the demanding man who'd just ravished her.

Long fingers tangled in her hair, then pulled her head back so he could look down at her face. He was frowning, and for a moment, she fully expected him to tell her to get off of him so he could be on his way— she had no idea what the protocol for this sort of thing was, and she hadn't meant to come across as clingy—but he didn't seem anxious to part ways.

"Are you okay?" he asked, loud enough to be heard above the music.

She hadn't anticipated his concern, either—

29

certainly not in a place like this, where a little rough play was common. Expected and encouraged even. His ability to command her body so thoroughly just moments ago, then switch gears to check on her mental and physical well-being changed everything about him—made him go from a hard-core sex object to something far more dangerous and appealing and *real*.

Not caring for the sudden heavy beating of her heart, she pushed away from his chest and gave him a reassuring smile that contradicted the odd twinge of regret forming in her chest. "I'm good."

She lied, and he didn't look completely convinced, either. That he even *cared* was something totally unexpected and confusing to her, and she needed distance to clear her head and put things back into proper perspective.

She used the best excuse she could think of. "Where is the ladies' room?"

"Over by the bar, just past the men's room," he said, jutting his jaw in that general direction.

"Thanks." Slowly, she stood, trying not to groan as their bodies separated—and very aware of the fact that he was still semi-hard. She straightened the hem of her dress and turned to go, but he caught her wrist and stopped her. Her pulse tripped all over itself—and she honestly hated that a man she'd just met had that much power over her self-control when she'd been so determined to treat tonight like a fun, no-strings-attached fling.

She glanced back at him, relieved to see that sexy, bad-boy smile of his making an appearance. The bad boy she could handle more than the caring man.

"I'll meet you back here," he drawled, looking so freakin' irresistible Raina had to resist the urge not to climb back onto his lap right then and there. "I'm not done with you yet."

His words were casual and flirtatious, but coming from a man like him, there was no doubt in her mind that they were more an order than a request. One she was certain that any other woman wouldn't hesitate to obey, knowing the kind of pleasure he was capable of giving.

She made no promises, just walked on shaky legs toward the women's restroom. She used the facilities, washed her hands, then paused in the lounge area, where a few other women were sitting around and talking. Her legs still felt like wet noodles, and her mind was still spinning, so she sat down in a chair off to the side. There was a counter in front of her, with a long, full-length mirror, and Raina stared at her reflection, shocked by what she saw—a woman who'd been well and truly fucked.

Her hair was a tousled mess from his hands, her

blue eyes a bit dreamy from two amazing orgasms. Her skin was flushed, and her mouth was pink and swollen. She licked her bottom lip, still tasting him there, and dear Lord, she wanted *more* of him.

Nothing and no one would ever compare to what she'd just experienced—the attraction and off-the-charts chemistry between them and the way he'd so instinctively mastered her body and tapped into her deepest, darkest desires, the ones she'd never shared with any man before. It was a sobering thought that struck a slice of panic inside of her, because she feared he was a man she could easily get addicted to. A man who could tear down her guard and melt her resolve to keep every emotional component *out* of sex.

She exhaled a deep breath and mentally shored up her fortitude to get out of this situation as gracefully as possible. In her favor, he knew nothing about her. Not her past, her present life, nothing. She had to admit that it had been so nice to have that anonymity, without any expectations, just mutual pleasure. And that's exactly how she wanted to keep tonight's encounter—as a hot tryst between strangers. Her emotional well-being depended on it.

Now, she just had to figure out how to leave the club without running into him again, because one touch and she knew her willpower to resist him would crumble.

She stepped out of the ladies' room and glanced in the direction of the alcove they'd shared, relieved to find the area vacant. Assuming he'd make a similar trip to the men's room, Raina dodged her way through the throng of people still enjoying the Rave and toward the stairs leading to the upper level of the mansion. She reached the entryway without incident and continued out the main doors to the courtyard, then to the valet.

It was quiet outside compared to all the action going on inside the club, and as she waited for one of the attendants to bring her car around, she shifted anxiously on her feet while casting quick glances back toward the mansion's doors to make sure she hadn't been followed.

Just as her vehicle came around the curved driveway, she heard a very irritated male voice from behind her yell out, "Hey! *Wait!*"

Oh, shit. She didn't have to look over her shoulder to know it was him. The urgency and confusion in his deep voice spoke for itself. She willed the kid in her car to *hurry up*, and as soon as he brought the vehicle to a stop and exited, Raina quickly got behind the wheel before she changed her mind and did exactly as the man ordered and *waited for him.*

"Goddamn it, *stop!*"

He reached her car just as she shut and locked the

door. Because she couldn't bring herself to look at him, out of the corner of her eye, she saw him stop right by the driver's door.

"I don't even know your name!" he said, sounding both bewildered and extremely pissed off that she'd stood him up without an explanation.

No names exchanged, and she planned to keep things that way. She'd never see him again, so what did it matter? Self-preservation edged out the regret tightening in her chest, and she pressed her foot on the gas pedal and drove away, resisting the temptation to look in her rearview mirror to drink him in one last time.

She felt like Cinderella escaping her prince before the clock struck twelve and she turned into a pumpkin. But instead of leaving behind a glass slipper, she realized he still had her *panties* tucked away in his pocket.

Well, at least she'd left him with a sexy souvenir of their one night together.

Chapter Three

RAINA DIDN'T KNOW what she'd been thinking to visit The Players Club on a Thursday night, a work night, knowing she'd have to be up early the next morning since Fridays were her day to open the store. To make matters worse, she'd agreed to meet her girlfriends for breakfast before work, because they'd insisted on hearing all about the sexy, illicit details of her evening at the club while everything was still fresh in her mind.

As if she could *ever* forget those heated green eyes, that rock-hard body, and being possessed so thoroughly she knew that no other man would ever come close to satisfying her the same way ever again. Even now, she was sensitive and sore between her legs, a decadent reminder of how a person could hurt so good.

With a soft groan, she rolled to her back and stared

at the ceiling, her eyes scratchy and tired. After the earth-shattering orgasms her sex god had given her, she should have slept like a baby, but instead, she'd spent most of the night tossing and turning, alternately feeling bad for ditching the guy without an explanation and knowing she'd done the right thing for *her*. It had been a long time since she'd felt so exposed with a man, *a stranger, no less*, and she'd certainly never let any man have that much control over her body.

The worst part? She'd *liked* him being in charge, and that was a very dangerous realization for a woman who'd learned the pitfalls of trusting men in general— that doing so usually came with a wealth of heartache and disappointment.

Her iPhone pinged from where she'd left it on the nightstand, and she picked up the device, punched in her code to unlock the screen, and read the text that her best friend, Paige, had just sent to her.

Rise and shine, baby! Our Coffee and Cocks Club meeting is in thirty minutes, and you'd better not be late. We're all dying to hear what happened last night!

Paige's message made her laugh and lightened her mood. Leave it to her outrageous friend to rename their monthly Cocktails and Cocks Club meeting to reflect the morning hour.

Don't worry, I'll be there. Raina added a smiley face and hit send, then got out of bed and took a quick, hot shower. She didn't have time to wash her hair, so she pulled it back into a ponytail, applied minimal makeup, and chose a pretty pink summer dress that buttoned down the front and a pair of white strappy heels. Twenty-five minutes later, she was heading for the door, with ten minutes to get to the café in Old Town that was located a few blocks from her shop. She was going to be a few minutes late, and no doubt Paige was going to give her shit about it.

She unarmed the alarm system that came as part of the apartment building security and opened her door, startled by a loud clanking sound against the metal surface, and it took her a moment to figure out what had made such a clamor. She frowned in confusion at the metal handcuffs dangling from her doorknob just outside of her apartment, one end secured tight around the round handle so that she'd need a key to remove it. Tied to the handcuffs with a thin red ribbon was a piece of paper, which Raina removed so she could read the note, which had been written in a barely legible masculine scrawl.

I know you like it rough.

Raina's stomach lurched, and a trickle of unease scurried down her spine. *Holy shit.* Who would leave something like this on her door? Her heart raced as she mentally ran down the list, coming up empty except for the one thing that made any sense—that maybe the man at The Players Club had somehow followed her home last night. Which meant he knew where she lived and obviously hadn't taken her rejection well if his little present, and ominous message, was any indication.

Nausea swamped her. She felt violated and scared. If he'd had the nerve to leave the cuffs on her door, what else was he capable of? And worst of all, how had she misread him so badly?

Trying to calm the rush of fear coursing through her veins, she glanced around the second-floor landing just outside of her apartment, but there was nobody around. It was eerily quiet, and her car was parked right where she could see it, so she locked her door, having no choice but to leave the cuffs where they were for now. She quickly walked down the flight of stairs to her vehicle with her car keys in one hand and the small canister of mace she always carried in her purse clutched in her other hand, armed and ready for any surprise attack.

She made it to her car safely and wasted no time getting the heck out of there. Within minutes, she'd arrived at the café, walked inside, and found the girls already sitting at a table in the back of the restaurant. All five of them were talking and laughing, already enjoying their various coffee drinks as they waited for her to arrive.

"There you are!" Paige said enthusiastically, her green eyes as bright as her personality. "I was just about to send you another text. I thought maybe you ditched us for something, or someone, better."

Raina knew her friend was joking, but she couldn't bring herself to respond with a teasing reply like she normally would. "Umm, no," she said, her voice faint even to her own ears as she slid into the vacant seat between Jillian and her other friend, Stephanie.

From across the table, Kendall frowned as her gaze searched Raina's face. "I was expecting you to be glowing from your night of hot, wild sex, but you look pale and a little panic-stricken. Are you okay?"

Raina shook her head, her system still in shock over what she'd discovered. Her girlfriends were anticipating titillating stories about The Players Club, but after coming to the realization that she had a stalker, it all felt so wrong, and she needed to tell them the truth so they could help her figure out what to do.

"Something unexpected happened this morning that still has me shaken up," she said and swallowed to ease the dryness in her throat. "When I opened the front door to leave, there was a pair of metal handcuffs attached to the doorknob, along with a note that said, 'I know you like it rough.'"

Kendall gasped. "Oh, my God."

"What the hell?" Paige said, her outrage on Raina's

behalf coming through loud and clear.

"Who would do such a thing?" Stephanie sounded equally indignant.

"I don't know." Raina looked at each one of her friends, noticing how calm and collected Jillian was, that she'd yet to speak, but she was listening very intently. "The only thing that makes any sense was that the guy I was with last night somehow followed me home."

"Well, that certainly isn't a reassuring thought," Summer added, her tone concerned. "I thought The Players Club did an in-depth background security check on all their members to make sure things like this don't happen."

"They do," Jillian said, finally speaking up. "But that doesn't mean someone with issues can't slip through the screening process. This isn't good at all. What was his name?"

Raina shook her head. "I don't know. We didn't exchange names." She felt her face flush as she revealed the truth. "I kind of ran out on him after we were together, he followed me out to my car, and he was a little pissed off that I left so suddenly." She didn't feel the need to elaborate on the fact that she'd had an emotional panic attack that had sent her bolting.

Jillian's lips flattened into a grim line as she picked

up her cell phone from the table. "I'm calling Dean."

"Wait." Raina grabbed her friend's arm before she could place the call. She knew Jillian's husband owned a security firm, but she wasn't sure what he could do about her having a possible stalker from the club. "Why are you calling Dean?"

"Because if some guy from The Players Club is harassing you, Dean will look into it and find out who the guy is. He's a security specialist. It's what he does," Jillian said, her firm tone allowing no room for an argument. "And his partner, Mac, has been a member there for years, and he knows a lot of guys at the club, too. They'll find out who this guy is and make sure he leaves you alone. They'll also make sure the club knows that he's a threat to their guests and let them deal with him accordingly."

She sounded so certain of her husband's abilities, and very determined to involve him. Clearly, Jillian was in mama-bear mode, something Raina hadn't had much experience with even with her own mother, who'd always been too weak to stand up for herself, let alone her daughter. At thirty-nine, Jillian was a little over ten years older than the rest of them, had raised two sons who were grown and in college and the military, and now that she was a part of their group, she didn't hesitate to use her personal resources to help her friends.

"I'll be right back." Cell phone in hand, Jillian left the table and went outside to call her husband.

Left alone with her four other friends, Raina gave them an apologetic look. "I'm sorry, I know this isn't what you all were expecting to hear this morning."

Stephanie clasped Raina's hand and gave it a gentle squeeze. "Trust me, we're way more concerned about you and making sure you're safe. That's the *only* thing that matters to us."

"Thanks." Raina was grateful to have such supportive friends. They were all like sisters to her, and the closest thing to family she had.

Jillian returned a few minutes later, her high heels tapping on the wooden floor of the restaurant as she approached the table. As soon as she arrived, she looked directly at Raina and said, "Dean wants you at his office immediately, so he can talk to you about what happened, get a description of the guy you were with, and assign one of his security agents to look after you until the threat has been taken care of."

It all sounded extreme and like overkill to Raina, and she started to second-guess the entire situation, that maybe she was blowing everything out of proportion. "I'm sure I don't need a bodyguard. Besides, it's my morning to open up the shop, and I don't want to be late."

"This isn't a polite request, Raina," Jillian said,

crossing her arms over her chest in an intimidating manner. "It's an *order*. Get your ass over to Noble and Associates *now*, because if I have to call Dean back to tell him you're making light of a serious situation, he's going to be pissed off, and you do *not* want to deal with a pissed-off Dean."

Resigned, Raina scooted out her chair and stood. "What is he going to do, turn me over his knee?" she said with sass.

"No, but he might make Mac or one of his other guys do it for him," she said, her mouth twitching with a teasing smile. "They're all overbearing alpha males and like to assert their dominance whenever the opportunity presents itself."

At the mention of hot men, Paige popped up from her seat enthusiastically. "Can I go with Raina? I'm suddenly feeling very, very bad."

Raina laughed, grateful for her friend's bit of humor. "No. You need to open up the shop for me because I have no idea how long this is going to take."

Paige feigned a pout. "Spoilsport."

Raina rolled her eyes. "Aaron is scheduled to come in at noon," she said of her store manager. "But hopefully I'll be back before then."

"That's fine," her friend said, serious now. "I can handle things until he gets there. Besides, I have a few new corsets I want to take to the shop and put on display, so I'll do it this morning while I'm there."

Jillian walked Raina out to her car, then handed her a business card with Dean's office address and information on it. "Until Dean figures out what's going on and who's responsible for the handcuffs and note, please take this seriously. I don't want anything happening to you, and I feel partially responsible since I'm the one who gave you the invitation to The Players Club."

"None of this is your fault," she assured the other woman.

"I know, but since my husband's business is security, I'm going to make sure you're safe and protected." Jillian gave her a warm hug. "Now go."

Raina got into her car and drove to the address, which was located in downtown San Diego. Dean's offices were based in a modern glass and chrome building, and she took the elevator up to the twenty-eighth floor. When the double doors slid open, they led directly into Noble and Associates' plush reception area. She stepped up to the desk, and the older, pretty woman sitting there offered her an amicable smile.

"You must be Raina," she said and pushed away from her desk to stand up.

Raina nodded. "Yes, I am."

"I'm Gail," she said by way of introduction. "Dean told me to expect you. He's finishing up a call with a client, so I'm going to get you settled in the conference room. It's right this way."

Raina followed Gail down a short hallway and into a spacious room with a large boardroom-type table, leather chairs, and warm wood paneling on the walls. Floor-to-ceiling windows overlooked the city, showcasing the blue, cloudless spring sky, and provided a stunning panoramic view of the ocean. The office was a prime piece of real estate, speaking to the success of Dean and Mac's company.

"Go ahead and make yourself comfortable," Gail said as she opened the blinds on the windows that looked back into the reception area, then headed toward a refreshment bar off to the side. "Can I get you some coffee, tea, or water while you wait?"

Considering breakfast had been cut short, Raina missed her normal morning cup of caffeine and needed it badly. "I'll take a coffee. Cream and sugar, please."

She sat down facing the door that also gave her a view of the outer offices, and a moment later, Gail set a steaming mug of fragrant brew in front of her. "I'll let Dean know you're here. He shouldn't be long."

"Thank you." She'd only taken a few sips of her coffee when Dean and another good-looking man walked into the room. She was friendly with Dean because of her relationship with Jillian and the man's frequent trips into Sugar and Spice.

"Hey, Raina." Dean took her hand in his and gave it a warm squeeze before turning to the other man who'd joined him. "This is my partner, Mac. He's more familiar with The Players Club and a lot of the members there, so I'd like him to sit in on our conversation if that's okay with you?"

"Yes, of course, that's fine." She shook Mac's hand, his long, strong fingers engulfing hers. He was in an incredibly attractive man—former military like Dean, according to Jillian—and though his dark blue gaze was kind, there was no mistaking this man's intensity and the power latent in his every movement. "It's nice to meet you."

"Same here," he replied with a polite nod.

Both men sat down at the table. Mac clasped his hands on the surface, and Dean opened the leather-bound portfolio he'd brought with him to jot down notes from their discussion, then met her gaze. "Why don't you tell us what happened last night at The Players Club and we'll go from there."

She took another fortifying drink of her coffee. Both men were members of the club, and knowing that neither one of them would judge her for having a sexual encounter with a stranger made it much easier for Raina to share the details without any embarrassment. "I met a guy at the Rave party down on the dungeon level and we had sex. It wasn't rough, like the note attached to the handcuffs indicated, but it was definitely…intense. The music was loud and we didn't exchange names. Afterward, I decided to leave the club without telling him, and he found me just as I was getting into my car to go. He was definitely annoyed that I slipped out on him."

Dean wrote something down on his note pad while Mac asked, "Did he hurt you or threaten you in any way, either physically or verbally?"

Out in the courtyard, he'd yelled at her to stop and wait. She'd heard the confusion in his voice, but nothing that could even remotely be construed as intimidating. "No, he didn't. I think he was just genuinely upset that I bolted on him without giving him an explanation or my name." She absently rubbed her fingers along her forehead, suddenly feeling a little silly about being here over a pair of handcuffs and a note attached to her doorknob. "This probably is nothing more than someone's idea of a stupid joke. It could even be totally unrelated to anything that happened at the club with the guy I was with."

Dean arched an uncompromising brow at her. "Don't downplay something that could be *very* serious. Jillian made it clear that we're to put a security detail on you until we know for absolute certain that this guy isn't a threat of any kind, and I already put a call in to one of my men who has the next few weeks free before his next assignment."

A babysitter and a shadow. Ugh. "Dean, I have a security system on my apartment, and I really hate to—"

Dean held up a hand, effectively cutting her off with that firm gesture. "Security system or not, I'm not giving you a choice in the matter, Raina. Not only do I insist that you're protected while Mac and I talk to the manager of the club to see if they've had any reports of other guests being stalked or threatened, but I do *not* want Jillian busting my balls for not following *her* orders."

Mac smirked at that, and Raina wanted to laugh, too. Dean possessed such a dominant personality, and it was amusing to think that Jillian had that much power over her husband. Then again, theirs was a rare marriage, one that was based on equality and respect and, ultimately, love. It was the kind of relationship that Raina secretly envied.

The phone in the conference room buzzed, and Gail's voice came through the intercom. "Dean, Logan Cruz is here."

"Great." Dean shot Raina a pointed look informing her that her appointed bodyguard had just arrived. "Send him into the conference room."

The line disconnected, and Mac sat forward in his seat. "You don't have a name for this guy you were with, but could you recognize him if you saw him again?"

"Absolutely." The man's gorgeous features were seared into her memory, and would be for a very long time. Forgetting *anything* about him was impossible.

Through the open blinds covering the windows, Raina saw someone walking toward the conference room. Definitely male. Definitely tall and big with a body that was built out of lean muscle. A crisp pair of jeans hugged his narrow hips and long, lithe thighs, and his broad shoulders filled out a light blue shirt— the first few buttons at his throat undone, and the sleeves cuffed to reveal strong forearms.

Curious to know if his face was as attractive as the rest of him, she lifted her gaze, and her breath literally caught in her lungs, and her blood seemed to drain from her face. "Oh, my God," she said, her voice a startled rasp of sound. "That's him."

Mac frowned in confusion. "That's who?"

"*Him*," she said, pointing to the man who came to an abrupt stop in the open doorway leading into the conference room, his own shock at seeing her there evident in his eyes and expression. "*That's* the guy I was with at the club." *And he obviously worked for Dean!*

"You were with *Logan* last night?" Dean asked, seemingly a little thrown off by the huge coincidence, as well.

Logan's surprise quickly evaporated. Every inch of his big body tensed, his demeanor turning guarded as he tried to assess the situation he'd just walked into. "Mind if I ask what's going on and what *she's* doing here?" His tone was deceptively calm.

Mac studied the other man intently. "So, you know her then?"

"Yes." Logan gave a curt nod and braced his hands on his hips, his stance defensive. "I met her at The Players Club last night. She left before I could get her name, though I *did* try."

She winced inwardly as he aimed that last part directly at her. Okay, so he was still a little miffed about her exit strategy. She supposed she'd wounded his male pride and he was still smarting over the sting of her rejection. But even annoyed at her, he still had the ability to make her pulse flutter and made her body remember every wicked thing they'd done together.

"Were you so pissed about her brushing you off that you followed her home and left a pair of handcuffs on her doorknob, along with a threatening note?" Mac asked, his sharp gaze leveled at Logan's face.

Logan stared at his boss as if he'd lost his mind, his bewilderment over Mac's question genuine, then he shook his head. "*What* are you talking about?"

Mac glanced at Dean. "It wasn't him."

"Agreed," Dean said, looking equally certain.

The two men were former Navy SEALS and security experts. Whatever test they'd just issued Logan, he'd passed to their satisfaction, and Raina trusted their experience and judgment.

"What the hell is going on?" Logan said through clenched teeth, his gaze flashing with exasperation. "Is that what she *claimed* I did?"

"Nobody is claiming you did anything," Dean said in a calm tone meant to diffuse the other man's irritation. "It was a question we had to ask, not that I ever thought you were responsible for the cuffs or note. Come in and sit down, and we'll explain everything."

Reluctantly, Logan entered the room and sat down next to Mac, which put him directly across from Raina. He placed his clasped hands on the table, exhaled a deep breath, and she watched as his annoyance ebbed, thank goodness.

"Since names weren't exchanged between the two of you last night, this is Raina Beck," Mac said, a hint of amusement in his voice. "Raina, this is Logan Cruz."

Raina nodded politely at the man sitting opposite her, and he actually had the nerve to *smirk* at her. God, could this situation get any more awkward? Logan Cruz already knew her body intimately, was searing her with his gold-green gaze, and the formality was so out of place.

"Cruz has been with our firm for over three years," Dean said to Raina. "He's a former Marine, his credentials are impeccable, and he has a spotless record with us. I would trust him to protect Jillian, that's how confident I am in his abilities as a security agent."

It was an impressive, reassuring recommendation from someone whose business and reputation was based on the quality of men he hired, and Dean's endorsement of Logan put Raina at ease.

Dean turned his attention to Logan and began filling him in on the threat she'd received that morning. A deep frown formed on Logan's brow, his jaw clenched, and the muscles across his broad shoulders tightened as he listened to the details she'd shared earlier with the two other men at the table.

Once Dean was finished, Logan shifted his darkened gaze back to hers, clearly disturbed by what he'd just heard. "Was there anyone else at the club, before you met me, who said or did anything that made you feel uncomfortable?" he asked, surprising her with the depth of his concern.

She gave his question serious consideration and realized she'd overlooked another possibility. "Actually, yes, there was a guy who followed me around the club before I met you. He was tall, with blondish hair and brown eyes. Very arrogant and persistent. We didn't exchange names, but he asked me to do a scene with him, which I turned down and he wasn't happy about. He didn't physically threaten me, but he definitely made me feel uneasy."

Dean wrote another note on his pad of paper. "We'll definitely check with the club to see if any complaints against any members have been issued lately. In the meantime, until we're absolutely certain that Raina is safe and the threat is diffused, Logan, you'll be assigned as her security detail, since your schedule is the most flexible for the next few weeks." He glanced from Logan to Raina, his gaze direct and businesslike. "Do either of you have any issues with this arrangement?"

Logan was much too quick to speak first. "Not at all. You?" He glanced across the table at Raina, an unmistakable challenge in his sinful eyes. The kind of look that dared her to say *yes*, to him, to them, together.

She barely suppressed a shiver. Even from across the table, the sexual tension between them was palpable. The slight curve to his sensual mouth spoke volumes and made her shamelessly wet and aching, because she knew the kind of exquisite pleasure this man was capable of giving her.

He was temptation personified. Despite knowing how dangerous this situation was going to be to her, both physically and emotionally, Raina wasn't about to show any weakness where Logan was concerned. She'd just have to prove that she could handle him being her temporary bodyguard, that she could maintain control and not be swayed by the heat in his eyes or the memories of how amazing he'd felt thrusting so deep inside her body.

Yeah, good luck with that, girlfriend.

"I'm fine with Logan," she said, determined to be equally professional about the situation.

"Good to hear," Dean said with a succinct nod of his head. "He'll escort you to your store and stay there during the day as surveillance and security, and he'll make sure you get home safely in the evenings. He'll do a sweep of your apartment, and since you have a security system, he'll make sure it's armed and in working order before he leaves."

She understood Logan making sure she made it to work and home without any incidents, but the last thing she wanted was the distraction of him being in her store all day long, too. "That's a bit over-the-top, isn't it? I have my manager, Aaron, at the store during the day, so Logan really doesn't need to be there, too."

"Logan's only job is to look after you and protect you," Mac said, his voice firm and inarguable. "And that means at work, too. If someone is watching you, they'll see Logan and be less likely to approach you or take this to a more physical level. And if anyone does try anything, Logan is well trained in martial arts, and that other person won't stand a chance against him."

Raina believed every word that Mac spoke, and knew that she'd lost this battle.

Dean stood up and grabbed his portfolio. "Mac and I have a meeting with a client we need to head out for. We'll be in touch as soon as we get the chance to talk to the manager at the club. In the meantime, don't take any of this lightly, Raina."

With that, Dean headed for the door, followed by Mac, who stopped and glanced back at them with a devilish look in his eyes. "Play nice, kids," he said, clearly referencing the undercurrents of attraction still simmering between her and Logan.

Then he was gone, leaving Raina alone with the one man she'd thought she'd never see again.

Chapter Four

THE CONFERENCE ROOM grew quiet, with Raina refusing to look at Logan now that Mac and Dean were gone. She shifted in her seat and placed her purse on her lap to rummage through the contents—for what, he had no idea. Now that it was just the two of them, she was obviously nervous, even a little flustered, and that knowledge gave him a whole lot of satisfaction considering the way she'd left him high and dry the evening before.

He was also placated by the realization that she wasn't as unaffected by what had happened between them at the club as she'd like him to believe.

But as much as her abrupt departure last night had chafed him, that really wasn't what concerned him right now. Knowing she was in danger, that she had a potential stalker pursuing her to the point that the person knew where she lived, raised every one of his protective instincts. Ensuring her safety was his main focus, and if that meant being able to spend more time with her, well, he wasn't about to complain about that bonus.

She withdrew her car keys from her bag and stood. "Are you ready to go?"

"Sure." He scooted out his chair and straightened to his full height, watching as she headed for the door with her gaze averted and her chin thrust out a bit too stubbornly.

In two steps, he reached her and caught her arm, gently but firmly bringing her to a stop. That got her attention, and she sucked in a quick breath and quickly turned her head to look at him, her long blonde ponytail swinging over her shoulder and her expression startled by his bold move. Her lips parted, and he was momentarily distracted by thoughts of how that soft mouth would feel sliding along the length of his cock and sucking him deep.

He definitely intended to find out.

"Tell me something," he murmured as he caressed the sensitive crease of her elbow with a stroke of his thumb, gratified to see the pulse at her neck flutter at his touch and her eyes darken with that same desire he'd witnessed last night. Even her nipples beaded against the pretty pink dress she wore. "Are you more afraid of me or the stalker?"

Her gaze turned guarded, contradicting the sugary-sweet smile she gave him. "I'm not afraid of you."

No, not in a threatening sense, but physically he could feel her resistance. Hell, the way she'd bolted on him last night was a clear indicator that the combustible chemistry between them had spooked her. Given this second chance, he planned to take full advantage of their time together and the attraction that hadn't dissipated one iota. But first, he needed to knock down some of those walls she'd erected between the two of them.

"Maybe you *should* be afraid of me," he said, giving her a wolfish smile. "Because I'm itching to put you over my knee and spank you for being so insubordinate last night."

Her brows shot up, and then the most beautiful thing happened—that strong, confident woman he'd met last night at the club reappeared right before his eyes.

Fire and sass sparked in her gaze, making him hard in a flash. "Oh, I'd like to see you try."

He flat-out grinned, welcoming this more flirtatious side to Raina. He lowered his head closer to hers, so that his mouth was near her ear. "Sweetheart, it would be my greatest pleasure to feel your smooth ass beneath the palm of my hand. But I don't think that Dean or Mac would appreciate me doing so right here in their conference room. However, if you'd like to wrestle it out later to see who comes out on *top*, I'm certainly game."

She gaped at him, though there was no misinterpreting the amusement in her gaze. With the awkwardness between them finally dispelled, he released her arm but didn't step away. "Now let's get you to work before I change my mind and give everyone in the office a titillating peep show, with your bare ass as the main attraction."

She opened her mouth to say something, thought better of it, and instead walked out of the conference room and toward the elevators. He fell into step beside her, deliberately placed his hand on the base of her spine, and wasn't at all surprised to feel her body tense at his unexpected touch.

"Sweetheart, you're really going to have to learn to relax around me," he said in a low voice. "I swear I don't bite, unless you want me to."

She glanced at him and sighed. "You're not going to make any of this easy on me, are you?"

"Why should I?" Reaching the elevator, Logan pressed the down button, glad that Gail wasn't at her desk at the moment so they could finish this private conversation. "You certainly didn't make it easy on me last night."

She winced, her expression filling with contrition.

"I'm sorry about that. I know I should have handled things differently. What do you say we start fresh and new?"

Oh, hell no. Logan wasn't about to allow her the luxury of wiping the slate clean and pretending their erotic, sizzling encounter at The Players Club had never happened. "That's impossible. There is no forgetting *anything* about last night." Not the way she'd ridden him or the soft, wet heat of her body enveloping his cock or the flush on her lovely face when she'd come for him.

She was saved from responding when the doors to the elevator opened and they stepped inside with two other women already there. Logan leaned against the brass railing along the side wall while Raina stood a few feet away from him, looking straight ahead as the elevator stopped on various floors on the way down to drop off and pick up people.

He was certain she was grateful for the reprieve, and he really couldn't blame her. From the moment they'd seen one another in the conference room, they'd both gone through varying degrees of emotion, but the strongest one that remained for him was a renewed lust and need for this one particular woman. And considering how he'd lived his life the past six years, he wasn't sure how he felt about her pull on him.

When it came to The Players Club and his choice of women, he was never impulsive. He'd always been much more calculated in his pursuit of sexual pleasures, finding women who were far more malleable and submissive than Raina—women he knew he could walk away from because they were easy and a one-time challenge because a long-term relationship wasn't what he was in the market for. Not when he could still feel the burn from the way his high school sweetheart/fiancée and his best friend had so completely devastated him with their betrayal.

But from the moment he'd seen Raina dancing up in that gold-gilded cage at the Rave party, so uninhibited in her sensuality and that long, gorgeous blonde hair begging to be wrapped around his fist, he'd been riveted. And even though his gut told him she was different, that she was the exact opposite of docile and pliable when it came to his demands, his cock had wanted her.

The moment he'd crowded into that cage with her and pressed her against the bars, he'd known that she wasn't a pushover, that her ability to yield to him would be based on him being stronger and more dominant—a prospect he'd found incredibly arousing. He'd managed to keep her fingers wrapped around those bars while he'd slid his hand beneath her dress to make her come, and had restrained them again behind her back when she'd straddled his lap on the chair and he'd sunk balls deep into her silken pussy.

But both times, he'd been well aware of the defiance and rebellion in her body's movements, along with the struggle and need for *her* to be in charge. She'd been passionate, full of fire, and an exciting challenge in terms of him maintaining control of her and the scene. She was clearly a woman who liked being on top, and he'd allowed her that position at the club because it had been convenient to have her sitting astride his lap because of the chair. But make no mistake, he intended to make sure she knew that *he* was the top when it came to sex, and he welcomed the challenge of that particular power play between them.

As he watched her lick her bottom lip, something deeper stirred within him, and he was struck with the realization that he didn't merely want to fuck her. No, he wanted to unravel her, figure out what made her so guarded and wary beneath her tough facade, and ultimately, he wanted to possess her.

He ignored the warning in his head, the one that was telling him he was breaking all his self-imposed rules and he'd be much smarter to keep their association all about business, instead of pleasure.

But it didn't matter what his logical mind was advising him, because he wasn't even close to having his fill of her. And until he sated this deep, addictive craving he'd developed for Raina, he was going to pull out the heavy artillery and seduce the hell out of her mind and body and make sure she enjoyed what he already knew was a mutual, and undeniable, desire for one another.

They finally reached the lobby level, and as they walked out of the elevator, he deliberately splayed his palm against the small of her back, just because he wanted her to get used to him casually touching her. She didn't stiffen or pull away, and he suppressed a smile, chalking it up as a small victory.

They stepped out of the building into the bright, warm sunlight, and he followed her to her car, realizing he didn't even know where she worked or what she did for a living.

"Where do you work?" he asked. Since he'd be following her in his own car, it would be good to know what direction they were headed.

She hesitated a noticeable moment before replying. "At a store in Old Town called Sugar and Spice."

The name was familiar, and it took Logan a moment to put two and two together and remember what type of business Sugar and Spice was. "Isn't that an adult toy store?"

She stopped at a small compact car, unlocked the door, but didn't get inside. Instead, she met his gaze straight on. "I prefer the term *adult boutique*," she said, the defensive note to her voice matching the tilt of her chin. "And I *own* the place. If you dare to call it a *porn shop*, I'm going to have to knee you in the groin."

He couldn't have been more surprised, or intrigued, that she owned a place that sold erotic novelty items. And judging by her comment, her rebellious stance, and the fire in her eyes, she'd clearly expected some kind of crude or derogatory comment about her business, which was something she probably encountered often with more narrow-minded people.

"I'm not about to degrade what you do for a living," he said, softening his tone, wanting to make sure she knew he wasn't the type of person to judge or criticize. Considering he enjoyed incorporating various grown-up toys to increase sexual pleasure, he wasn't about to be a hypocrite. "I'm actually fascinated. I've always wanted to check the place out but just haven't made the time."

She visibly relaxed. "Well, here's your chance." She opened the car door, then gave him a sly, teasing glance. "Just please, no playing with the merchandise."

He feigned a sigh of disappointment when he really wanted to laugh. "You're no fun. Do I at least get a discount on any purchases I make, because I'm sure there's going to be *something* I won't be able to resist?" *Like leather restraints or a spanking paddle*, he thought. *Or maybe use both on her at the same time.*

The corner of her lovely mouth twitched as she fought to contain her amusement. "Since you'll essentially be working as security at the store, you can have the employee discount."

"Excellent." Feeling bold and daring, especially in a very public place, he reached out and skimmed his thumb along her smooth jaw. Satisfaction filled him when she didn't jerk back or slap away his touch, and he tipped his head, pleased that all the awkward tension from the office upstairs had vanished. "And does whatever I buy come with a personal demonstration?"

Amusement danced in her blue eyes, and she shook her head. "Absolutely *not*." The breathless quality of her voice underscored the conviction she no doubt had been striving for.

After tucking a wispy strand of hair behind her ear that had come loose from her ponytail, he let his fingers fall away and arched a brow. "I think I'm going to have to lodge a complaint with the owner about changing that policy."

She laughed, the sound light and real and so damn sexy. "Good luck with that. From what I hear, the owner's a real ball-buster."

He grinned, thoroughly enjoying this light and easy banter between the two of them. "I guess I'll just have to take my chances."

✧　✧　✧

BY THE TIME Raina pulled into her parking spot at the back of Sugar and Spice, where all employees kept their vehicles, she was *smiling* and feeling light and flirty, something she hadn't expected to feel considering how strained things had been between her and Logan when he'd walked into Dean's conference room.

But somewhere along the way, they'd both calmed down and relaxed, and by the time Logan had escorted her out to her car, the intense, aggressive man she'd met the night before, the same one who'd all but glared at her when he'd seen her again at Noble and Associates, was playfully teasing her and coaxing her to do the same.

The man's charming side was just as lethal as his bad-boy persona, but there was absolutely no doubt in her mind that the power and depth she'd witnessed at The Players Club, along with all that raw sexual energy he'd exuded, was barely leashed below the surface, just waiting for an opportune moment to assert itself.

She shivered at the thought as she slipped out of her car, even as she realized that she wasn't completely opposed to seeing that sexy, dominant side to Logan again.

He met up with her at the steel door that led into the back of her boutique, where she swiped a key card, then entered a security code that allowed the door to give a quick buzzing sound and unlock.

"Who all has a key card to unlock the store?" he asked as he followed her into a sectioned-off area of the shop, where her office was located, along with a sizeable storage room she used for excess stock and inventory to fulfill the orders that came through on her website.

"Just the full-time workers, which would be myself, my manager, Aaron, and the assistant manager, Callie, who also handles the packaging and mailing of the Internet orders. Part-time workers don't have key access. And my best friend, Paige, also has one, for emergencies." Raina used the same key card and code to unlock her office door, then stepped inside and placed her purse in the bottom drawer of her desk, then used a small, regular key to lock it inside. "We all have our own card and code, specifically assigned to us, so there's always a log of who came in the back door or the office, and at what time."

He nodded approvingly. "That's a solid security system to have."

"I had a problem with an employee in the past who had a regular key to the store," she said as she faced him again, his formidable size in her small office a bit overwhelming to her senses. "Security footage caught him coming in after hours through the front door, and inventory went missing on the night shifts when he closed up the place. When I let him go, it just seemed smarter to upgrade the security system and make everyone accountable."

He glanced around the office, his sharp gaze seemingly missing nothing, including the security monitor on the wall that showed a live feed of different angles and sections of the store. "How long ago did you fire this employee?"

"About three months ago."

"Do you think he'd be disgruntled enough to start threatening you?" he persisted.

"I'm pretty sure he didn't leave the handcuffs and note," she said with a shake of her head. "He moved to Vegas about a month ago."

Logan let it go at that, but Raina had no doubt that he'd mentally filed away the information for future use.

"I'd like to get a key card for myself before the end of the day, so I have one in case of an emergency while I'm protecting you," Logan said.

"Sure," she said, understanding his reasons. "Come on, I'll show you the rest of the store." She led the way out of the office and through a framed doorway covered in a brocade curtain, used to separate the back of the shop from the boutique's retail floor.

There were a few customers browsing in the store,

her manager, Aaron, was up at the register helping a young man with a purchase, and Raina headed over to the lingerie section, where Paige was preoccupied with lacing up a mannequin in one of her newest corset designs—a gorgeous, one-of-a-kind creation made of sapphire silk, trimmed in black ruffles, and embellished with dark blue crystals.

As she made her way around racks of sexy negligees, lacy baby-dolls, and barely there panties, Raina was very aware of Logan just a few steps behind her, his wholly masculine presence such an extreme contrast against all the frilly, feminine items on display.

"I'm back, Paige," Raina said as she neared her friend. "Thank you for opening the store and handling things for me until I got here."

"Oh, hey, no problem," Paige replied, and after tying the corset's ribbon into a perfect silk bow, she turned around to face Raina. "I, uh…"

Paige's words trailed off as if she'd forgotten what she was going to say, her eyes nearly popping out of their sockets when she caught sight of Logan standing beside Raina. Her friend was rarely at a loss for words, but she understood the kind of impact Logan had on a woman's brain cells. He was gorgeous, with seductive green eyes and a body built for sin.

After a moment of silence, she swallowed hard, gave her head a small shake to regain her train of thought, and glanced back at Raina. "I, um, called Aaron in early so he'd be here when you arrived."

"Thank you. I appreciate that." Knowing Paige was dying to discover who the man beside her was, she introduced the two of them. "Logan, this is my best friend, Paige Moore. Paige, this is Logan Cruz, a security agent with Noble and Associates."

Logan extended a hand toward Paige in a professional greeting, but there was no mistaking the glimmer of amusement dancing in his eyes. "Nice to meet you."

Paige slid her hand into Logan's much larger one. "You, too," she said so breathlessly Raina nearly laughed at her friend's obvious infatuation with Logan.

Clearly, Logan was used to women falling all over him because he handled Paige with grace, charm, and an irresistible smile.

He tipped his head toward Raina, his expression back to business. "If you don't mind, I'd like to go and introduce myself to your manager, Aaron, and fill him in on any details he might need to know about why I'm here. I'd also like to ask him some questions about that previous employee you let go."

"Sure, go right ahead," she said, waving her hand toward the front of the store, where Aaron had just finished up with the paying customer.

He walked away, and Paige blatantly stared at his

perfect ass encased in a pair of expensive-looking jeans. Her mouth hung open, and when she looked back at Raina, her eyes were glazed with lust.

"Oh, my *God*," she said, her whispered voice tinged with female admiration and awe. "I think my panties just hit the floor."

The comment was so outrageously Paige that Raina could only laugh. "Well, while you're putting them back *on*, you can put your tongue back in your mouth and wipe the drool off your chin, too."

"I'd rather use my tongue to lick him instead," Paige said, only half joking.

There had never been any kind of jealousy between her and Paige, but Raina had the sudden and odd urge to mark her territory—or at least let her friend know that she and Logan already had a history.

"Dean assigned Logan to be my bodyguard while they figure out who left the cuffs and note on my door," she said as she rearranged a silk chemise on a hanger. "Logan is also the guy I was with at The Players Club last night."

"*What?*" Paige shook her head in confusion. "But I thought the guy you were with last night was—"

"He's not the stalker," Raina clarified and went on to explain what had happened at Noble and Associates and why she trusted Dean and Mac's judgment when it came to Logan.

"God, he's so freakin' *hot*," Paige said as her gaze went back to Logan again. "Please do *not* tell me that you're going to let that fine piece of male specimen go to waste while he's guarding your body."

Raina wasn't making any promises—either way—because while her head was telling her to keep her distance from this man, her body wanted to get as close as possible and do all sorts of down-and-dirty things with him. And yeah, she was leaning toward enjoying her time with Logan, because it was an ideal and temporary arrangement that suited her perfectly.

"I will keep your opinion under advisement," Raina said with a grin. "Now, don't you need to be somewhere? Like work?"

Paige made a face at her. "I'm my own boss, remember? I could stay here all day…"

"Not gonna happen." Raina raised a brow and pointed toward the front door. "Thank you for your help this morning, but I can handle things from here."

"Well, if you need help handling *him*, just let me know." Paige gave her a sassy little finger wave as she headed toward the front of the store. As she passed behind Logan, who was still talking to Aaron, she placed the back of her hand across her forehead and feigned a swoon that made Raina laugh.

As soon as her friend was gone, Raina met up with Aaron and Logan. "Everything good here?" she asked, wanting to make sure her manager was comfortable with the situation since Aaron, who was a competing body builder and looked like a linebacker, normally provided security for the store.

"Absolutely, boss," Aaron said, a troubled frown furrowing his dark brows. "Your safety is my main concern."

She placed her hand on Aaron's muscular arm and didn't miss the way Logan's gaze zeroed in on that familiar touch—though he had nothing to worry about. Aaron was like a brother to her, nothing more. "Well, with the two of you in the store, I don't think I have much to worry about."

Aaron excused himself to go and help another customer who walked in, and Raina turned to face Logan, who was still frowning at her, his chest puffed out a bit more than usual.

"Something wrong?" she asked, though she definitely had an idea what had agitated him. She just wasn't sure if she was more amused or annoyed that he was suddenly asserting a bit of alpha dominance in her workplace, and in public.

"Anything going on between you and Aaron?" he asked, a clipped note to his voice.

She deliberately rolled her eyes, making sure he saw her act of insolence. "He's my employee and a friend, nothing more."

"Good." He gave her a hot, lingering, possessive stare that made her stomach muscles flutter and accelerated her pulse. "Do whatever you need to do work-wise. I don't want to be a distraction or get in the way, so pretend like I'm not even here."

Was he serious? As if ignoring the fact that he was in her store was even a remote possibility. He sauntered off to check out the placement of the security cameras and to familiarize himself with the layout of the store.

As she surreptitiously watched him, she saw the boutique through his eyes—the clean, modern design, the elegant, upscale décor, the luxurious, high-end items she carried and sold. She'd worked hard to make the place warm and welcoming and a comfortable environment for her customers. And despite those people who looked down on her for what she did for a living or judged her without even *knowing* her, she was proud of what she'd accomplished with Sugar and Spice. Seeing that Logan was impressed with the store, too, made her feel ridiculously pleased.

But Raina was a realist, and experience had taught her that while he might be initially fascinated with her and her shop filled with bondage toys and erotic lingerie, chances were that his intrigue would shift to embarrassment if he ever had to introduce her to his family or friends and had to openly explain that she owned an *adult* boutique that sold vibrators, anal beads, and sex swings. It was all well and good enjoying a bit of kink in private and on the sly, but she was a secret most men liked to keep well hidden.

She shook her head of those depressing thoughts and went behind the front counter to check the computer there, to see what kind of online orders had come in overnight. While her store held its own and turned over a nice profit, her website sales were nearly double the boutique's, and it was almost time to hire another employee to help Callie with packaging and mailing orders.

Raina spent the rest of the day working on the floor, which she enjoyed the most since it allowed her to interact with her customers. Logan mostly kept to himself, but when the store was empty, he didn't hesitate to peruse her inventory and seemed intrigued by the items located down the aisle displaying all things *bondage*.

Over the course of the afternoon, each one of her "Cocks and Cocktails" girlfriends stopped by the store…in the pretense of either needing something from the shop or just wanting to say hello, since their places of business were close to Sugar and Spice. But it became obvious that they were really there to check out and meet Logan, which told Raina that Paige had called each one to spread the news about her new bodyguard—who was also the guy she'd hooked up with at The Players Club. Much to Logan's credit, he handled the ogling and each introduction with amusement and charm.

By the time the clock struck six in the evening, Raina was truly exhausted after the day's events. She made her way to Aaron, who was stocking a shelf with some new leather riding crops that were becoming a hot selling item thanks to the popularity of *Fifty Shades of Grey*.

"Hey, Aaron, I think I'm going to take off for the night, if that's okay with you?"

He glanced over his shoulder at her with a nod. "Absolutely, boss. I've got Callie and Desiree here until closing time," he said of the other part-time girl who worked the evening shift. "So, we should be fine."

"Thanks. Call me if you need anything. I'll be home all night long."

"On a Friday night?" he drawled teasingly. "Now that's a shame."

As if she had anywhere to go or anything to do. "You forget that I'm on lock-down until we figure out who put those handcuffs on my door."

The corner of Aaron's mouth tipped up in a devil-ish smile. "You can always have your *bodyguard* take you out. You can go let loose and have some fun, knowing you're safe and protected."

Aaron also knew about her night with Logan—Jesus, who didn't?—and clearly had no qualms about pushing her and Logan together. "I'm sure Logan has better things to do with his evenings than to entertain me."

Her manager arched a dark brow, his gaze gleaming with too much knowledge and a whole lot of humor. "From the looks he's been giving you when you're not paying attention, that man wants to *entertain* you, big-time."

There was no mistaking the insinuation in his words or tone, but Raina chose not to reply to his comment. "I'll see you tomorrow, Aaron."

He grinned and winked at her. "Night, boss."

Chapter Five

RAINA DROVE TO her apartment building, with Logan following. She parked her car in her assigned slot, and per Logan's instructions when they'd left the shop, she waited for him to walk to her car after he parked his own vehicle in the guest area. He knocked lightly on her window when he arrived, and she unlocked and opened her door to get out.

Now that it was dark outside, with only the building lights on and shadows in every corner, she was extremely grateful that Logan was there to walk her safely to her apartment and that Dean had insisted he also do a sweep inside her place just as an added precaution. His hand was pressed to the small of her back, keeping her close to his side, and while she'd always professed to be an independent woman, she had to admit that he made her feel safe and protected—and that was something she'd never felt throughout her life.

Having grown up with a father who was seriously bipolar and never stayed on his meds for long, she'd constantly been on the receiving end of his manic phases, which tended to lean toward the more aggressive, irritable, and angry types of mood swings. As a child, and even as a teenager, she'd been terrified by his rages, and during those episodes she'd always seemed to be the center of his blowups. His attacks had been more verbal than physical, but the fear he'd instilled had been just as intense and painful.

And with a mother who'd been weak and passive when it came to her husband, Raina learned very early on to do whatever it took to protect herself—and survive on her own when her father had thrown her out of the house with nothing but the clothes on her back.

She'd come a long way since that frightened teenage girl, when she'd sworn she'd never allow any man to control her life or decisions or strip away her dreams, as her father had done to her mother. Which was why she'd walked away from the only man she'd ever fallen in love with when he'd issued her an ultimatum that meant giving him all the power and control in their relationship.

It had been an excruciating decision, but she had no regrets. She'd never marry a man who couldn't accept every aspect of who and what she was, and unfortunately she'd found it extremely difficult to find someone who was able to see past the Sugar and Spice businessperson to the heart of the woman who just wanted to be loved unconditionally.

"Did you tell Dean about the security cameras in the parking lot so he can check last night's feed for anyone suspicious heading toward your apartment?" Logan asked, his deep voice bringing her back to the present.

"No." She shook her head as they followed the walkway past the main entrance into the complex, then started up the stairs to the second level. "I was so unsettled this morning that I forgot all about the cameras around the outside of the building."

"Once we get inside your place, I'll call Dean and let him know. He'll contact the apartment manager in the morning, explain what happened, and I'm sure they'll cooperate. With luck, we'll be able to get a glimpse of someone heading in this direction between the time you arrived home last night and this morning."

Yes, she hoped so, too.

They reached her apartment, and she watched Logan's brows snap into a dark frown as his gaze lit on the handcuffs still dangling from her doorknob. "After I know everything's okay inside, I'll go and see if the maintenance guy has some bolt cutters to remove the cuffs."

"No need." She dug into the side pocket of her purse and withdrew a small, flat silver key. "They look like the novelty handcuffs I sell at the store, so I took one of the keys from a set out of my stock. The keys for these things are fairly common and universal, so it should work."

"Smart girl." Taking the key from her, he inserted it into the lock. With a quick twist, the one side of the handcuffs unhinged, enabling him to remove them from the knob. Dangling the cuffs by his index finger, he gave her a slow, sexy smile. "I'll just hold on to these. You never know when a pair of handcuffs will come in handy."

The heat in his eyes told her that he wasn't referring to capturing a perpetrator. She already knew he had a penchant for being in control and for restraining her, and the image of her being cuffed to her own bed while he pleasured her was enough to make her shift restlessly on her feet.

God, she'd never been submissive to a man, so why did the thought of being at Logan's complete and total mercy cause her entire body to clench with need?

Trying to maintain her composure, she unlocked her door, opened it, then stepped inside and punched the code to disengage the security system. Logan followed her into the kitchen off to the right of the entryway, and she waited there, per his instructions, while he checked the rest of the apartment.

He came back a few moments later. "Everything looks fine."

Which she'd figured since her alarm had still been set, but it was still nice to know that once he left, she'd be safe. "Would you like a glass of wine?" She needed one, if not two, after the day she'd had.

He shook his head and grinned. "I don't drink on the job. But I'll take a water if you have one."

"Sure." She opened the refrigerator and passed him a chilled bottle of water, then retrieved the unopened Moscato she'd bought a few weeks ago and a crystal wineglass from the cupboard.

As she extracted the cork and poured herself a generous portion of the sweet white wine, he made a call on his cell phone. Glass in hand, she walked over to the sliding glass door in her small dining area and pulled it open, allowing a cool evening breeze to sweep through the place and flutter gently against the skirt of her dress. Being on the second level of the complex, she had a lovely balcony and was able to see the ocean in the distance, even though she lived a few blocks away from the beach. The beautiful, peaceful view was one of the things she loved the most about her apartment.

She drank her wine while she listened to Logan's deep voice as he talked. Judging by the conversation, Raina assumed it was Dean or Mac on the other end of the line as he gave them a brief rundown of the day, then told them to call the apartment manager to review the building's security feed.

He answered with a few yeses and okays and finally disconnected the call. Slipping the phone into his jeans' front pocket, he joined her by the open slider. He cracked open his bottle of water, guzzled down half of it, then glanced at her to share the details.

"Mac spoke with the manager at The Players Club, and the last complaint they received about a member was three months ago," Logan told her. "Apparently, the guy had a problem stopping when his partner used the club's safe word, and after two written warnings, the third time he was banned from the club and hasn't been back inside since. So, whoever approached you last night, it was someone different."

She exhaled a deep breath. "Okay," she said, even though that didn't give them much to go on, when she'd been hoping for some kind of lead.

He must have heard the disappointment in her voice, because he was quick to reassure her. "Mac wants to review the security feed around this building for last night and this morning to see if he can get a glimpse of the person who put the cuffs on your door.

That might take a few days, so in the meantime, it looks like you're stuck with me for a while."

He winked at her, his light and playful demeanor chasing away some of the tension inside of her. Logan and the wine made for a great, relaxing combination. "My girlfriends will be thrilled," she teased him right back. "You're nice eye candy to have around."

He chuckled, then moved so that he was standing right in front of her, tall, imposing, and sexy as hell. She wasn't a petite woman by any stretch of the imagination, yet his height, the width of his broad shoulders, and his presence in general dwarfed even her. He tipped his head to the side, his eyes suddenly serious and very hot. The blast of heat—in his gaze and radiating off his body—was seductive and mesmerizing, as were his words when he murmured, "How do *you* feel about having me around?"

There was no denying the sudden shift between them, from discussing business one minute to him turning her comment into something far more personal and intimate the next. A wild, heated thrill flared through her, and she could feel her own traitorous body sway toward his, felt her nipples harden and her sex pulse in answer to his question.

"We're not talking about you just being my bodyguard, are we?" she asked, unable to disguise the breathless quality of her voice.

He shook his head slowly. "No, we're not." His voice was low and soft, like the finest of silk rubbing against her skin.

Anticipation simmered deep inside of her. Absently, she licked her bottom lip, and his jaw clenched as he watched the slow swipe of her tongue. Now that all aspects of business were taken care of, that professionalism and decorum he'd exuded all day long were gone, replaced by that tempting, irresistible man she'd met at the club last night, and all she could think about was his mouth on hers, his fingers stroking between her thighs to ease the building ache there....

He stepped closer, until the front of his hard body touched hers and gently pushed her backwards with nothing more than the pressure of his muscular thighs against hers. Her heart rate accelerated, and she took a step back, then tried to take another but came up against the wooden edge of her dining table. Trapped between two very unyielding objects, she felt a moment of panic. All that sheer strength overwhelmed her, and Raina's first instinct was to push him back so every breath she inhaled didn't make her dizzy with the scent of *him*.

Even before she could raise her free hand to his chest to keep him from crowding her further, he anticipated her move. "*Don't*," he said, soft yet commanding.

Her stomach flipped, and their gazes connected. Just one simple word that held a wealth of meaning, one of which she read in his dark, glittering eyes. *Trust me*, and Lord help her, she did. Probably more than was wise when she knew he was a man who liked to be in control—and that control had the ability to strip away all those protective barriers until she lay physically bare.

He took her wineglass from her fingers and set it on the table away from them, along with his bottled water. Encircling her waist with his big, strong hands, he effortlessly lifted her and scooted her bottom back so that she was sitting on the table. His palms gripped her knees and gently but firmly pushed them wide apart to make room for him to step in between her spread legs, which he did as he slowly pushed up the hem of her dress so it didn't get caught between them.

Her thighs bracketed his hips, the scratch of denim against her tender skin so arousing she had to swallow back a moan. Only a few inches separated the crotch of her panties from the bulge she'd glimpsed beneath the zipper of his jeans. Resisting the urge to wrap her legs around his thighs to draw him closer so she could rub herself against the hard length of him took extreme effort.

He braced just the tips of his fingers on the table on each side of where she sat, making her aware of the fact that he was deliberately holding back from touching her—which only increased the desire and need building within her.

And he knew it, too.

"From the moment I saw you in the conference room this morning, there's been one question I've wanted to ask you," he said, his tone suddenly serious.

"Okay," she whispered, both curious and a little nervous about said question.

"Why did you run out on me last night?"

There was no anger in his voice, just a quiet intensity that compelled her to be completely honest with him. "I never meant for anything that happened at the club to be more than a one-night stand with a stranger," she replied truthfully.

Because she wasn't prepared for him to delve deeper into her answer, which would mean explaining too much of her painful past, she turned it around on him. "Why did you come after me? Because I bruised your male ego?" It was the only explanation that made sense to her.

An amused smile touched the corners of his mouth. "Going after you had *nothing* to do with my ego, although I have to admit you are the first woman I've ever chased after."

Why did that admission make her feel ridiculously pleased? "Should I be flattered?"

"Oh, yeah," he said huskily, confidently. "*Very* flattered."

He softly tapped his fingers against the table next to her hips, reminding Raina that he *still* wasn't touching her. And she wanted him to. Badly. "If you don't chase after women, then why me?"

"Because fucking you once wasn't nearly enough, and I want a helluva lot more."

Her breath caught at his frank, uncensored statement. The explicit words caused a rush of warmth to spiral low and moisture to dampen her panties. "Oh."

He smirked at her startled response. "Do you remember me telling you last night that I wasn't done with you yet?"

"Yes," she whispered. How could she forget? That possessive, hungry vow had been one of the catalysts that had sent her running from the club, and him. Along with the way he'd instinctively known her secret desires, the ones that made her much too vulnerable to a man like him.

"I meant what I said, Raina. I'm not even close to being done with you."

Finally, he touched her. Splaying his hands on her knees, he gradually skimmed his palms up her thighs and beneath the hem of her dress, the cotton material pooling around his wrists the higher he went. She could feel her body and her resistance to him completely melting away.

His gaze, glittering with pure sin, hypnotized her. "There are so many more ways I want you. So many more things I'm dying to do to you and with you. Things that will make you scream and beg and come harder than you ever have before."

With any other man, she would have rolled her eyes and pushed them away, turned off by such a cocky, arrogant claim. She wasn't a screamer, and she never begged. But it was Logan's easy *confidence* that set him apart and made her want everything he offered and more.

"Things like what?" she asked, needing to hear all the sexy details.

"So many wicked, erotic, *filthy* things," he promised.

Oh, yes, please.

His hands reached the apex of her thighs, just inches away from her throbbing sex. But instead of his fingers pressing against the wet silk covering her, he moved his hands higher and grasped the waistband of her underwear and tugged them down with just enough force and finesse that they slipped off her bottom and he could drag them down her thighs. She gasped in surprise and pressed her hands to his shirt-covered chest as he removed the scrap of fabric and tucked it into the front pocket of his jeans.

Curling his fingers around the backs of her knees, he pulled her all the way forward on the table, until her thighs were straddling his hips and her bare pussy was pressed against the thick erection straining against the front of his pants. He shifted, just slightly, and the friction of denim against her sensitive clit nearly unraveled her from the inside out.

A knowing smile touched his lips as he removed her hands from his chest and flattened her palms on the table behind her so she was reclined at a slight angle, making her very aware of the fact that he was back in charge. Then, with agile fingers, he began unbuttoning the top of her dress, all the way down to her stomach, until both sides fell open and she could feel the cool air from the open slider caress that newly bared skin.

"I want to see you naked." He continued listing those *things* he desired as he traced his fingers along the strap of her bra, up to her shoulders, then dragged that strip of satin, along with both sides of her top, all the way down her arms and just past her elbows. Oh-so-slowly, he pulled down the lace cups of her bra, and she couldn't stop the moan that escaped her when her breasts spilled free, full and tight and aching for him to caress.

Lust etched his features as he took in the sight, and she could only imagine how wanton she looked, leaning back with her breasts thrust out, her nipples rock hard, her legs spread wide, and her pussy gleaming with slick arousal.

"*Fuck me*, you're beautiful," he murmured appreciatively, his searing gaze making her burn hotter. He cupped her breasts, firmly kneading the soft flesh before sweeping his thumbs across both taut crests, then pinching and rolling them between his fingers.

She felt as though her nipples had just received an electric jolt, and she inhaled a sharp intake of air, unable to remember a time when she'd ever been so on edge just from her breasts being stimulated. The harder he plucked, the harder her pussy clenched. It was as if the two were connected and each tug caused her sex to pulse and swell.

"Logan..." She was close to begging and didn't care.

He leaned more fully into her and grazed his warm, damp lips against the shell of her ear. "I'm not done telling you all the bad, depraved things I plan to do to you, unless you want me to stop?"

He was deliberately toying with her. But she also recognized that he was giving her a choice...to either admit how much she wanted to hear all those juicy details and experience them, too, or put an end to all this insanity right then and there.

The latter wasn't an option. Not with Logan...and

she wasn't about to analyze why she was so willing when it came to him. "Don't stop," she said before she came to her senses and changed her mind.

She felt him smile triumphantly against the side of her throat and couldn't help but feel like she'd just given him way too much power over her mind and body. "I want to tie you up, hold you down, and taste you *everywhere*," he breathed into her ear, as if he were sharing his deepest, most illicit fantasies of her. "I want to lick your neck and run my tongue along the gorgeous curves of your tits."

His skillful fingers gave life to his narrative, brushing along her collarbone as soft as the lick he described, then gliding down to her breasts and swirling along those mounds like a velvet stroke of his tongue.

Raina shivered and closed her eyes, completely seduced by his brazen words and his clever touch and so very anxious to hear and feel what came next…especially when his hands came to rest on her splayed thighs, then started inching upward.

He gently bit the lobe of her ear as he dragged his thumbs along the slick folds of her sex, gradually delving deeper, his own breathing harsh. "When I'm done sucking on your tight nipples, I want to kneel between your legs and French kiss your cunt, *right here*, until you come hard against my mouth." Those wicked thumbs pushed into her channel, just far enough to tease and make her wild.

She was vaguely aware of one of his hands pulling away from her thighs, his arm reaching up and behind her. She felt a tug on her ponytail, and it took her a moment to realize he'd wrapped that rope of hair tight around his fist and she couldn't move.

Her lashes fluttered open just in time to see the carnal heat blazing in his eyes now that she was under his command. Her heart pumped hard in her chest. Raina had already witnessed this dominant side to Logan at the club, but she had a feeling she was going to experience it on a whole new level now that they were alone.

With an unrelenting tug on her ponytail, he pulled her head back farther, exposing the length of her neck. He licked across the rapid pulse at the base, then gently sucked a patch of skin the same time he pushed two long, thick fingers deep inside of her. The dual sensation was so primal, so animalistic, she could no longer think, just *feel*.

But Logan wasn't done tormenting her, and he continued filling her imagination with more of his own dark, forbidden desires. "I want to fuck your soft, wet mouth and come against the back of your throat while you suck me off." His lips slid back up to her ear while his fingers pumped slowly in and out of her. "I want to slide my cock into your tight body and ride you until you're raw and you can't walk the next day without thinking about me being inside of you."

She whimpered, the arms bracing her now shaking with the effort to hold her up. If she dared to move, she'd collapse backward, and she wasn't about to lose this battle of wills between them. The ache between her legs was now a needy, demanding pang, and her hips began to push against his hand and penetrating fingers, seeking a desperate relief. "Logan…"

Ignoring her plea, he brushed his thumb over her clit in a slow, rhythmic circle, keeping her orgasm just out of her reach. He loosened his grip on her ponytail, and she lowered her chin and met his hot, unrelenting stare. "I want you, Raina, in every conceivable way I can have you," he said, his voice sandpaper rough. "But I need you to know right up front that I like to fuck hard. I like it aggressive and rough with a bit of kink and nothing held back. I think, deep down inside, you like it the same way, don't you?"

How did he manage to make her feel as though he could see straight into her soul? Yes, she liked it the same way, but she'd always harbored a deep fear about revealing those darker cravings to any man. The stigma of owning a sex toy shop was hard enough to deal with emotionally, with the words *slut* and *whore* being bandied about by the one man she'd allowed herself to fall for, that she'd been extremely cautious about allowing those more forbidden thoughts and needs to become a reality.

But there was no judgment in Logan's eyes, just an undeniable hunger for her as well as a perceptiveness that chipped away at her reserve, leaving her at a fork in the road that would either end with a reply of *no* or give him the permission he was waiting for to continue by answering *yes*, she did like sex with a bit of an edge.

And she wanted it with him. "Yes," she whispered, and the one word seemed to set something free inside of her.

His masculine features softened, as if he knew how hard that was for her to admit. But he also looked immensely satisfied with her honest response, too. He curled the fingers still filling her and rubbed the tips against a sensitive spot inside of her that made her gasp and squirm—her G-spot—which she'd only been able to find with a curved vibrator. No man had ever touched that patch of nerve-laden tissue, and Logan was using the knowledge to his advantage, relentless in his pursuit to make her beg and scream.

And oh, God, she was so damn close to doing both.

"You also like to be in control," he said, talking to her as though he weren't slowly driving her mad with the need to climax, as if he weren't building this huge tsunami of sensation with his stroking fingers and the skillful drag of his thumb across her pulsing clit. "And that's where the challenge comes in because I have this need to dominate, to be the *top*, to make you open up to me and submit and *feel*."

She couldn't remember a time she'd felt *so much*, yet her mind came to a screeching halt at the word *submit* and what it implied—a weakness she refused to allow. "I'm not submissive," she said, somehow managing to sound insistent, despite her flushed, extremely aroused state.

"No, you're not," he agreed in a silky tone. Amusement glimmered in his gaze, contradicting every bit of the lazy, exquisite chaos he was causing with his fingers. "Not by nature, anyway, and *that's* why I chased after you last night."

Her lashes had fallen half-mast, and she struggled to keep the lust sweeping through her from completely fogging her brain as he withdrew his fingers, then pumped slowly back inside her. "You chased after me because I'm a challenge for you?"

"No, because you fucking excite me," he growled roughly. "You stimulate me and make me so fucking hot with this push-pull between us."

Her head fell back on a moan, every nerve ending in her body drawing tighter and tighter with every word he spoke, with every slide of his fingers and thumb against her slick, aching flesh.

He pushed his hard, muscular body up against hers, his hips mimicking the thrust and grind of his hand between her thighs. "I want you to let go and give in to me." He dipped his head and licked her breast, pulled her nipple into his mouth, and bit gently before soothing the sting with his tongue. "Let me take care of you and your desires. Trust me to know what you need and to give it to you."

She closed her eyes and whimpered, feeling herself free-falling for his promises, for him. The excruciating need to come was a pool of heat shimmering and undulating in her blood, just out of reach.

"Tell me yes," he rasped against her neck. "Tell me *yes*, and I'll show you how good it can be. How good I can make you *feel*."

She'd never wanted, no, desperately *needed*, an orgasm so badly in her life. "Yes," she panted shamelessly, *begging* for it just how he wanted. "Oh, God, Logan, please, *yes!*"

Once again he dragged his fingers along that responsive spot inside of her while his thumb pressed and rubbed against her clit. The tension inside of her multiplied, then burst through her with such force she *screamed*, uncaring that the sliding door was open and her neighbors might hear. Her back arched, her hips lifted, and her arms and thighs shook as he relentlessly drove her higher, the pleasure so overwhelming her entire body shuddered with a series of orgasmic aftershocks.

When her breathing finally evened out and her heartbeat slowed, she felt his fingers ease from her body, leaving her feeling oddly empty inside, and not just physically. She was still leaning back on her hands—just barely—and she forced her eyes open and found Logan's smoky-eyed stare taking in her disheveled state, her flushed breasts, her swollen sex—while he was still fully, completely dressed.

He lifted his gaze to hers, his expression etched with a dark, carnal hunger…and a whole lot of male satisfaction. "That was so fucking beautiful to watch." Then a slow, arrogant grin curved his sensual lips. "At least we got the begging and screaming out of the way."

Her complexion heated at the reminder. "Stop gloating," she said, and pushed her dress back down her legs. "A *gentleman* wouldn't have pointed that out."

She readjusted her bra, then started to refasten her top, but he gently brushed her hands aside and did the task for her. "You should know by now that I'm not a gentleman when it comes to dirty, messy sex," he drawled softly, his eyes dancing with mirth. "And I'm coming to realize that you like it dirty and messy, too, don't you? Admit it."

She raised a brow, refusing to provide him with that much leverage. "And give you something else to brag about? I don't think so."

He gave her a smile, a flash of sexual promise that made her hot all over again. "By the way, you said yes."

Yes to letting go and giving in to him. *Yes* to letting him take care of her and her desires. *Yes* to trusting him to know what she needed, and for him to give it to her. All things she never would have agreed to if he hadn't held her orgasm for ransom, the rogue.

And now he was looking at her as if he wanted a whole lot more of all those things. "That was completely under duress."

He chuckled, the sound a sexy rumble in his chest. "I figured you'd try and find a loophole after the fact." He lifted his hand and oh-so-tenderly grazed his thumb along her jaw, the one action melting every bit of her resolve. "I want you bad, Raina, and considering we're going to be together for at least the next week, why not take advantage of that time and enjoy what we know will be some really great, dirty, messy, kinky sex?"

He was presenting her with an ideal situation—sex that she already knew would be off the charts and no complicated strings. He wasn't asking for a commitment or forever, only to later decide she wasn't good enough, that a woman who owned a boutique that sold sex toys wasn't marriage material.

Been there, done that, and had the heartbreak to prove it.

He was just offering her pleasure, and lots of it. He was being open and honest about what he wanted—and *honesty* was more than most of the men she'd dated in the past had ever given her. She knew exactly what to expect with Logan…a temporary affair until she no longer needed his bodyguard services. A practical way for the both of them to get this wild attraction to each other out of their systems, without any emotional entanglements.

He was asking for her body, not her heart, and *that* was something she could give him without any regrets.

Giving him a coy smile, she placed her hands on his chest, thinking it very unfair that she hadn't seen him naked yet. "I'm all for having a bodyguard with benefits for the next week." Leaning in close, she ran her tongue along his throat as she skimmed her flattened palms down his torso, then cupped the stiff rise in his pants and gently squeezed, more than willing to return the favor he'd just bestowed upon her.

He pushed his erection against her fingers and groaned, except when she started to unbutton his jeans, he grasped her wrist and pulled her hand away.

Confused, she glanced up at his face. "What about

you?"

He exhaled a harsh stream of breath and shook his head. Clearly, it had taken extreme effort for him to stop her. "What just happened wasn't about me, or you repaying a sexual favor. It was about you trusting me enough to give yourself over to me, which you did beautifully."

His explanation stunned her, left her in awe, and Raina wasn't sure how to respond to such a selfless act. She couldn't ever remember a man giving her an orgasm and not expecting one in return. And here was Logan, who'd just redefined the word *foreplay* with his erotic words and the way he'd seduced her body with his clever fingers and touch. He'd taken her on an exquisite, mind-bending journey of sensation and pleasure, all in the name of securing her trust.

"Don't look at me like I'm a saint, Raina," he said gruffly. "I'm far from it. I have every intention of seeing you restrained and spread out for me, panting, wet, and willing to do anything I ask. Tonight was easy. Next time, I won't be so gentle or accommodating."

Yes, he'd already warned her that he liked to fuck hard and dirty, that he was dominant and aggressive— and the thought caused an undeniable thrill to ripple through her.

He helped her down from the table, and it took

her a moment for her still jellified legs to stabilize. Clasping her hand in his, Logan walked them both to the front door, then turned to look down at her, his features serious. "You're in for the night, right?"

It was a statement more than a question, and she couldn't help but grin at him. "I promise I won't be a bad girl and sneak out after you leave." Honestly, she was exhausted and planned to take a long, hot bath and then go to bed.

"I just want to make sure you don't go out alone *at all*, not until Dean or Mac figures out what's going on." He rubbed his thumb along her knuckles, then let go of her hand. "If you need anything at all, no matter what time it is, call my cell and I'll be right over."

God, how long had it been since anyone had taken care of her or worried about her? The answer made her throat tighten. Even if it was part of Logan's job description as her bodyguard, it felt good to know that if she needed him, he was only a phone call away.

"Thank you," she said.

He nodded. "I'll be here at eight thirty in the morning to pick you up." That was a good hour and a half before she had to be at the store to open for the day. "Why so early?"

"Because we're going to breakfast." He gave her an adorably boyish grin that contradicted how masculine and *big* he was, a far cry from a boy. "After I work out in the mornings, I'm ravenous."

The image of his body all hot and sweaty, muscles flexing as he exercised, made her stomach tighten. "Okay, I'll be ready."

"Excellent." He lowered his head and brushed his lips along her cheek in a too-chaste kiss after everything he'd just done to her. "Have sweet dreams, *sugar*," he drawled huskily.

"Sugar?" she asked as he pulled back and straightened, wondering where that endearment had come from.

Humor curved his lips and he arched a brow. "Would you rather I call you *spice*?"

Ahh, Sugar and Spice, for her shop. "Cute, but I'd rather not be referred to as a Spice Girl."

He chuckled, the sound deliciously wicked. "You could be Kinky Spice."

She couldn't contain her own laughter. "No, thank you," she countered just as playfully—another thing she enjoyed about being with Logan. Their ability to flirt and tease one another. Everything about being with him was so effortless and easy.

"Then sugar it is." Winking playfully at her, he opened the door and stepped outside, giving the area a quick glance before looking back at her. "Lock the door and set the alarm," he said in a tone very much like an order.

"Yes, *sir*," she replied and saluted him, not thinking about the implications of what she'd just said.

In the next instant, his gaze darkened, turned a blistering shade of green. "Fuck, that sounds so hot coming from your mouth." He took a deliberate step back, when Raina suspected he wanted to do the opposite. "Close and lock the door *now*, Raina, before I change my mind and you're saying the word *sir* under much different circumstances."

She shivered, and a jolt of renewed desire spiraled deep and low. Obeying his command was more difficult than she imagined when she was so tempted to let those other tantalizing circumstances play out with him, right here and now.

But after the day she'd had and that much-needed orgasm he'd so generously given her, Raina really was tired and not in the right frame of mind to engage in those dominant games her protector wanted to play.

"Good night, Logan," she said instead and finally shut the door.

She secured the deadbolt, then closed and locked the slider in the dining room before she set the alarm for the evening. It wasn't until she was in her master bathroom, stripping off her clothes to get into the hot, steaming bath awaiting her, that she realized Logan had stolen yet another pair of her panties.

Chapter Six

THE FOLLOWING MORNING, after a hard-core session of cardio and strength training, Logan took a shower, changed, then picked up Raina right on time at eight thirty. He drove them to Perry's Cafe, his favorite place to have breakfast in Old Town and only a few blocks away from her store. He ate there a few times a week, usually with one or two of the guys from the office, and everyone there pretty much knew him by name.

When they arrived at the restaurant, the young, pretty hostess—who was very shy and sweet but always eager to greet him—seated Logan and Raina in a booth by a window. As soon as they sat down across from one another, June, one of the older waitresses who had been working there forever, came up to the table with two mugs in one hand and a coffeepot in the other.

"Hey good-looking," she said, greeting Logan with a bright smile as she set a ceramic mug down in front of each of them, then began filling the cups to the brim with the steaming brew as she eyed Raina curiously. "What's the special occasion, Logan? You've never brought a woman here other than your sister. Or is this one special?" she asked and gave Raina a sassy wink that made her blush.

Surprisingly, Logan *did* consider Raina a special exception, and not because she was a client of Noble and Associates. For the first time in a long time, she was a woman he actually *enjoyed* being around outside of The Players Club, which was normally the extent of his "dating" someone. "I think she could be very special, right, *sugar*?"

Raina rolled her eyes at the pet name he'd given her last night and glanced up at June. "Is he always such a sweet-talker?"

"Always." June waved a hand in exasperation. "Half the girls in here swoon like Southern belles every time he comes through those doors or he says hello to them. I think he broke some hearts when they saw him walk in with you today."

Smiling, Raina poured fresh cream into her coffee, added a packet of sugar, and stirred it all together. "Tell them not to worry, he's still on the market."

June sent a frown Logan's way. "Then you're not

trying hard enough to impress her," she said, chastising him. "You're gonna need to step up your game with this one and not rely on just your good looks and charm if you want to keep her around."

The woman was old enough to be his grandmother, and she liked to bust his chops. Logan didn't mind—June's personality reminded him of growing up and his own feisty grandmother, who'd raised him and his sister after their parents had died in a car accident.

"Yes, ma'am," he drawled, trying to keep his amusement under wraps. "No worries. I have every intention of stepping up my game with Raina." In fact, he couldn't wait until Raina saw what he had in store for her tonight—shameless, erotic *games* that would have her at his complete mercy.

Probably not the romance and flowers that June was insinuating, but it worked for him and Raina and the affair they'd agreed to.

June moved on to a nearby table to refill other customers' coffee mugs, and Raina laughed lightly and shook her head. "Wow, she's a real firecracker."

"Yes, she is." He added a splash of cream to his own coffee and took a drink. "She's always threatening to find me a nice, sweet, good girl to date and settle down with."

"And why not?" Raina's tone was flippant yet laced with something he could only describe as caustic.

"That's exactly the kind of girl every guy wants to take home to meet the family."

"Not me," he said, suddenly feeling as though he were treading through an emotional mine field of some sort and uncertain as to what might set her off. "I'm not into sweet or good girls." Not since he'd been burned by one. "I like them bad and wicked," he teased.

"Most guys do, until the novelty wears off." She gave him a tight, forced smile, then picked up her menu so he could no longer see her face, but not before he caught a glimpse of hurt in her eyes.

He resisted the urge to pull the menu down and ask her what she meant by the comment, because he'd bet everything he owned that it had come from a place of personal experience. He really wanted to know what had prompted such a sharp reply, but he didn't feel like this was the time or place to push for an answer that clearly was an emotional hot button for her.

He already knew what he wanted for breakfast, so he set aside his menu and waited for Raina to do the same. June came by again, took their orders, refilled their coffee cups, and continued serving her other customers, as well. The phone Raina had left on the table pinged, and she picked it up, punched in a passcode, and read whatever message had come through.

After a moment, she lifted her gaze to him. "I'm sorry. I hate being one of those people who are constantly checking their phones at a restaurant, but I need to answer this email from a customer who has a question about wanting to order something off the website."

"Go right ahead." He leaned back in the booth and drank his coffee while she typed out a response.

Actually, he didn't mind having a couple of minutes to just take in everything about her. Today she'd worn her blonde hair down in soft waves, just like she had at The Players Club, and he could easily remember how those silky strands had felt sliding through his fingers and wrapped around his fist. She wore minimal makeup, her smooth, rosy complexion giving her a girl-next-door kind of appearance that attracted him just as much as the temptress she'd been that first night he'd met her.

Her brow was furrowed in concentration as her fingers tapped across the phone's keyboard and tended to a customer online. Having spent all of yesterday at Sugar and Spice, Logan had seen firsthand just how hard she worked, how dedicated she was to her job, and how serious she was about maintaining a respectable adult toy store that was classy, tastefully decorated, and one that customers found warm, friendly, and inviting.

She had a great connection with her customers, chatting with regular clients and helping new ones with their purchases in a way that made them feel comfortable and at ease. While he was impressed by her obvious success, he was curious to know what had prompted her to open up a business in an industry that provided adult products and erotic toys that ranged from the mild to triple X-rated.

As soon as she sent off her email and set her phone back on the table, he posed the question. "What made you open up an adult boutique?"

She eyed him guardedly, as if debating whether or not to have this discussion with him. It was the same hesitant response she'd had when he'd asked her yesterday where she worked and she'd at first been defensive about her shop. He supposed it was a knee-jerk reaction, because she probably dealt with narrow-minded people who didn't hesitate to criticize or condemn her.

"I'm not judging you, Raina. Remember, I'm the guy with a membership to The Players Club that features more kink and fetish items than your store," he teased good-naturedly and watched as her stiffened shoulders relaxed. "Everyone has a motivating factor in life that leads them down a certain path, whether it's planned or not, and I'm genuinely curious to know what the catalyst was for how you ended up in the business."

"Opening an adult toy store wasn't something I'd planned on doing with my life," she said with a too-casual shrug. "It just happened out of necessity."

He tipped his head, refusing to let it go at such a vague answer. "What was the necessity?" He was no longer just curious…he had this burning need to know everything about her. She fascinated him on so many levels and drew him in ways no woman ever had with her combination of feminine strength, independence, and determination.

Which shocked the hell out of him. At one time in his life, he would have sworn he preferred a more passive, docile type of woman, the kind who would be happy to stay at home and be a wife and mother to their kids. The kind of soft, gentle woman he could take care of and she'd want for nothing because he would provide everything. Just as his father had treated his mother.

Except his *everything* hadn't been enough for the woman he'd thought he'd marry.

He pushed those thoughts from his head and watched as Raina reached out and toyed with her fork, mulling over the question he'd just asked her. Then she gave him a half-hearted smile. "It's actually a pretty depressing story."

The shadows he glimpsed in her gaze made his

chest squeeze tight. "Doesn't matter. I want to hear the story. All of it."

Raina stared at Logan for a long moment, completely swayed by the genuine sincerity in his voice and eyes. She couldn't recall the last man who'd been interested in knowing about her past, about her personally, or beyond the woman who owned an adult novelty store. Not even her fiancé had known the gritty, painful details of her family's dysfunctional dynamics—he'd never asked, and she'd always been too ashamed to bring it up herself.

Looking back, she should have seen that as a huge red flag, but she'd truly wanted to believe that Derek was different. Instead, he'd proved that he was no better than the other man in her life, her father, who'd judged her, condemned her, and ostracized her.

She exhaled a deep breath, and before she changed her mind, she spoke. "The summer after I graduated high school, about two weeks after I turned eighteen, my father kicked me out of the mobile home we lived in at a trailer park with nothing more than the clothes on my back."

"Why?" he asked, looking as appalled as he sounded.

"Because he caught me making out with my boyfriend on the living room couch."

She saw Logan's confusion and went on to explain,

because her father's illness had led up to that dark, horrible night when her entire life had changed. "My dad was bipolar, but he never stayed on his meds for long, so he was constantly going through severe mood swings from extreme depression to these horrible manic episodes that sometimes lasted weeks. The depression was difficult enough to deal with, because when he was going through one of those phases, he was suicidal and would just sleep for days. During those times, it was easier for my mother and me to get him back on his medication, but as soon as he started feeling better, he'd insist he was fine and didn't need any treatment, and the manic-depressive cycle would start all over again."

"Jesus," Logan said and scrubbed a hand along his clenched jaw. "That sounds intense."

"It was." She wrapped her hands around her coffee mug, figuring she'd come this far, why not share the rest of her family's nasty secret? "Those manic phases were awful," she went on, feeling her stomach churn when she thought about the terrifying things her mother, and her, had gone through. "He'd become paranoid and delusional, and it didn't take much to set him off into a rage, which was always focused on me and my mother. He'd yell and throw things, and sometimes it even got physical. We just never knew when he was going to explode, and it was a constant cycle of crazy and madness."

She gave a bitter laugh and shook her head. "Most of the time, he was mean and controlling. He was always accusing my mother of cheating on him and screamed at her that she was a slut and a whore, when I knew for a fact *he* was screwing another woman who lived in the trailer park where we lived. Whatever he was paranoid about, he'd turn it around on my mother and blame *her* for his shitty behavior."

June came up to their table, startling Raina since she was so wrapped up in their conversation and the past. She placed a plate of scrambled eggs, bacon, and fresh fruit in front of Raina and served Logan his chicken-fried steak, eggs, and biscuits and gravy. The man hadn't lied when he said he was ravenous in the mornings after his workouts.

Their waitress topped off their coffees, made sure they had everything they needed, then was gone again.

Logan cut into his crispy fillet and didn't hesitate to ask a personal question. "Why didn't your mother leave your father and take you with her?"

Despite the oppressive memories, Raina was hungry and needed something in her stomach for the long day ahead at the shop. She ate a bite of eggs and answered Logan's question.

"My mother was meek and mild and scared of my father and the threats he made when he was manic."

Now that she was years removed from the situation, her mother's weakness just made her feel sad. "She constantly made excuses for my father's mood swings, and even when I told her about my father screwing the trailer park whore, she didn't react. I think she was honestly relieved that he was getting it elsewhere so he would leave her alone."

"What happened that night with your boyfriend?" he asked as he dug into his biscuits and gravy.

"Well, that night my parents were at church," she said and nearly chuckled at the incredulous look on Logan's face, because that image totally contradicted the man she'd just described. "Yeah, he was a hypocrite and wanted everyone else to believe he was a good Christian. And I suppose, in his deluded, bipolar mind, *he* believed it, too."

"That is *so* fucked up," Logan said and shook his head in disgust.

She laughed at his succinct reply, and the release actually felt good. What also felt good was how relaxed and comfortable he made her feel, even when she was dredging up the most painful events of her life. Talking about it lightened something in her chest, made her breathe easier and feel as if she was gradually setting something horrible free from deep inside of her.

"I'd been dating this guy for a few weeks, and that

night he came over and we started making out like teenagers do," she said and took a bite of melon, the sweet taste counteracting the bitterness to come. "My parents came home early, my father saw the two of us on the couch with Tyler on top of me and his hand under my shirt, and my father went into a rage. Tyler couldn't get out of the house fast enough, and as soon as I stood up, my father slapped me hard across the face and called me a filthy whore. Before I could recover from that assault, he grabbed me by the hair and literally dragged me across the living room and threw me out of the house, yelling loud enough for the whole trailer park to hear that he was disowning his slut of a daughter and I was no longer welcome in his home."

Logan's brows furrowed into a deep frown, his eyes dark with banked anger on her behalf. "And your mother? Where the hell was she when all this happened?"

"She was right there, watching the whole thing play out. She was too afraid to interfere." Yeah, that part still hurt, but Raina also knew if her mother had tried to intervene, she would have paid dearly for it once she was alone with her manic husband. "So, I stayed with a friend that night, and the next day when I knew my father was gone, I went back to talk to my mother. I begged her to leave with me, but she refused. She told me that she'd married him for better or worse, and I was so angry at her for being so timid and submissive, but I refused to stay anywhere near him. She gave me about four hundred dollars she'd squirreled away over the years and told me to go."

Her mother's last words to her were still engraved in her mind and heart. *Go and make a good life for yourself. Better than the one I was able to give you. And find a man who'll treat you well and with respect. Don't settle for anything less.*

She'd desperately tried to find a man who'd met those qualifications, had thought she *had*, but she'd misjudged just how much a man was willing to accept of a woman he wanted to make his wife. And accepting the fact that she made a living selling sex toys was distasteful and offensive and not something he was willing to tolerate on any level.

Swallowing back the tightness in her throat, she finished off her eggs, taking a few extra moments to get her emotions back under control before she continued. "I decided I wanted to start over somewhere bright and sunny and as far away from Nebraska as I could get. I bought a bus ticket to San Diego and got a job at T & A's Bar and Grill as a waitress within a few days of arriving."

"Also fondly known as tits and ass," Logan said, his eyes twinkling with mirth.

She grinned at him, because it was well known that the owners, Ted and Adam, had used the initials of their names as a double entendre and to deliberately compete with that *other* restaurant chain that featured skimpily clad waitresses. "I take it you've been there?"

"Maybe a time or two," he admitted and gave a boyish shrug. "For the beer and wings, of course."

"Yeah, sure." She rolled her eyes. A guy like Logan would undoubtedly enjoy the *visual* aspects of T & A's and the tight, clingy uniforms the girls wore. "I have to admit that the skimpy shorts and super snug, low-cut tank tops were great for getting nice, big tips."

He smirked. "For me, tipping was all about personality and service."

She pointed her fork at him and called him out on his fib. "You are so full of shit."

"Okay, maybe a little." Done with his entire breakfast—where did he put everything in that lean, tight stomach of his?—he pushed his empty plate aside. "If you were my waitress and you bent over in that scanty uniform, I probably would have emptied my entire wallet out on the table."

His gaze, now hot and hungry—and not for food—dropped leisurely to the scoop neckline of her red lace top that showed a discreet amount of cleavage, since she didn't like wearing anything too revealing at the shop. The top wasn't overtly sexy, but she quickly realized her mistake in selecting this particular garment with the stretch knit fabric when she felt her breasts respond to his heated stare.

"Eyes up *here*, mister," she instructed humorously while trying not to squirm in her seat as her lower body tingled, too.

Oh-so-slowly, he lifted his gaze back to hers. "Your nipples are hard," he pointed out shamelessly, making her face flush at his brazen comment. "But I digress. I still want to know about the necessity that led to you opening Sugar and Spice."

She hadn't realized how far she'd veered off from the question he'd originally asked, and just how much she'd revealed about herself in the process. He'd been so easy to talk to, and genuinely interested in knowing about her past, that it was like talking to someone she'd known a long time and trusted.

Trust wasn't something she gave easily, especially to a man, yet she'd given it to Logan as if he was a close confidant and someone she *could* trust.

Not wanting to ponder that realization too deeply, she sat back in the booth and instead rerouted her thoughts to what he wanted to know. "Like I said, the tips at T & A's were decent, but I was just making ends meet, so when one of the waitresses I worked with asked me if I wanted to make some good extra money on the side doing in-home Passion Parties for women, I decided to give it a shot."

One of Logan's dark brows lifted with male interest. "What's a Passion Party?"

"It's basically an in-home, private presentation of sex toys and products for women, but in a fun, party-type atmosphere where girlfriends can let loose, have drinks, play a few sexy games, and check out the merchandise without having to walk into an adult toy store," she said and grinned. "And let me tell you, after they've had a few cocktails and the toys and products are being passed around, it would get wild and crazy, and these women wanted to buy one of everything."

He chuckled. "Sounds like my kind of party."

"Actually, I did some parties for men, usually around Valentine's Day, so they could buy stuff for their wives or girlfriends for gifts. And good Lord, I could easily make a couple of grand in commission in one night because these guys wanted their partners to have great sex and multiple orgasms with them. I was making so much money that I was able to quit working at the restaurant, and after a few years of working at this full-time and saving everything I could, I decided to open Sugar and Spice—the store *and* website."

He looked very impressed. "So, you found your niche."

She nodded. "I did."

Before he could reply, June came by their table. "Can I get either of you anything else? More coffee?" she asked, lifting the fresh pot she held in her hand.

"No, thank you," Raina said, placing a hand on her full stomach.

Logan shook his head. "I think we're good, June. Just the check."

"Got it right here." She pulled a slip of paper from her apron pocket and set it on the table. When Raina automatically reached for the bill, the older woman quickly snatched it away and pushed it toward Logan. "You're stepping up your game, remember?" she said pointedly to him.

"Yes, ma'am," he drawled politely, the corner of his mouth twitching with laughter. "Though I'd *planned* to pay for breakfast," he said in his own defense.

"Good, because that's what you do when you take a nice girl out on a date," June said, then winked at Raina, and Logan didn't argue that they weren't linked *romantically*. "He might be a bit rough around the edges, but if the sweet, caring way he treats his sister and cute little niece is any indication, he does have some redeeming qualities you don't want to overlook."

Raina tried very hard not to laugh at just how serious June was about them as a couple. "I'll keep that in mind."

"Good. I hope to see you again." June picked up

their empty plates and headed back toward the kitchen area of the restaurant.

Logan glanced across the table at her. "Ready to go?"

"Umm, no. Not yet." She quickly checked the time on her phone. They had about fifteen minutes before they had to leave, and she decided since she'd pretty much just given him her life story, and way more than she'd ever intended at that, it was his turn to share. That and she truly wanted to know more about Logan Cruz and the man he'd become.

"I want to know what *your* motivating factor was for joining the military," she said, remembering Dean's comment about him being a former Marine. "Following in family tradition?"

"No." He tipped his head to the side, his expression wry. "Definitely out of necessity."

"Sounds like a familiar theme between the two of us," she teased lightly. "What was the necessity?" she asked, repeating the same question he'd posed to her.

Logan hesitated for a moment, thinking about his response and modifying before he replied. "I needed a steady income to help support my sister, and joining the military ensured that, considering there weren't many high-paying jobs in the small town where we lived in Iowa."

"What about your parents?" she asked, her gaze

filled with a sweet and kind interest.

"They died when I was eight and my sister, Emily, was six," he said, still feeling a pang of sorrow in the vicinity of his chest when he really thought about his parents' death. "Their car was hit by a semitruck on the highway late one night when they were coming home from a dinner date, and it killed both of them instantly."

She sucked in a horrified breath. "Logan...I'm so sorry."

"It was definitely a tough time," he said, unwilling to lie or be macho about such a painful loss. "Both my mother and father were only children, so the only living relative who could take us in was my grandma Betsy, who raised us on her own until she passed away. I was twenty at the time, and my sister had just turned eighteen, and I was making a little over minimum wage working at an auto shop in town. Even at full-time, I barely made enough to support myself, let alone my sister, too. It just made sense to me to join the military and send home my salary to make sure she had everything she needed, and for me to be able to save for the future, too."

That was the short, succinct version, and he'd deliberately left out a whole lot of details that didn't seem necessary to the conversation. Like the fact that he'd been engaged at the time to a very *sweet* girl—his high school sweetheart—and had been adamant about not marrying her until he knew he could give them a financially secure life.

Joining the Marines had been twofold—in helping to provide for his sister and to give Logan the opportunity to save up enough money to make sure that he and Charlotte wouldn't have to scrimp and save and go into debt up to their eyeballs in order to be able to buy a house and start a family. His plan had been smart, strategic, and logical…but he'd *never* expected to have his fiancée and best friend betray him just a few months after he'd been shipped off to Afghanistan.

The incident had changed his whole mindset about love. He'd been angry and bitter, and while he'd eventually buried the pain, he knew it had affected his relationships with women going forward, and especially the ability to trust them enough to allow his emotions to get involved, which hadn't happened since Charlotte. His membership at The Players Club assured that he could keep things light and fun and uncomplicated, so long as he was the one in control and the woman he was with knew exactly what to, and what not to, expect from him. He was all for hot sex and mutual pleasure, but that had been the extent of his involvement with the opposite sex for the past six years.

"How long were you in the military?" Raina asked,

bringing his mind back to the present.

"I spent six years in the military and served four tours of duty during that time, including three of them in Afghanistan." For him, once he'd discovered Charlotte's deceit, there had been nothing left to leave the military for—no fiancée, no future with a wife and family, and it had been much easier to just remain in the service for those six years and keep building up his savings.

"You grew up in Iowa," she mused out loud. "So what made you move out to San Diego once you were out of the Marines?"

"My sister, Emily. She met a guy while I was in the military and ended up marrying him. His name is Pete and he's one of those IT geeks," he joked, though he was truly impressed by his brother-in-law's intelligence. "Supersmart and a wiz at software design and applications, and he was offered a high-level position at a company here in San Diego with a six-figure salary. They moved and loved it here, and since we have no family left in Iowa, it was an easy decision for me to follow them and settle down here, too. Besides, who in their right mind is going to turn down gorgeous beaches, warm weather, and winters without snow?"

"Not me," she said with a laugh. "That's exactly why I moved here, too."

Raina glanced at her phone, and a startled look transformed her features. "Damn, those fifteen minutes went by way too fast. Now we definitely need to get going so I'm not late opening the store."

"Let's go then." He tossed a generous tip onto the table and paid for the bill at the register, then walked with Raina out to his black Chevy Camaro.

His hand automatically went to the small of her back, the tips of his fingers touching her lightly yet in a way that was familiar. When he'd decided to take Raina to breakfast, it had been a deliberate attempt to get to know her better, but he never would have anticipated all the things she'd shared with him about her past. Deeply intimate things that showed her in a whole different light and made him like her even more for being such a fighter and a survivor.

She was fierce and strong and independent, yet it was the glimpses of vulnerability he'd seen when she'd talked about the situation with her mother and father and how she'd been banished from her own home that cracked open a piece of his own heart and made him want to be the kind of man who'd take care of her the way she deserved and never hurt her.

Yeah, that was a huge revelation for him, but he had to admit that the possessive, protective streak wending its way through him had nothing to do with the unknown force stalking her and everything to do with the urge to make her completely and utterly his. The impulse was insane, but there was nothing he could do to change the way he felt.

And quite honestly, he wasn't sure he wanted to, either.

Chapter Seven

A S SOON AS Logan pulled out of the parking lot of the restaurant, his cell phone rang. Raina watched as he checked the caller ID before slipping on his Bluetooth earpiece, then answered the phone.

"Hi, sweetheart," he said in greeting.

The affectionate endearment, along with the warm tone of his voice, startled Raina.

"I know it's been a while since I've seen you," he went on, a smile on his lips as he drove toward her store—one hand on the wheel and the other on the gearshift. "I've been busy with work."

The realization that he was talking to a woman, and so sweetly, too, made her chest tighten in a way she didn't care for at all. She'd never thought about him having another woman in his life that he was intimate with, even if she was a "friends with benefits" perk. Despite having sex at the club and Logan seducing her on her dining table last night, it wasn't like the two of them were exclusive—for all she knew, he could be a player who juggled a few females at a time depending on who and what he was in the mood for. But damn if the slow burn in her belly didn't feel a whole lot like *jealousy*, and she was so *not* the jealous type.

He chuckled softly at something the other woman said. "You're cute, you know that?"

Ugh. Raina shifted uncomfortably in her leather seat and glanced out the window, hating that she felt even a little bit possessive of a man who wasn't even hers. What the hell was up with *that*?

"I know, honey, I miss you, too." He went silent, clearly listening to the woman's response before replying. "Tomorrow for dinner? And you'll even bake me brownies? Wow, you know I can't say no to brownies, or you."

Raina inwardly cringed. Good, God. Could this get any more awkward?

"Yep, I'll be there," he said as he brought the car to a stop at a red light. "And I'll be bringing a friend, too."

Raina's head snapped around so fast she was certain she'd given herself whiplash. She looked at him, horrified at the thought of being a third wheel on his date—his bodyguard services didn't need to extend to his one day off on Sunday, which was her day off at Sugar and Spice, as well, since the store was closed that one day a week.

She shook her head furiously and mouthed the word no, but he merely grinned wickedly at her and continued his conversation through the Bluetooth.

"Yes, she's very nice," he said and returned his attention back to the road when the light turned green, ignoring any silent attempts Raina made to try and make him retract the invitation. "I think you'll like her."

Raina shook her head in frustration. All she could do was wait until he was off the phone to make it *very* clear she wasn't joining him tomorrow evening with whomever was on the other end of the line.

He turned into the back lot for the store, parked the car, then turned off the engine. "Hey, sweetheart, I have to go, but I'll see you soon, okay?"

They said their good-byes, and Logan turned off his phone and removed the earpiece. He glanced at Raina, and there was no mistaking the playful sparkle in his gorgeous green eyes. "That was my five-year-old niece, Hannah. I swear that little girl has me completely wrapped around her finger."

"Your niece? I thought…" Relief trickled through her, and she closed her mouth before the silly words escaped. She wasn't about to tell him what she'd believed and *look* like a jealous woman.

He blinked at her, much too innocently for an incongruous bad boy like him. "You thought what, sugar?"

Oh, he knew exactly where her mind had gone, the rogue. "Doesn't matter." She released her seat belt and grabbed the handle to open her door, but he caught her arm in his big hand and stopped her before she could escape.

"Look at me," he said softly, his hold on her arm loosening, but he didn't let go.

The words weren't a demand but rather a gentle overture she couldn't help but respond to, when she should have asserted her own fortitude and gotten out of the car. Instead, she schooled her expression and glanced back at him…and nearly melted at the sweet, caring look in his gaze.

"Just in case it *does* matter, I just wanted to clarify that I'm not seeing anyone else right now," he said as his thumb stroked along the soft skin of her arm. "Just you, Raina."

God, she hated that it *did* matter, and that was a very, very bad sign when she knew their affair would only last as long as his temporary assignment to protect her. "You don't need to worry about me tomorrow or feel as though you have to entertain me, especially when it's your only day off. I have plenty of things to do to keep me busy."

He frowned at that. "If you have errands to run, I'll take you. I don't want you going anywhere alone."

She shook her head. "No, it's stuff I can do at home with my laptop. You go and have a nice time with your family."

"My niece is excited to meet you," he said oh-so-persuasively. "I can't show up without you."

She arched a brow in a silent *yeah, right* kind of statement.

He chuckled, the sound as warm and coaxing as the fingers stroking her arm. "Okay, so I *could* show up without you, but I really would like it if you came along. You'll be cooped up in your apartment for most of the day, so it'll be a nice break for you. Dinner at my sister's is always low-key and casual, and tomorrow they're barbequing burgers. Nothing fancy."

"Logan—"

"I'm not taking no for an answer," he cut her off in a suddenly stern tone of voice that got her full attention. "And I really don't think you want to challenge me on this."

A frisson of heat spiraled through her, and she cursed how easily her traitorous body responded to the authoritative gleam in his eyes. But that stubborn part of her decided to defy him right back. "Or what?"

He leaned across the console so that he was invading her personal space. So close she could smell the clean, masculine scent of him and see the gold specks in his green eyes. So close there was only a few inches separating their lips.

"Tell me no again, and we'll sort this out in the bedroom tonight with a spanking paddle and see who comes out on top." He smirked, making it very clear who the victor would be in that tussle. "Say yes, and I'll actually *let* you have an orgasm or two tonight. What'll it be, sugar?"

So, he was resorting to sexual blackmail. She bit the inside of her cheek to keep from laughing. He was so cocky, so arrogant. So irresistible, and she had no doubt that he'd withhold her release until she screamed the word *yes*. But her acquiescence wasn't about making sure she got an orgasm tonight… No, it had more to do with the fact that he truly seemed to want her to accompany him to his sister's in a way that had nothing to do with his protective services.

"Fine," she said. "I'll go with you."

"I knew you'd see things my way." He kissed her softly on the lips, much too quickly for her liking, and moved back to his side of the car.

He got out of the vehicle, and she did the same, marveling at this man's skill in manipulating her. She'd agreed to dinner with his family, but she definitely had reservations about it. It wasn't a date, but she knew the million-dollar question *what do you do for a living* would undoubtedly come up during the course of the evening, which was a normal part of a casual conversation with a person you were trying to get to know, but always seemed to put her, and the recipient, in an awkward and uncomfortable situation.

Not that it mattered, considering Raina didn't need anyone's approval for what she did work-wise. Her affair with Logan was short-term, and his sister and brother-in-law would probably never see her again, so what did it really matter what they thought of her?

They headed into Sugar and Spice, and from the moment she unlocked the front door at ten a.m., the store was bustling with a steady stream of customers, which was normal for a Saturday. Raina worked the front counter with Aaron and assisted clients to find whatever they needed, while Callie put together website orders to mail out when the delivery guy arrived later that afternoon. At one point, it was so busy that even Logan, who was standing off to the side watching the store and patrons, was approached by a young woman who'd never been in the shop before and needed help finding a few items.

Instead of informing her that he was the store security as Raina would have expected, he went ahead and escorted the woman throughout the boutique, showing her the items she requested and upselling her on a few other things that intrigued her. He was surprisingly knowledgeable about the various products in the store, as well as engaging and incredibly persuasive. It was an irresistible combination, and clearly Raina wasn't the only one who wasn't immune to his masculine charm.

By the time the woman checked out, she'd spent over three hundred dollars in a surplus of sex toys, lubricants, bondage gear, and even some frilly lingerie.

As soon as she was gone, Raina turned toward Logan, who was standing near the register. "If you ever need another job, you're hired."

He chuckled. "Nah, I like sleeping with the boss too much to give that up." He winked at her, then went back to patrolling the store and keeping an eye on the customers.

Technically, they'd yet to *sleep* together, but his comment still tugged at something deep inside her, made her feel as giddy as a smitten teenager—and put a smile on her face and a sway in her walk for the next few hours.

The afternoon continued on, the store constantly filled with customers, which made time go by quickly. While she was helping a longtime client select a G-spot stimulator for him to use with his wife, Raina heard the back door to the store buzz, indicating that Jared, their delivery guy, had arrived to pick up the website orders.

The store had gotten so busy that Callie had come out to work the floor as well, which she often did once the online packages were ready to go—which was one of the reasons Raina had given Jared a key card to the back door to use during business hours, so that he could start loading the parcels onto his truck until someone came and signed off on the pickup.

Once she finished with her customer, Raina headed to the back of the shop. As she neared, she heard Logan's deep voice as he demanded to know who Jared was and what the hell was he doing in the office and storage area of the store. She quickly slipped behind the heavy curtain separating the main floor from the private area of the boutique and found the two men glaring at one another—with Logan looking far more intimidating with his muscular arms crossed over his broad chest and his assertive, domineering stance. In comparison, the sandy-blonde-haired delivery guy was a few inches shorter, his body not nearly as built or solid as Logan's.

"Is there a problem here?" she asked, stepping up to where the two men were having a Mexican standoff.

"This jerk here seems to think there is," Jared said angrily as he squared his shoulders in his beige knit shirt with the ICS logo, which stood for Independent Courier Service, clearly taking offense to Logan's aggressive third degree. "Who the hell is he, anyways?"

"I'm the *jerk* who's going to toss you out on your ass if you don't answer my questions," Logan growled and took a step closer to Jared, his gaze snapping with animosity.

Raina immediately moved in between the two men and placed a flattened hand against Logan's hard chest. "Logan, stop," she said and was surprised when he actually listened to her, though he never took his narrowed gaze off of Jared. "He's our delivery and courier guy. He's contracted to drop off packages and pick up the website orders that need to be mailed out. He's here three times a week. Tuesdays, Thursdays, and Saturdays."

Jared gave Logan a too-smug smile.

Logan's jaw clenched and he finally glanced at Raina. "He was back here, *alone*, and I didn't see him come through the front door."

"That's because he didn't," she said calmly and explained the system they'd established. "Jared has his own separate key card to the back door because I don't want him traipsing through the store when customers are here, and especially on a busy Saturday. It's easier for him to load and unload packages from back here anyway. He backs up his truck, opens the door, and does everything quickly and efficiently."

Then she turned back to Jared, who was eyeing

Logan with disdain—not that she could blame him after the heated and unexpected confrontation. "I'm sorry for the misunderstanding," she said and gave him a smile to smooth things over. "You can go ahead and get those packages loaded." She waved a hand at the big pile of boxes and padded envelopes stacked against the wall that were filled with website orders.

Jared did as she said. He turned away and got to work, starting with propping open the back door so he could use a dolly to load the parcels in bulk and wheel them out to his truck.

Raina grabbed Logan's arm and attempted to pull him away so he wasn't in Jared's personal space as he worked, but the man remained immovable.

"I'm not going anywhere while he's back here," he stated firmly, and if Raina wasn't mistaken, there was a possessive note to his voice, too, which was ridiculous because there was zero chemistry between her and Jared.

She rolled her eyes but kept her voice low so Jared wouldn't overhear what she said. "Yeah, well, you don't have to stand here breathing down the poor guy's neck like a rabid pit bull while he works, either."

"Fine." Logan moved away, but only as far as the wall that separated the two sections of the store. He still had an unobstructed view of Jared, and as soon as the other man wheeled the handcart out to his truck to load the boxes and was out of earshot, he said, "So, this bozo can come and go as he pleases?"

Raina ignored the name calling and now wished she'd remembered to tell Logan about Jared so the two of them wouldn't have gotten off to a bad start. "During normal business hours, and as long as one of the key management employees is here, yes, he can come in the back door for deliveries and pickups. Once the store is locked down for the night, our exit pass code overrides his, so it's not like Jared can come and troll through the store at midnight when no one is here. And just like the rest of us, his key card has a code that gets logged in every time he uses it."

It was a solid security system, and Logan didn't argue over the setup they had in place. But that didn't mean he wasn't done interrogating her just yet, either. "How long has he been your delivery guy?"

She thought about the time frame of when Jared had started as the new delivery guy. "About three months now."

Logan frowned, and she knew his mind was turning over all sorts of scenarios and possibilities.

Before he could think the worst, she said, "He's a nice guy, and I've never had any issues with him or any reason to believe he's any kind of threat."

She didn't tell Logan that Jared had asked her out a few times—once for drinks, another time for dinner, and just last week for coffee. As nicely as possible, she'd turned down each of his invitations with the excuse that work kept her too busy, and that last time when he'd persisted and he'd told her that surely she could make time for coffee in the morning, she'd decided to tell him that she just wasn't in the frame of mind to date someone right now. It had been a partial truth, the other being that he really wasn't her type, though she hadn't been able to bring herself to say something that might hurt his feelings or make their working relationship strained.

"Hey, Raina," Jared called from just outside the back door. "Everything is loaded. If you want to come out and sign for everything, that would be great."

"Sure, Jared." She gave Logan a *wait here* kind of look, since he could still see the two of them where he was standing, then stepped outside to the back of the open delivery truck.

Jared stopped beside her, his arm brushing hers as he handed her the clipboard with the paperwork attached.

"Who is that guy, anyway?" he asked, annoyance infusing his voice.

Jared's head was very close to hers, so that his breath fluttered her hair against her cheek, and while it made her uncomfortable knowing that Logan was watching them, she assumed that Jared just wanted to be sure that Logan didn't overhear their conversation.

"He's temporary security," she said, signing the pickup order slip.

"Security?" His voice raised a notch. "Is everything okay?"

"Yes, everything is fine," she assured him with a smile. It was one thing for her employees and close friends to be privy to the details about her being stalked, but she wasn't sharing her personal business with anyone outside her trusted circle.

Jared glanced over his shoulder at Logan and gave him an insolent look before meeting Raina's gaze again. "He seems awfully protective of you, considering he's only the hired help."

Raina heard the thread of jealousy in his tone and refused to confirm or deny what Jared was insinuating. "He's just doing his job." She handed back his clipboard. "Have a good weekend, Jared."

"Yeah, you, too," he muttered as she turned and walked away.

Raina stepped back inside the store, closed and locked the door, then faced Logan, who was blocking her way back into the boutique. She nearly laughed when she saw his surly expression. "Wipe that scowl off your face, or you're going to scare away the customers."

He grunted like a caveman. "The only one I wanted to scare off was your *infatuated* delivery guy."

"Infatuated?" she repeated, unable to keep the amusement from her tone.

"Oh, yeah," he drawled. "There was a hell of a lot of posturing going on, and he was just a little too defensive for my liking."

She laughed at his poor reasoning. "Yeah, well, so were *you*."

He closed the distance between them and backed her up against the nearest wall, trapping her there with his hands braced on either side of her arms. He wasn't touching her at all, but she could feel the seductive heat emanating off of him. Her breasts tightened at his nearness, and her entire body melted and liquefied.

He dipped his head and brushed his lips against the side of her neck, just below her ear, in a slow, sensual tease. "I have every reason to make sure he, and any other man who looks your way, knows you're off-limits."

The gruff, territorial note to his voice thrilled her, but she wasn't about to let him know how much she liked that dominant side to his personality and give him that much emotional power over her. "I'm not off-limits to anyone."

"Yeah, you *are*." He lifted his head and stared down at her, his dark green gaze as intoxicating as a shot of hard liquor on an empty stomach. "While we're together, you belong to only *me*, no one else."

She opened her mouth to dispute his statement, but before she could argue, his lips covered hers in a hard, fierce, possessive kiss. The deep, sinful kind that stole her breath and made her instantly wet and aroused. One hand curled around her neck, his thumb pushing her chin up so she couldn't turn away—not that she intended to, despite the fact that she had a store full of customers and employees who could walk in on them at any second.

None of that mattered when she craved the addictive taste of Logan Cruz.

The man kissed like he fucked...down and dirty and without an ounce of shame. He kissed her like they were a couple, like they were exclusive, like she was *his*. Logan's mouth ate at hers, his tongue licked and stroked, and with a soft moan of surrender, she gave him everything he demanded, every hesitation stripped away in favor of the pleasure he offered.

Just when she was on the verge of pulling him into her office so he could bend her over her desk and ease the throbbing ache he'd ignited between her thighs, he lifted his mouth from hers, but not before he bit gently on her plump lower lip, then soothed the sting with a slow lick of his tongue.

"*Mine*," he growled adamantly.

The heady, masculine claim made her shiver—and

what did it say about her that she couldn't even bring herself to refute something she was beginning to want very badly—to belong to him, and no one else?

Chapter Eight

T HE EVENING COULDN'T arrive soon enough for Logan. After a busy Saturday at the store, Raina finally announced at six that she was ready to head home, and Aaron would work until closing time. Since she'd ordered in sandwiches and potato salad from the deli down the street at five, neither one of them were hungry, so stopping for dinner wasn't on the agenda.

Getting Raina alone and naked as soon as possible was.

As he escorted her out the back door to his car, she curiously eyed the black Sugar and Spice shopping bag he held.

"What did you buy when I wasn't paying attention?" she asked and playfully tried to reach for the bag.

He was quick to keep his new purchases out of her reach. "That's for me to know and for you to find out." He waggled his brows at her. "Trust me, we're gonna have a good time tonight, sugar."

She made a cute face at him. "Tease."

Enjoying this flirtatious side to Raina, he walked to the passenger side of the sports car and opened the door for her. "Oh, you have no idea how much of a tease I can be, but you'll find out soon enough."

Her gaze warmed in anticipation of his seductive promise right before she slid into the leather seat and buckled in.

He went around to the driver's side, placed the package behind his chair, and started the car. Heading out of the parking lot, he drove toward Raina's apartment, his mind planning out tonight's activities. After that hot, deep kiss with her in the back of Sugar and Spice and her sassy comment about not being off-limits to anyone, he intended to prove her wrong. By the time he was done with her tonight, her body would belong to him.

And if he was lucky, the rest of her would follow.

There was no denying that he was in way over his head when it came to Raina. She was the extreme opposite of all the submissive women he'd been with since walking away from Charlotte, which had been a deliberate decision on his part in order to keep his encounters with women all about sex, the power of being in control, and physical release. Nothing more.

Being with Raina that first night at The Players Club had been the start. Spending more time with her since had flipped a switch inside of him and made him want something beyond a string of one-night stands. Her confidence had drawn him in, and her fire and passion had consumed him. She was the furthest thing from an easy lay, and the fact that she was a constant challenge, that she wasn't afraid to be defiant and push back and make him work for her surrender, made him so fucking hot and hungry for her. All the damn time.

And he had a strong feeling that this burning need for Raina wasn't going to be sated anytime soon. Surprisingly, he was okay with that. Now it was just a matter of gradually convincing her that this thing between the two of them was more than a temporary itch for them to scratch. That once his stint as her bodyguard was over, they didn't have to go their separate ways.

"Was Dean able to get ahold of the security tapes from my apartment manager?" Raina asked, effectively pulling him from his personal thoughts.

He glanced over at her, surprised to see the hint of vulnerability in her gaze. Despite her brave front, her stalker definitely had her concerned, even though the person had yet to make another move beyond the handcuffs and note. But that didn't mean Raina wasn't being watched, that the person stalking her wasn't just waiting for an opportune moment to strike again.

Logan was determined to make sure nothing happened to her on his watch.

"I talked to Mac about an hour ago," he said as he turned down the street leading to her place. "He told me that they should have the tapes in their office by Monday morning. They'll review them right away and let me know what they come up with."

She released a heavy sigh. "I'll be so glad when this is over. I hate having to constantly look over my shoulder to see if someone is watching me."

At least she didn't complain about him being her permanent shadow and bodyguard, and he took that as a positive sign. "I guess I'm growing on you, huh?" He grinned.

She rolled her eyes, though a smile tugged at the corner of her mouth. "Maybe a little."

Arriving at her apartment building, he parked his car in the guest lot, and they both got out. He grabbed the black shopping bag, came around to Raina's side of the vehicle, and automatically clasped her hand in his. She looked at first startled by his bold move, but she didn't pull away as they walked toward her unit, and he reveled in that small intimacy between them— as well as it being a silent gesture that claimed her as his.

It had been years since he'd held a woman's hand

for the sheer pleasure and affection of it, but having Raina's slender fingers entwined with his just felt *right*. Like they'd been dating for months instead of only knowing each other for days, and he wasn't about to question or analyze why.

As they neared the stairs leading up to the second landing, he felt her stiffen beside him and assumed she was bracing herself to see yet another threat left on her doorstep. But when they arrived, there were no surprises, and she visibly relaxed.

And that's exactly how he wanted Raina to-night...relaxed, pliable, and very, very willing.

He took the key from her and opened the door. While she punched in the code to turn off the security alarm, he did his normal patrol through the entire place. Once he was satisfied that the apartment was fine, he met back up with her in the kitchen area, where he noticed that the handcuffs he'd taken off the door last night were still where he'd left them on the counter. He'd considered using them tonight, especial-ly after insinuating he would, but he'd bought something much better and more suited to his own liking from her shop.

She was leaning against the counter, watching him with a look of pure anticipation as he approached her, the black bag of sexy toys still in his hand since he wanted to be certain she didn't look inside while he'd been checking her apartment. He stopped in front of her, his body less than an inch away from hers, and stared directly into her big, sultry eyes.

"You ready to play my way, sugar?"

Her chin tipped up slightly, and she raised a blonde brow. "*Your* way?"

That subtle show of defiance had his dick swelling in his jeans. "Hard. Rough. And very, *very* dirty."

Lust flickered in her gaze, and she licked her bottom lip and nodded eagerly. "Oh, yeah."

"With me in charge and you obeying my orders and calling me sir?" He was pushing his luck, big-time, but he wanted to make sure Raina knew exactly what she was agreeing to before they got down to business. Because once he had her consent, it gave him the permission he needed to open the door to a whole other level of ecstasy and push her past her personal limits.

"What's it going to be, sugar?" he murmured when she paused longer than he liked. "Plain ol' vanilla sex or trusting me to give you the kind of searing pleasure you've only fantasized about?" *Trust* being the key word, he realized. That's what he wanted from her most of all.

And she didn't hesitate to give it to him.

"I trust you," she whispered.

He was humbled by that precious gift, and elation

flowed through him, but he kept his expression neutral and his mind focused. "The same safe word from The Players Club applies here, as well. If you want me to stop at any point, just say *red*."

"Okay." The word came out breathy and, if Logan wasn't mistaken, *excited*.

God, she was so fucking perfect, and he couldn't wait a second longer to get this party of two started. Grabbing her hand, he led the way into her bedroom. As soon as they walked inside, her queen-sized bed was to the immediate left, and in front of that were double French doors leading out to the same balcony that wrapped around to the dining area. The drapes were open, and he didn't bother closing them since she lived on the second floor and no one could see into her place. Besides, he wanted as much light as possible streaming in so he could see every single inch of her once he had her stripped naked.

The room was decorated in soft shades of purple and green, with whitewash furniture and a matching bed frame with a sturdy headboard and thick slats that would help keep her restrained, when the time came. Setting his black shopping bag on the nightstand, he strolled over to a pretty floral chaise lounge and reclined comfortably on the elongated chair, hands clasped over his stomach, though he was anything but relaxed. The thick bulge already straining against the zipper in his jeans attested to just how aroused he already was.

Raina turned around to face him but didn't move from where he'd left her standing by the bed. The fact that she was awaiting his direction pleased Logan immensely, and he didn't hesitate to mete out his first demand.

"Take off your clothes," he ordered succinctly. "All of them."

She gave him a slow, sensual smile and started with her red lace top. She pulled it over her head and dropped it on the floor, then slipped out of her three-inch-high wedge sandals. Next, she shimmied out of her white, straight-leg jeans and added those to the growing pile, leaving her standing in a sheer, white lace bra and matching thong panties, which did little to conceal the rosy hue of her areolas and the enticing shadows at the V of her thighs.

With her long, wavy blonde hair tousled around her shoulders and her pure white lingerie, she looked like an angel—albeit a naughty, tempting one he was eager to corrupt.

"The bra, sugar," he prompted in a deep, husky drawl.

She reached behind her back, unclasped the hooks, and let the bra slide down her arms to the carpet, proudly displaying a pair of gorgeous, firm breasts with pink, melt-in-his-mouth nipples he couldn't wait to taste again.

He loved her confidence, that she could stand in front of him so openly and without reservation or embarrassment. Her lack of inhibition boded well for the more wicked things he had planned for her tonight.

"Your panties," he said and held out his hand. "Take them off and give them to me."

Arching an incredulous brow at him, she hooked her thumbs into the waistband of the barely there underwear and pushed them down her endlessly long legs and off. Seeing her completely and totally naked for the first time was like a sucker punch to his belly. His mouth went bone dry as he took her all in. She was stunning, with generous curves in all the right places and skin that looked so soft and supple...everywhere.

She tossed the scrap of lace at him, which landed on his chest since he'd been leering at her delectable body rather than paying attention to her throwing arm. "You keep taking my panties," she accused in a tone more teasing than indignant. "This is the third pair. Just how kinky are you?"

The insinuation in her tone made him chuckle. "I'm not a cross-dresser, if that's what you're worried about." He stood up and strolled slowly toward Raina, her panties in his hand.

"I'm so relieved." Amusement laced her voice, but her gaze darkened with awareness as he neared. "So why do you keep stealing them?"

He brought the lace to his nose and inhaled her addicting, musky scent that went straight to his head and made his dick rock hard. "Because they smell like you." Stopping behind her, he leaned in and brushed his lips against her ear. "And when I'm jacking off, like I did last night when I got home after finger fucking you on your dining table, I like to imagine you being there with me, that it's your hand stroking my cock and making me come."

She shivered, and from over her shoulder, Logan watched the tips of her breasts pucker into tight, firm points. Satisfied that his words had the desired effect on her, he tucked her panties into the front pocket of his jeans and placed his hands on the feminine swell of her hips. He moved closer, aligning the ridge of his denim-clad cock against her bare bottom and skimmed his fingers down to her sex, burrowing into the damp folds with a slow, gliding stroke that made her thighs tremble and a needy moan escape her lips.

"I can't wait to see you completely spread open for me, panting and wet and eager," he rasped along the side of her neck before lightly sinking his teeth into the tender skin there to mark her with a love bite, while his finger grazed her taut clit. "*Begging.*"

She whimpered, spread her legs farther apart to give his fingers more access, and rubbed her ass oh-so-temptingly against his erection. She lifted her arm and reached back, twining her fingers in his hair as her head fell back on his broad shoulder.

Enjoying her rising lust, and not done teasing her, he slowly slid his large, warm hands over her soft belly, then up along her rib cage. "I'm dying to taste your pussy, to lap up your sweet juices with my tongue. And just when you think I've wrung every last bit of pleasure out of you, I'm going to make you scream for more."

Reaching her breasts, he lifted them in his palms. He scraped his thumbnails across her rigid nipples, then flicked the sensitive tips with his middle fingers, *hard*.

Her entire body jerked at the jolt of burning sensation he'd just inflicted, and she sucked in a shocked breath. He knew a bit of pain would heighten her response but wanted to make sure he hadn't just surpassed her comfort zone.

"Too much?" he asked, even as he gently rubbed her sore nipples between his fingers to soothe the sting.

"I, uh, just wasn't expecting you to do that," she said breathlessly.

It wasn't a complaint, and that was all he cared about. "Wouldn't want tonight to be predictable," he murmured and dropped his hands back down to his sides before giving her his first command. "Kneel on the bed, facing the wall."

She settled on top of the mattress on her knees as he'd ordered, her spine straight and her hands resting on her thighs in a perfect submissive pose—not that he was going to inform her of that, he thought in amusement. She did exactly as he asked without argument or resistance so far, but there was no denying the sudden tension in her body because she knew it was the start of her giving herself, and her pleasure, over to him. For a woman who liked being on top and in control, it was a huge statement of trust, and it made him all the more determined to show her how good her eventual surrender could feel and be.

He reached into the black bag on the nightstand and withdrew a pair of leather bondage restraints with a long adjustable strap in between to allow a bit of movement between her arms, if needed. "Give me your hands."

Again, she obeyed, lifting her arms to him in the sweetest offering. "I thought you'd use the handcuffs," she said, a half smile on her lips.

He secured one of the leather cuffs, which lined in soft velvet, then started on the other. "For what I have in mind, those metal handcuffs would chafe the tender skin on the insides of your wrists with all your thrashing." Once the restraints were fastened, he splayed his hand on her spine. "Now lay just your upper body down on the mattress, hands above your head and knees spread a foot apart."

As if realizing what a very vulnerable, sexual position that would put her in, she paused for a fraction of a second, exhaled a deep breath, and assumed the pose. He unclipped one of the straps, looped it through the slat in her headboard, then reattached it to the wrist cuff. Another quick adjustment had her arms stretched taut above her head. With her still on her knees, her back sloped downward, her delectable, bare ass was raised nice and high in the air.

Her flushed cheek rested on the floral comforter, her face toward him as he stood next to the bed, a heated awareness glowing in those deep, sultry blue eyes of hers. Logan's dick throbbed like a fierce motherfucker at the erotic sight, and it was all he could do not to rip off his own clothes and take her fast and furiously to slake his building lust. Needing a moment to rein in his hunger, he reached out and ran his fingers through Raina's soft, silky hair, brushing the long strands off her cheek and letting it spill like silk around her head.

Her lips parted on a soft sigh, her body relaxing

only for a handful of seconds before he decided to ramp up the tension and begin the process of pushing her beyond any pleasure she'd ever experienced before. He stroked a hand along her spine, then up the graceful incline leading to the tantalizing globes of her ass, which he had some dirty, naughty plans for, he thought with a wicked grin.

Soon. Very soon.

He slid his fingers between the two halves of her bottom, following the crease until he came in contact with her slick, warm flesh. Her soft nether lips were already swollen with arousal, and he pushed one thick finger into her tight sheath, withdrew, then returned with two digits tunneling deep.

She closed her eyes, shuddered, and moaned.

Time to introduce the next surprise.

From the shopping bag, he pulled out a high-end spanking paddle—a strip of supple leather on one side and luxurious faux fur on the other. Two drastically different textures, depending on whether he wanted to mete out pain or pleasure—or a bit of both.

Using the soft, sensual side, he ran the plush pelt along her back, over her upturned bottom, and down the backs of her legs. He swept the silky material along the inside of her thighs, up one side and down the other, caressing her delicate skin and heightening her senses.

"Where do you keep your toys?" he asked, curious to know what kind of sexy devices she liked to use to enhance her pleasure.

Her lashes fluttered open, and a wary frown marred her brow, which wasn't an emotion he wanted to see. "What...what toys?"

She was clearly hedging, and it earned her a sharp smack of the leather side of the paddle against her ass. She gasped, her eyes widening in shock as she instinctively yanked on her wrist restraints.

"Sugar, you own a sex toy shop," he drawled as he stroked the soft fur over the red splotch forming on her smooth, pale backside. "I know you must have some playthings you like to use for a little added stimulation. You hesitate again, and I will double your punishment. Now, where do you keep your toys?"

She swallowed hard and answered quickly. "In the nightstand drawer."

He slid the drawer open, impressed by the variety of items awaiting him inside. There were a wide array of traditional and more exotic vibrators and dildos in different sizes and shapes, clit stimulators, Ben Wa balls, lubes and lotions, anal toys, and even a few pairs of nipple clamps.

He grinned at her. "This is quite an assortment."

Her cheeks turned a rosy shade of pink. "I need to know what the toys are like in order to effectively sell them."

He felt like a kid in a proverbial candy store, but there was one item that intrigued him more than the others—a vibrating anal plug in a phallic shape that came with a remote—and he picked it up for her to see. "Do you like this toy?"

"I…" She bit her bottom lip, her face flushing crimson red because of what he was forcing her to admit. "Umm…"

He leveled two more firm swats to her ass that made her yelp. "Answer me, sugar."

Her hands curled into the comforter above her head, her arms pulling on the sturdy shackles keeping her in place. "Yes!"

Thwack. This smack landed on her thighs, just below her pussy. "Yes, *what?*"

"Sir," she said on a catch of breath, immediately knowing what he was asking for. "Yes, I like that toy, *sir!*"

He awarded her obedience with a soft stroke of the fur against her searing flesh, and she moaned her gratitude. "Spread your legs wider," he demanded as he prepped the toy with a generous amount of lubrication.

She widened her knees, giving him the access he needed to insert the penis-shaped plug inside of her back entrance. He watched the vibe slide deep, his own cock throbbing at the thought of taking her so intimately. Once the thick device was all the way in to the hilt, she arched, tensed, and whimpered, and a sudden curious possibility dawned on him.

"Has anyone ever fucked you here?" he asked, his voice sounding as though he'd just swallowed crushed glass.

She shook her head, panting. "No…sir." She could barely get the words out.

Playing with a toy and experiencing the real deal were two totally different things—different sensations and different levels of pleasure—and he wanted to be the one to share that with her. "I'm looking forward to being the first." Not tonight, but over time, he planned on having her every way imaginable.

He picked up the remote and switched it on, and the toy inside her vibrated to life with a soft buzzing sound. With a wild groan, she tossed her head back, her hips instinctively jolting against the humming device, her arms thrashing against the cuffs buckled around her wrists. There was no doubt in his mind that he'd just given her a nice little push toward what would eventually be a momentous orgasm, *when* he finally allowed her to climax.

"Oh, God, Logan…I need to come now, *please.*"

"Not yet." He stroked the soft fur along her back, her bottom, and thighs in a mollifying caress, even as his own body pulsed with a furious need of its own. "We still have your punishment to deal with."

"Punishment?" Her voice was as bewildered as the look in her glassy eyes. "What for? I said yes to dinner tomorrow night with your family."

Yes, he had threatened her with a spanking in order to secure her agreement for dinner at his sister's, but there was still the matter of chastising Raina for her defiant behavior the night they'd first met. "This disciplinary action has nothing to do with that. This is about you running out on me at The Players Club."

Her mouth gaped open in disbelief. "You've got to be kidding!"

"Do I look like I'm joking?" He bent closer to her face so she could see the wicked grin that matched his equally shameless mood. "I think five firm swats with the leather side of this paddle should be sufficient penance."

"*Seriously?*"

"Oh, I'm very serious," he assured her and straightened, noting that she hadn't said the safe word, which told him she wasn't completely opposed to feeling the sting of the leather against her tender flesh. "In fact, make it *six* swats. Protest again, and I'll keep raising the amount." He positioned the flat side of the paddle right against her supple bottom. "Count them out loud, sugar."

He swatted her ass, and the word "one" rushed out of her on a sharp gasp. Another landed on her thighs, and another came precariously close to her gleaming sex. In between each consecutive strike, he soothed the flash of heat with the faux fur. A bite of tingling pain, followed by a delicious stroke of pleasure...six times in a row. By the time he was done, she was quivering all over.

Moaning incoherently.

Thrashing uncontrollably.

Begging shamelessly for him to give her the relief she so desperately needed.

She was so fucking gorgeous like this...with her head tipped back and her long blonde hair tousled around her face. Her skin was flushed everywhere, and a light sheen of perspiration gleamed along her spine. Logan was so thick and hard he was surprised he hadn't split open the seam of his jeans.

He touched a palm to her warm bottom, then slid two fingers along her drenched slit and pushed them deep inside her tight, hot, creamy channel. She undulated brazenly against his invading fingers, and he could feel the fluttering vibrations of the anal toy pulsating against her vaginal walls and knew it wouldn't take much to send her skyrocketing into a euphoric orgasm.

Before he triggered her release, he withdrew his

fingers, and she whimpered at the loss and glanced over her shoulder at him, her eyes dilated with lust. "Logan, please…"

"Please what, sugar?" he prompted, wanting to hear her express her desires out loud.

"Please fuck me," she said, the words raw and uninhibited and completely uncensored. "I need you inside me. I need to come so badly."

He was dying for the same thing and done teasing them both. Retrieving a condom from the box he'd bought at the store today, he moved onto the bed and positioned himself behind her. He was still fully dressed, and he impatiently tore open the front of his jeans, pushed the rough material down to his thighs, and quickly sheathed his fierce erection. The second he dragged the head of his cock through her slick folds, he knew this was going to be a fast, rough ride. He pushed into her just an inch, then leaned over her from behind, wrapped her hair in his fist, and drew her head back until his lips brushed her cheek.

"You want to come, sugar?" he whispered hotly against her ear. "Ride my cock and take what you need."

She reared back against him, so hard and quick that he slammed all the way into her and his balls slapped against her pussy. They both groaned at the same time, and she didn't stop there. She pistoned her hips against his, rocking her body back and forth and gyrating her ass in a way that had his shaft thrusting so fucking deep into her, without him doing anything at all.

Despite her restraints, she was greedy and aggressive, and Logan belatedly realized just how much power he'd given her with that challenge to ride him and take what she needed in order to climax. He was suddenly a slave to the demands of her body as *she* fucked *him*, and holy shit, the reverberations from the vibrator inside of her made the friction surrounding his dick even more intense.

She started to pant, her hips grinding hard and frantically against his groin. "Oh, God, *Logan!*"

She started to shudder and cried out, and her internal muscles did a tight, rhythmic give-and-take around his cock as she came, destroying the last of his control with those rippling contractions. Everything in him tensed, and he grabbed on to her hips and took over, driving into her with rough, ruthless strokes, shoving his way deeper with every unbridled thrust until he possessed her completely.

The orgasm that tore through him was huge and overwhelming, a pleasure so all-consuming it blew his mind and left him reeling, more than just physically.

With a low, rough groan, he withdrew from her body, switched off the remote, and gently pressed a hand to the base of her spine and pushed her hips down, so she was lying in a flat, prone position on her stomach. She was boneless and languid, and he let her rest for a few minutes while he went into the adjoining bathroom to take care of the condom and clean up.

When he returned, he easily rolled her over so that she was now on her back, her arms still stretched above her head and cuffed to the headboard, her eyes closed. Her expression was sated, but Logan wasn't done with her yet. He trailed his fingers down her stomach, swirled one digit lazily around her navel, and watched as her nipples puckered tight and hard from his touch.

Her lashes fluttered open and she frowned at him. "You're still dressed."

"Not for long," he promised with a smile.

"I've yet to see you completely naked." She pouted adorably.

"Then let's remedy that right now." His shoes and socks were already off, so he quickly peeled his shirt over his head, tossed it to the floor, then shucked his jeans and briefs.

She sighed appreciatively as her hungry gaze slowly traversed his nude body, taking in his muscular chest, his toned abs, and when she reached his semi-hard cock, she licked her lips in anticipation.

"God, you're so big...everywhere." Her husky

voice sent another shot of heat straight to his dick. "And absolutely gorgeous, too."

He moved up onto the bed between her legs, then pushed her knees wide apart so he could see every inch of her pink, glistening pussy. "So is your cunt," he murmured reverently. "So fucking gorgeous, and damn, I'm dying to taste how sweet you are and eat you up."

She sucked in a breath and tried to move, but he had her right where he wanted her...pinned to the mattress and completely at his mercy. He gave her a wicked grin and touched his lips to the inside of her silky, smooth thigh, slowly nuzzling his way higher with a series of love bites alternated with long, wet laps of his tongue.

She gasped and tensed as he neared her weeping sex, pulling once again on her shackles. "Logan..."

Her hips thrashed, and he wedged his shoulders tighter between her spread thighs, subduing her erratic movements with his size and strength. "Just relax and enjoy yourself, sugar. This is where it's going to get good and messy," he whispered against her flesh and settled in to feast on her for a good long while.

The moment Logan's mouth opened over Raina's pussy and his tongue glided through her slit, her breath caught in her throat. Raina enjoyed good oral sex—*what woman didn't?*—and Logan was a master. He parted her folds with his thumbs, exposing her completely, and proceeded to go down on her in a way that was so freaking hot and erotic she feared he was about to ruin her for all other men.

His mouth was ravenous, his tongue utterly wicked as it licked all the way from her seeping hole to the hard knot of her clit, then sucked ruthlessly on that taut bundle of nerves. He added a soft scrape of his teeth, making that delicate flesh swell and ache before he started the process all over again. Making her moan and beg and grow increasingly delirious for release.

Ignoring her demands, he continued tormenting her with another slow lap of his tongue that ended in a suctioning swirl of heat around her clit. Her hips bucked against his mouth, and a nearly overwhelming wave of desire rippled through her veins. He slid two long fingers inside of her, fucking her slow and deep while grazing that sensitive spot just inside her channel, causing her body to clench around his fingers.

The simmering burn inside of her escalated as he repeatedly ramped her up with his mouth, tongue, and fingers, then cooled her down, until she was arching off the bed, her thighs trembling on either side of his head, and she was alternately cursing him for being so cruel and sobbing for the orgasm he denied her.

"Tell me you want it," he teased in a deep, husky voice, his warm breath caressing her sex as he looked up at her from between her spread legs, his eyes bright with his own searing passion.

"I…I want it," she pleaded raggedly.

With his free hand, he reached up and pinched a nipple hard between his fingers, and she felt the electric jolt of pleasure-pain all the way down to her pussy. "Tell me you *need* it," he rasped, depraved man that he was.

If she weren't so desperate to come, she would have rebelled against his commands, but he held her orgasm in his hand—or his talented mouth, as the case would be—and if she wanted it, she had to give herself over to him. "I need it, *please*," she railed at him.

With a devilish grin, he buried his face between her thighs once again and delivered an open-mouth assault that was all about giving her what she wanted, what she needed. *Finally.* The kiss was intimate, his mouth hungry, with his firm tongue replacing the thrust of his fingers inside her core.

That's all it took for her orgasm to gather, coalesce, and peak, fast and furiously, injecting its way through her system like wildfire. The pleasure was so enormous, so intense, she screamed as sensation upon sensation assailed her, ravaging her body, sizzling across her skin, and stripping away everything but the sublime ecstasy infusing her entire being.

Feeling as though she'd been drugged, she floated

on an incredible plane of bliss. Her skin was warm and damp and flushed, her breathing still erratic, and she was vaguely aware of Logan moving and shifting between her slack legs. She waited for him to remove her cuffs, but instead, he shoved a pillow beneath her ass, propping her hips up higher.

Momentarily confused by the action, she forced her heavy eyelids open and glanced down as he rolled on another condom, surprised to see just how reinvigorated he was. He took his granite-hard cock in his fist and rubbed the head between her drenched, sensitive folds, his jaw clenched with a barely leashed restraint, his nearly black gaze fueled by a carnal lust that made her shiver.

She gasped as he tucked the broad head right up against her entrance and worked his solid erection slowly into her body, which was still tight and tender from their first go-round, despite her recent orgasm. "*Again?*" she managed in an incredulous tone.

"Oh, fuck yeah, *again*. And this time, I'm going to last longer than twenty seconds," he said with a laugh as he shoved a little harder, shocking her system with the burning fullness of him sliding farther inside her. "This time, I'm going to fuck you long and hard and so deep you're going to feel me everywhere. I want your thighs quivering and your pussy sore, sugar, so all day tomorrow you'll think about me and how you're *mine.*"

His gruff, possessive tone aroused her more than she ever could have imagined, as did the avid way he watched his cock disappear completely into her molten center, inch by decadent inch, before he finally moved up over her body and seated himself to the hilt. His deliciously sinful mouth touched down on her breast, his hot, wet tongue licking its way to the center, where he sucked her taut nipple between his lips, then bit down on the stiff peak until her back arched and she cried out from the sharp sting. He repeated the process on her other nipple—lick, suck, bite—and this time he added a slow, deliberate grind of his hips against hers.

She moaned, realizing now why he'd used the pillow beneath her bottom. The upward tilt of her hips provided a deeper penetration for him yet also gave him better access to rub directly against her clit with every thrust inside her. The friction was maddening, mainly because he applied just enough pressure to arouse her but not enough to take the pleasure to the next level—deliberately, she was certain.

He raised his lips from her breast, those dark, wicked eyes staring directly into hers while he pumped his cock slowly in and out of her. "Everything about you is so fucking addicting," he said, his voice gruff with arousal and an honest reverence that softened her in places no man had touched in a very long time. "The way you smell…" He buried his face against her throat and inhaled her scent. "The way you taste…" The tip of his tongue trailed up to her ear, much in the same provocative way he'd licked her pussy not too long ago. "And the way your body responds so perfectly to mine."

He lifted his head again to stare down at her, the rhythm of his thrusts still too slow and lazy for her growing impatience. With every stroke inside of her, the restless need gathering deep within compounded, causing her hips to gyrate against his.

His masculine features were etched with too much control, while she was dying to push her fingers through the dark hair falling around his strong face and rake her nails down his back to mark him in her own way.

She tugged on the leather cuffs in frustration. "Release my hands, Logan."

He shook his head. "No."

She moaned as he tunneled into her again, making good on his promise to fuck her long and hard and deep when she was dying for something fast and furious. "I want to touch you."

"I said *no*." He flicked her nipple with his finger, delivering a stinging punishment for her persistence.

She gasped and glared at him. "Dammit, Logan,

this is so not fair!"

"I never said it would be," he murmured, every inch the bad boy she'd met at The Players Club just a few nights ago. "Another word, and I'll fucking gag you."

Her eyes widened at the threat. "You wouldn't dare!"

He chuckled, the sound dark and devious. "Oh, I would *so* dare, sugar, so do *not* challenge me."

Not willing to test him further, she bit back another sassy retort and instead did the only thing she could, since he'd banned her from speaking without suffering severe consequences. He wasn't the only one who held the power, and she proved as much when she wrapped her legs tight around his waist and began moving against *him*.

He shuddered, his eyes rolling back in his head as he reached even greater depths with his next sliding stroke inside her. "Oh, fuck," he breathed raggedly. "Obviously, I need to restrain your legs, as well."

"No. This feels too good. You feel so deep this way." She licked her bottom lip, needing even *more*. "Fuck me harder."

With a deep-throated growl, he lunged against her, the strength and power of his accelerating thrusts pushing her body up the bed a few inches. Sweat slicked both of them, providing a tantalizing friction at every point of contact—her breasts against his chest, her stomach against his firm abdomen, all the way down to where they were joined. The taut line of his wide shoulders flexed, and the ropes of muscles strained up and down his arms as he fucked her with a barrage of rough, relentless strikes.

Above her, his gaze was dark and dilated, unfocused, and there was one more thing she wanted from him. "Kiss me, Logan," she rasped, needing that connection.

Without hesitation, his mouth slammed down on hers, his lips forcing hers apart and his tongue sinking deep. He fisted his hand in her hair and tilted her head back so he could ravage her mouth in a blistering kiss, the same way he was plundering her body, as though he couldn't get enough of her.

Her heart raced as she reveled in the all-consuming passion enveloping her, at the extreme ecstasy rippling through her veins, at Logan's sheer dominance that with any other man would have had her rebelling but, with him, made her feel so free in places she'd kept a tight rein on for so long.

With that thought, she emptied her mind of everything but the exquisite sensations building inside her and gave herself over to Logan once again with utter abandon, which was becoming increasingly easier to do. Her orgasm milked him, her inner contractions clamped down on his cock, and he tore his mouth from hers as his own climax blasted through him.

He threw his head back as he came, a hoarse cry escaping him as he pounded savagely into her, making good on his promise to leave her sore and aching in the best possible way.

Chapter Nine

RAINA HAD BEEN sleeping by herself for a very long time, so why did waking up in bed the following morning without the warmth of Logan's body wrapped around hers make her suddenly feel so cold and alone? Especially after the incredible night they'd spent together and all the ways he'd branded her with his wicked mouth, his clever hands, and his hot, hard body.

She had only herself to blame for Logan being gone. Once he'd had his fill of her and she'd been limp and sated with pleasure, he'd gotten out of bed and said, "It's getting late and I should go," and she hadn't argued, even knowing if she'd asked him to stay, he would have. Last night, she'd appreciated that he was respecting her space—having hot, mind-blowing sex with him was one thing, but spending the entire night cuddled against him established an intimacy that had no place in their short-term affair.

So, after ensuring that her apartment was locked up tight for the night, he'd left and she'd returned to bed, where she couldn't stop thinking about all the bad, wicked, and wonderful things Logan had done to her.

Those illicit memories flooded her mind, and with a soft groan, she buried her face in her pillow, inhaling the decadent scent of sex and Logan still lingering on the linens. The heady fragrance shot through her system like an arousing drug, making her tingle in very tender places, reminding her just how thorough a lover Logan was. He had no qualms about pushing her beyond those sexual and physical boundaries she'd erected with other men, in ways that made her wild for him. In ways that made her *beg and scream*, which clearly stroked that masculine ego of his.

God, he was the epitome of an alpha male, she thought with an indulgent smile. He was confident, aggressive, and dominant, with a dirty mouth and a penchant for a bit of kink, and Lord help her, she was quickly becoming addicted to the intense pleasure that he always, *eventually*, provided.

She'd never felt so utterly and completely con-sumed with passion for a man, to the point of letting go of her inhibitions, all because she trusted him...with more than just her body, she realized.

There was no way she could let Logan do the things he did to her without trusting him with her emotions, as well, and that startling realization made her heart jolt hard in her chest.

Until she remembered Logan's sister and brother-in-law, who he'd coerced her into having dinner with later that afternoon. A sweet, seemingly conservative family who would probably be shocked, possibly even appalled, to discover exactly what she did for a living.

Yeah, she was being pessimistic, but her past experiences had proven that most people who'd never used erotic toys or sensual accessories to enhance their sexual pleasure viewed her shop as lewd and depraved, rather than a tasteful boutique. It was a crappy stigma she'd learned to live with, and normally she didn't give a damn what other people thought of her. She hated that Logan's sister's opinion of her mattered so much when this visit was nothing more than a one-time deal because Logan didn't want her spending the entire day and night alone, cooped up in the apartment.

Even though she was having second thoughts about meeting his family, she knew if she tried to back out, Logan wouldn't let her. He'd show up at her door, and being the pushy, take-charge guy that he was, he'd no doubt toss her over his shoulder and carry her out to his car if necessary.

Yeah, that was just his style—pure Neanderthal.

The thought made her laugh and lightened her mood, which was exactly what she needed. She rolled out of bed, raised her arms over her head, and stretched all the kinks from her tight, sore muscles. She took a long, lingering shower, washed her hair and shaved her legs, and dressed in a comfy pair of cotton shorts and a tank top. After eating a quick breakfast, she headed into the second bedroom in her apartment, which she'd made into a home office, and worked on the store's payroll, and paid product invoices and checked inventory.

The afternoon went by quickly. Before she realized it, it was nearly time for Logan to pick her up, and she headed back into her bedroom to get ready. Wanting to look as conservative as possible so she fit in, she curled her hair in soft waves, applied a light application of makeup, and chose a modest sundress in a pale green color, with a flared skirt and pearled buttons fastening up the front to cover any cleavage. Just as she finished slipping her feet into a flat pair of white leather sandals, the doorbell rang.

She glanced into the peephole to make sure it was Logan, then opened the door, her traitorous heart fluttering like an infatuated school girl at the gorgeous sight of him. He was wearing a navy blue USMC T-shirt that outlined the breadth of his wide shoulders and solid, muscular chest and a pair of dark jeans that molded to his lean hips, thighs, and the soft, substantial bulge beneath the button fly.

A shameless heat trickled through her, and she bit the corner of her lip and raised her gaze back to his. "Hey," she said breathlessly.

A lazy smile curved his sensual mouth. "Hey, yourself," he murmured as he strolled into her apartment, the light, woodsy scent of his cologne adding to the other arousing chaos swirling deep inside of her.

She closed the door after him, and he turned around, his hooded gaze now taking in *her* attire. His heated stare made her feel stripped naked, and her breasts responded to his visual caress, beading tight in her lace bra and against the cotton material of her dress. He licked his lips hungrily, and knowing just how good his mouth felt sucking on her breasts, she went weak in the knees.

She pointed a direct finger at him. "Stop looking at me like that."

He smirked. "I can't help it. You look so pretty and sweet in that prim and proper dress, when I know just how wild and wanton you *really* are." He moved toward her, slow and purposeful. "I think I might need to dishevel you a bit before we go."

Her pulse leapt with a startling clash of panic and excitement. She shook her head and flattened her palm on his chest, *trying* to resist him. "No." As much as her body would enjoy the quickie he was suggesting, she wasn't about to arrive at his sister's post-sex, looking tousled and completely debauched.

He tipped his head and arched a commanding brow. "*No?*" he questioned in that deep, dominant tone of his, the one he used in the bedroom with her. The one he expected her to obey. The one that made her wet, because she secretly loved how confident and assertive this man was when it came to the sexy games they played.

She lifted her chin with enough disobedience to get him hot and bothered, too. "No," she repeated, both defiant and firm.

The heat and amusement flashing in his narrowed eyes was an arousing combination. He jammed his hands on his hips, when Raina suspected he wanted to put them all over *her*, instead. "Then be prepared to make up for your insubordination tonight when I bring you back home."

The sexy threat started a slow burn deep inside of her, and she added a bit of fuel to the wildfire he'd just ignited between them. "Anything you want, *sir*," she promised oh-so-sweetly, knowing whatever kind of kink he had in mind would ultimately be her pleasure.

A low, toe-curling growl rumbled up from his chest, and as much as Raina knew that Logan wanted to pounce and assert that bad-boy authority of his just to prove he could, he refrained from doing so and respected her request. "Let's go, before I change my mind and fuck you right here, up against the nearest wall, until you come all over my cock and you smell like *me*."

She shivered, and her pussy clenched from the mental images his statement created. God, the man had a way with words that completely disarmed her, and if making a good impression on his family wasn't so important to her, she would have let him shove her up against the nearest wall and claim her so primitively.

Not wanting to risk pushing him to that snapping point, she retrieved her purse and ushered them out the door before they were late. It was a beautiful, warm sunny day out and very quiet around her apartment building, and it felt quite normal walking out to Logan's vehicle with him—not as her bodyguard but as a couple. It was at moments like this when Raina began to think that everything was fine, that whoever had left the handcuffs on her door had done so as a stupid prank.

Nothing else had happened in the three days that had passed, no intimidating gifts or notes or anything remotely threatening, and she was fairly certain that the building tape would reveal some kid playing what he considered a practical joke.

And once that was established, there would be no need to see Logan on a daily basis any longer.

The thought caused a pang in her chest, one she was quick to shove away as Logan opened the passenger-side door of his black Camaro for her. She slid into the leather seat, buckled her belt, and waited for him to join her behind the wheel.

Once they were on their way, he glanced over at her and asked, "How was your day today?"

"Boring," she said honestly. "I worked on business-related stuff."

He sent her one of his patented wicked looks. "You know what they say about all work and no play…"

She laughed. "When you own your own business, the work is never ending. Besides, I've been playing way more than usual because of *you*."

He arched a dark brow. "Are you complaining?"

"Not at all," she replied with a shake of her head. "You're fun to play with." *In oh-so-many ways.*

"So are you, sugar," he drawled.

The low timbre of his voice made her shift restlessly in her seat. "How was your day?" she asked, curious to know how he'd spent his Sunday morning and afternoon.

"Busy." He merged onto the freeway and accelerated his speed. "I did some kickboxing this morning, then came home and got some yard work done. Mowing, edging, trimming."

She was surprised to learn he did his own land-scaping. "You don't have a gardener?"

"No. I actually enjoy doing it all myself," he said with a shrug. "Ever since I was a kid, it was my job to do all the yard work for my grandma, and I'm particular about how I like the lawn to look. I like being out in the sun, and I like to sweat."

The thought of him shirtless, his tanned chest glistening with perspiration and his muscles flexing as he mowed or trimmed, was a very heady image. It wasn't often that a guy actually enjoyed physical labor, embraced it even, and she loved that about Logan.

"After the yard was done, I spent a few hours at a friend's house," he went on. "Sawyer and I work together, and he recently bought a '69 Pontiac GTO that was having engine problems, and I've been promising to help him out. I love working security, but I miss working under the hood of a car, and I wasn't about to pass up the opportunity to tinker on a classic muscle car."

She smiled at his enthusiasm, remembering him telling her he'd worked at an auto shop for a few years before he went into the military. He continued talking about the GTO and spoke in engine lingo that she didn't understand, and because it was a topic that he was clearly passionate about, she let him talk while she listened and asked questions that he enjoyed answering.

Twenty minutes later, he exited the freeway in the city of La Jolla, an affluent area just outside of San Diego. As they drove through an upscale neighborhood, Raina felt the nerves she'd tried so hard to keep at bay start to swirl in her stomach. The anticipation of meeting the people who meant the most in Logan's life. The foolish need for them to like her. And that awful fear of ultimately being judged and rejected.

By the time Logan parked his car in front of a beautiful ranch-style home and turned off the engine, her unease must have shown on her face because he reached across the console, grabbed her hand, and gave it a squeeze.

"Are you okay?" he asked, his deep voice full of concern. "I lost you somewhere along the ride, and you suddenly look like you'd rather be anywhere but here."

She pasted on a bright smile, refusing to blurt out all her stupid insecurities. "I'm fine."

Clearly seeing through the fib, he turned his body toward hers and brushed his fingertips along her temple. "I think there's way too much going on in this head of yours," he said, much too perceptively as he lowered his mouth to hers. "So how about I help you refocus on something more pleasurable so you can relax?"

She knew what was coming, and she was helpless to resist him. Especially when he slid his hand around to the nape of her neck and gently gripped her hair so he could tip her head at just the right angle for his lips to seal softly, warmly, against hers. One touch, and she was completely and utterly his.

She had little willpower when it came to Logan and what he wanted.

Her lips automatically parted on a low moan, and he swept his tongue inside, tangling seductively with hers. The kiss was slow and deep and hot. Teasing and tempting her. Making her melt and draining the tension from her body and replacing it with the delicious, arousing thrum of pleasure.

Too soon, he lifted his head, his heavy-lidded gaze capturing hers. "Much better," he murmured huskily. "Though I'd be happy to provide an orgasm to *really* make you feel relaxed."

His free hand slid beneath the hem of her dress, his fingers skimming up the inside of her thigh. She caught his wrist before he touched her and she no longer cared that they were parked right outside his sister's house. "*Red*," she whispered weakly, somehow managing to summon the one word guaranteed to make him stop.

He chuckled and withdrew his hand. "Well played, sugar. Well played. That's twice that you've cock blocked me in less than an hour. We'll continue this little power play later this evening."

She had no doubt they would.

He got out of the car and came around to her side of the Camaro and opened the door for her. She stepped out, inhaled a deep breath, and smoothed her hand down the front of her dress to make sure she looked presentable. They started up the pathway leading to the front of the house, and Logan grabbed her hand and threaded their fingers together, startling her with the intimate, and possessive, gesture.

She pulled her hand back, but he held tight. "Logan, I don't want them to think—"

"That I actually *like* you?" he interrupted, his tone wry.

She sighed. "I don't want to give them the wrong impression, that we're dating or a couple."

They reached the front door, and Logan rang the doorbell, her hand still secured in his. He glanced at her and grinned. "I like the idea of dating you, so how about we make this our first official date."

Before she could argue, the door swung open, and a pretty young woman with dark brown hair and friendly green eyes was standing there, with a mini five-year-old version of her peering up at the two of them with bright, curious eyes.

He finally released her hand to give the woman a warm hug and ruffle the child's silky-looking hair. "How are my two favorite girls doing?"

"We're good," Emily said at the same time Hannah hopped from foot to foot and said exuberantly, "I've been waiting for you all day, Uncle Logan!"

"Well, I'm here now," he said with a grin. He turned back toward Raina, introducing the two as his sister, Emily, and his adorable niece, Hannah, before doing the same with her. "And this is—"

"Your girlfriend," Emily said before Logan could finish, a mischievous look in his sister's eyes as she extended her hand in greeting.

Startled by the assumption, Raina quickly shook her head as they clasped hands. "Oh, no, I'm not his—"

Emily held up a hand to interrupt her. "Too late. Your cover has already been blown," she said, laughter threading her voice. "Hannah already tattled on the two of you. She was looking out the front window when you drove up and parked outside. She informed me that the two of you were kissing, then holding hands on your way up to the house. In her words, 'Uncle Logan has a girlfriend.'"

Raina felt a mortified flush sweep across her cheeks.

"My mommy and daddy kiss a lot, too," Hannah

said, adorable and precocious as only a five-year-old could be. "They told me that's what two people do when they really like each other."

Logan swooped down and picked up his niece, holding her in the crook of his strong arm so they were face-to-face. "Anybody ever tell you that you're a smarty pants?"

"You do!" she said and giggled, clearly enamored of her uncle Logan.

"That's because it's true." He tapped her affectionately on the nose.

"She's *way* too smart and inquisitive for her own good," Emily said, glancing at Raina with a welcoming and amicable smile. "And it's very nice to meet you, Raina."

Raina smiled back, already liking Emily and her easygoing personality. "Nice to meet you, too."

They stepped inside the beautifully decorated home, and Logan set Hannah back down on her feet. He sniffed the air and gave his niece a wide-eyed look that was animated for her benefit. "Do I smell brownies?"

"I made them for you! I told you I would!" She jumped around and clapped her hands in delight. "Come and have one."

Hannah grabbed Logan's hand and pulled him toward the kitchen. He glanced over his shoulder and gave Raina an impish grin so unlike the hot, sexy, alpha guy he was with her. "She clearly has her uncle Logan wrapped around her finger, doesn't she?"

"Oh, yeah," Emily agreed as they followed behind. "The feeling is mutual between those two."

They walked into the kitchen just in time to see Logan biting into one of the brownies from the plate on the counter as he handed one to Hannah.

The little girl shook her head, her expression wistful as she watched him eat the chocolate confection. "Mommy said I can't have one until after dinner."

He crouched down to her level. "Yeah, well, this will be our little secret, okay?" he said in a low voice.

Hannah grinned as she took the offered brownie. "Okay," she whispered, then took a big bite.

"Logan Whitney Cruz!" Emily scolded her brother in a playful tone. "You are such a bad influence on your niece."

Raina glanced at him with wide-eyed humor upon hearing the feminine moniker. "Your middle name is seriously *Whitney*?"

He groaned and scowled at his sister. "Are you trying to emasculate me in front of Raina?"

"I think she should know *all* about you," Emily said, clearly enjoying ribbing her older brother. "The good, the bad, *and* the ugly."

Logan exhaled a long-suffering sigh and explained.

"My parents gave me the middle name of Whitney, after my great-great-grandfather."

Raina bit the inside of her cheek to keep from laughing. "It's very…*pretty*. Do the guys you work with know about this lovely middle name of yours?"

He narrowed his gaze at her. "No, and I'd like to keep it that way."

"I'll *try* not to let it slip," Raina said. She definitely liked having something on Logan to tease him about later.

Emily laughed at the flirtatious banter between them. "Looks like my brother has met his match," she said gleefully, then looped her arm through Raina's to give it an affectionate squeeze. "I think you and I are going to get along just fine."

"Uncle Logan!" Hannah said, tired of the grown-up conversation and wanting his attention again. "Daddy bought me a ring toss game for the backyard. Wanna play with me?"

"Sure." He gave the little girl an indulgent smile as she tucked her small hand in his much larger one.

"Here's drinks for you two, and an extra beer for Pete, who's out back," Emily said of her husband as she retrieved two bottles of beer for the men and handed them to Logan, then gave her daughter a juice box. "Raina and I will join you in a few minutes."

Hannah, pleased to have her uncle all to herself,

pulled him toward the sliding glass door leading to the patio and backyard.

Once they were gone, Emily turned back to Raina and asked, "Would you like a glass of Chardonnay?"

Raina nodded, feeling very comfortable and relaxed with Emily. "That sounds lovely. Thank you."

Emily set a chilled bottle of white wine on the granite counter and grabbed two crystal glasses from the cupboard, filling them both before handing one to Raina.

"I wanted to apologize if I embarrassed you earlier about the whole girlfriend thing," Emily said, her tone suddenly serious and sincere. "You're the first woman Logan has brought around since Charlotte, and it's so nice to finally see him dating again and happy."

There was so much in Emily's comment that grabbed her attention—like Logan dating again, and being happy, and the fact that she was the first woman he'd brought to meet his sister since… "Charlotte?" she asked, the name a question in and of itself.

"His ex-fiancée," Emily automatically said as she took a drink of her wine, just as an *oh crap* look spread across her face when she realized her blunder. "Logan hasn't told you about Charlotte?"

Raina shook her head and took a sip of her own Chardonnay. "No."

"Oh, shit," the other woman muttered beneath her

breath, looking miserable. "I'm *so* sorry. Me and my big mouth. I just assumed that he would have mentioned her—"

Raina reached out and gently grabbed Emily's arm, not wanting the topic to make things awkward between the two of them. "Hey, don't worry about it. It's really not a big deal." It wasn't like she and Logan were in that kind of relationship, where they exchanged painful stories about exes and the emotional upheaval that came with those breakups. Lord knew she had her own baggage that had made her cautious and wary when it came to opening herself up to a man again.

Yet yesterday morning at breakfast, she'd told Logan about her awful family life, her father's manic episodes and abuse, and how she'd been alone and on her own since the age of eighteen. She'd revealed deeply emotional things with him that she'd never even shared with her own ex-fiancé, and he'd listened without judgment, and it had felt so damn good to finally get all that old crap out in the open with someone she was coming to trust. It had been a huge first step for her, and she was beginning to wonder if maybe, possibly, there really could be more between her and Logan. Yet he hadn't opened up to her.

"I'm sure Logan will tell you about Charlotte at some point," Emily went on, still trying to smooth things over. "But it's really not my story to tell."

"I understand." And Raina truly did. Whatever was in Logan's past, she didn't want the details from his sister. But she was definitely curious about Charlotte and what had happened between her and Logan.

"Come on, let's go sit out on the patio," Emily said, clearly eager to leave their current conversation behind.

Raina followed her out the sliding glass door to a large, beautifully landscaped backyard and a custom-designed patio, complete with a comfortable seating area, a fire pit, and built-in outdoor grill area. Between the exclusive area where they lived and the gorgeous house, Emily's husband obviously did *very* well as a software designer. As soon as they came outside, a nice-looking man who was playing ring toss with Hannah and Logan came up to the patio area, wearing a collared shirt and a pair of khaki shorts. He was tall and lean, with short blond hair and wire-rimmed glasses, looking very much like the IT geek Logan had called him.

He came up to Raina, hand outstretched in greeting and a warm smile on his lips. "Hi, Raina. I'm Pete."

"Nice to meet you," she said, liking him just as much as she liked Emily. They were both so friendly and welcoming, and she was suddenly glad she'd come. "Thank you for having me."

"It's our pleasure." He hooked a finger toward the kitchen. "I'm going to get Logan and me another beer. You two want anything?"

Emily raised her glass for him to see. "We have our wine, so we're all good."

Raina and Emily spent the next hour sitting on the patio, watching as Logan and Pete played endless games of ring toss with Hannah—and being competitive with one another on the side. Their conversation was light, casual, and easy, with Emily talking about how much she loved being a stay-at-home mom, but now that Hannah was in kindergarten and she had more free time on her hands, she was starting to dabble in graphic design, which was her major in college, and was selling custom stationary to friends.

Raina deliberately kept the steady stream of conversation focused on Emily, which was much easier and safer than her having to answer curious questions, and after two glasses of wine, she was feeling very comfortable and relaxed.

A squeal of laughter had Raina glancing out to the yard, where Logan was chasing Hannah and demanding in a gruff voice that she give him the red plastic ring she'd stolen from him. He let the child evade his grasp time and again, and the little girl giggled in pure delight each time she managed to escape his clutches.

"I swear, Hannah has boundless energy, and Logan has the patience of a saint when it comes to her." Emily finished off her second glass of wine and smiled as she watched her brother interact with her daughter. "Then again, he loves kids and has always wanted a big family of his own."

The comment was very matter-of-fact, but something in Raina's chest tightened in a combination of regret and envy when she thought of Logan with a wife and kids. She could easily see that he'd be a wonderful dad, and any woman would be incredibly lucky to have him for a husband—he was sexy as hell, chivalrous and caring, and inherently protective.

But for as much as she and Logan were currently enjoying a hot, provocative affair, she had the feeling that Logan was a man with very traditional values when it came to having a wife and family. And she was the furthest thing from traditional a woman could get.

Logan finally caught Hannah and hefted her over his broad shoulders, carrying her up to the patio like a sack of potatoes while she giggled and squirmed, loving every minute of her uncle's attention. Pete followed behind, grinning and shaking his head at the sight.

"Anybody getting hungry?" Pete asked when they reached Emily and Raina.

"Me, me, me," Hannah said as soon as Logan put

her down. "I want a burger!"

Emily laughed and stood up. "Raina and I will go and get all the fixings ready and on the table while you guys prep the grill and barbeque the burgers."

Back in the kitchen, Emily provided Raina with a cutting board so she could slice tomatoes while she took a platter of meat patties out to her husband to grill. When she returned, the two of them worked companionably while Emily rinsed lettuce leaves.

"Logan mentioned that the two of you met through Noble and Associates," Emily said casually as she placed the cleaned leaves into a colander. "But he never did say what you did for work."

Raina's stomach tightened and she exhaled a deep breath. The moment of truth had arrived. She'd honestly begun to think that maybe Logan had already told his sister what she did for a living, but obviously not, and she prayed that Emily's easygoing personality meant she was equally open-minded, because she truly liked her. A lot.

"I own a shop down in Old Town called Sugar and Spice," Raina said, being deliberately vague in order to see if Emily was familiar with the name.

The other woman tipped her head curiously. "Is that a bakery?"

A small, strangled gust of laughter escaped Raina. Clearly, Emily didn't venture down to Old Town often. "Umm, no. It's a boutique that sells adult toys and products."

"Oh…" She frowned for a moment, processing Raina's words, then as if finally realizing what she was alluding to, a shocked look transformed her features, and her cheeks turned a bright shade of red. "*Oh.*" Then she dropped her voice to a low whisper. "You mean you own a *porn shop*?"

Raina inwardly cringed at the derogatory and demeaning label but managed to remain outwardly calm as she finished cutting the last tomato, then glanced out the kitchen window to make sure that Hannah was still outside before she answered Emily. The last thing she wanted was for the little girl to overhear this conversation.

"No, it's not a porn shop," she said as nicely as possible as she washed her hands and dried them on a terry towel, her gaze on Emily. "It's an upscale boutique that sells sensual products to customers who enjoy using sex toys, or those who want to find other ways to spice up their sex lives and have fun in the bedroom."

"I'm sorry," Emily said with a shake of her head, her tone apologetic though her entire demeanor remained stiff and guarded, in a very prim and proper way. "I didn't mean to offend you."

"It's okay. Really." Raina managed a smile as she

picked up the plate of tomatoes, quickly changing the subject. "Would you like these on the table?"

Emily nodded and glanced away. "Yes, thank you."

In awkward silence, Raina helped Emily put the rest of the side dishes and condiments on the table. She couldn't deny that she was disappointed with the other woman's reaction, but it certainly wasn't the first time Raina's business venture had changed a person's view of her and made them see her in a scandalous light or perceived her as a slut or whore because she sold sex toys for a living.

It was a stereotype she encountered all the time, but she'd hoped that Emily would be different, that maybe she'd even be intrigued by the store and novelty items. Curiosity was so much easier to handle than aversion or distaste, and this situation was made even more uncomfortable by the fact that it was now a big elephant in the room between her and Emily, who was probably trying to come to terms with the fact that her brother was dating a woman with loose morals.

Been there, done that, and she had no desire to repeat that kind of scrutiny, judgment, and criticism. She knew from painful experience that if a man's family had an issue with her business, it would become a huge source of conflict between her and Logan at some point down the road. His family was extremely important to him, and what she did for a living obviously didn't sit well with the one person he loved and respected the most, his sister, Emily.

The reminder helped to shore up her emotional defenses and put things back into proper perspective, that this *thing* between them was all about great sex and erotic pleasures until his job was done, which would be soon.

With the table set, the guys brought in the grilled burgers, and everyone sat at the table and began passing around the various dishes to put items on their plates. Emily sat across from Raina and Logan; the other woman hadn't been able to look Raina in the eyes since their discussion in the kitchen.

Logan and Pete talked about work-related stories as they ate their dinner, and halfway through, when there was a lull in the conversation, Pete glanced at Raina and asked conversationally, "So, what do you do for a living?"

Emily shot her husband a startled look, and dread settled in Raina's stomach like a lump of lead. She was also more than a little annoyed that Logan hadn't told either of them about Sugar and Spice, which would have been so much easier than her being subjected to this torture *twice*.

Across the table, Emily's expression reflected pure panic that a sordid topic was about to be brought up in front of her five-year-old daughter, who was eating her hamburger and at the moment was blissfully unaware of anything else going on around her. To Raina's right, Pete stared at her expectantly, waiting for a reply, completely unaware of his wife's distress.

"I…um…" Raina couldn't bring herself to say the words.

"Raina owns a boutique in Old Town that sells adult toys and novelty items," Logan provided oh-so-helpfully, keeping his reply G-rated for his niece's ears.

"*Logan*," Emily hissed through gritted teeth.

He frowned at his sister's reprimand. "What?" he asked, oblivious that he'd said anything wrong.

Hannah glanced up at Emily, her gaze inquisitive. "Mommy, what are adult toys?" she asked guilelessly.

"*That's* what," Emily retorted, glaring at her brother.

"My bad," he said, though the corner of his mouth twitched with a grin.

Even Pete looked amused by his daughter's innocent question.

Emily, not so much.

Hannah tugged on Emily's shirt to get her attention again. "Mommy, I want to know what adult toys are."

"They're toys that adults play with, sweetie," she said, giving her daughter a bright, and forced, smile. "Just like you have your Barbie Dolls and My Little

Ponies."

Hannah's eyes widened with excitement. "Can *I* play with *your* toys?"

Emily exhaled a deep, calming breath. "No, honey, they're for adults only."

"That's not fair!" Hannah crossed her arms over her chest and pouted, big-time. "I let you play with *my* toys!"

Logan dared to chuckle, which earned him another dark, pointed look from his sister.

"This is so *not* funny," Emily said, clearly flustered and distressed, and Raina's stomach cramped even more.

"It is kind of amusing, Em," Pete said lightly, trying to diffuse the situation and his wife's exaggerated response. "It's not as though Hannah *gets it*, and I think you're making a bigger deal of this than it is."

Hating that she was the cause of the dissention that had settled over the dinner table, Raina sought to alleviate the strained atmosphere and hopefully distract the little girl in the process. "Hey, Hannah, I would love one of those brownies you made. Do you think you can bring a plate of them to the table for dessert?"

The child's eyes lit up at the mention of chocolate. "I can do that!" Hannah scrambled off her chair and scampered to the kitchen.

That easily, the little girl forgot all about wanting to

play with her mother's adult toys. Unfortunately, the awkward tension at the table with Emily lingered far longer.

Chapter Ten

I F LOGAN THOUGHT things were strained and cool at the dinner table after his sister's uptight reaction to Raina's business, the atmosphere in his vehicle on the drive home was even frostier, and he wasn't referring to the weather but, rather, Raina's disposition. She'd become quiet and withdrawn after that conversation, and while he felt bad that Raina had to endure his sister's backlash, he certainly didn't want the situation affecting them as a couple.

And yeah, he wanted that with Raina. Them as a couple. A relationship based on more than just hot, mutually satisfying sex. He knew things were moving at lightning speed with her, faster than any woman since Charlotte, but after seeing her interact with his family—Emily's meltdown at dinner notwithstanding—he realized that he was finally ready to settle into a real relationship with one special woman.

And he wanted that woman to be Raina. She was complex and independent. Strong yet vulnerable. Kind and compassionate despite the horrible things she'd endured growing up with a severely bipolar father and a mother who didn't have the backbone to get herself, and her daughter, out of such a volatile situation. Instead, Raina had picked up the pieces of her shattered life when her father had disowned her, and carved out a successful life for herself, all on her own, despite the odds.

And sexually, she was every fantasy he'd ever imagined, he thought with a private smile as he merged onto the freeway toward her apartment. A bit of a challenge, definitely, yet uninhibited in her desire and needs. She gave herself over to him beautifully, not in weak-willed submission like other women he'd been with at The Players Club but the kind of ultimate surrender that was so damn fearless and without reservation. The kind of passion that was fueled by emotion and trust.

And he'd bet everything he owned that if he pointed out those things to her, she'd deny every single one. Despite their strong connection, when it came to the two of them beyond their sexual escapades, he sensed she was holding something back that made her wary and cautious with him.

And tonight's incident hadn't helped matters in

that regard.

He cast a glance at Raina sitting in the passenger seat, her gaze turned toward the window and her hands clasped much too demurely in her lap. She was silent and too damn stiff and closed off, which was something he intended to change. He wasn't about to end their evening without discussing what was on her mind.

Reaching across the console, he placed his hand on her thigh, giving it a gentle squeeze. "You're awfully quiet. Are you still thinking about the whole fiasco at the dinner table with my sister?"

She turned her head toward him, her eyes flaring with annoyance. "How can I *not* think about it? Why didn't you tell them ahead of time what I did for a living so they at least knew in advance?"

He shrugged, kept his eyes on the road, and told her the truth. "It never came up in conversation, and I didn't think it was an issue."

"Obviously, it's a *big* issue with your sister," she pointed out. "She was completely scandalized. She thinks I sell hard-core porn. She probably thinks I'm a porn star, too."

Her words were laced with sarcasm, but there was no mistaking the deeper level of hurt reflecting in her tone. "She definitely overreacted," he agreed. "And I'm betting she regrets the way she handled things—"

"Don't worry about it," Raina said, abruptly cutting him off. "I'm used to being judged based on my business. I was just hoping…" Her tone grew soft, then as if realizing she'd been about to reveal something deeper and more emotional, she shook her head of the thought. "Never mind. It doesn't matter."

She tried to feign indifference, but he knew better. She might be able to brush things off when a stranger labeled her in a derogatory way, but she was truly upset, as if Emily's acceptance of her had been important, which he completely understood.

"Emily can be overly dramatic sometimes." He hated that he was making excuses for his sister's behavior when she clearly needed to apologize for her lack of finesse, but he also wanted Raina to know how *he* felt about the situation, which was vastly different from Emily. "I don't care about my sister being a prude about your shop. That's her problem, not mine."

"You *should* care," she said, her tone defensive. "I've learned that what a family thinks of me eventually matters to the person I'm dating. A lot."

There was so much more to her comment, a bad experience he was betting had shaped her way of thinking. "Care to elaborate on that?"

She crossed her arms over her chest and shook her head. "I'd rather not."

Okay. Her words didn't invite further conversation on the subject. He thought about pushing her to talk to him, *to let him in*, but decided that whatever had happened in her past needed to be told when she was ready, and on her terms. Forcing a discussion wasn't his style. "Maybe some other time," he said, leaving the dialogue open-ended. "I'll talk to Emily about what happened tonight."

"No." Raina's reply was immediate and adamant. "Please don't make this any more awkward than it already is. Just let it go." When he hesitated, she reached over and grabbed his arm. "*Promise me* you won't say anything."

It was a difficult promise for Logan to make, because it was equally important to him that Emily accepted Raina and everything about her. But ultimately, he had to respect Raina's request. For now. "Okay. I won't say anything to her."

She exhaled a stream of breath and seemed to relax. "Thank you."

He returned both hands to the wheel as he navigated the Camaro off the freeway and onto side streets. The interior of the car grew quiet again, until Raina's soft voice broke the silence.

"Who is Charlotte?"

The unexpected question hit Logan like a punch to the stomach, mostly because the inquiry had come straight out of left field. "How do you know about Charlotte?" he asked, even though he knew the culprit was most likely Emily.

"Your sister mentioned her, before things went south at the dinner table," she said, her tone lighter than it had been since the incident she spoke of. "She said she was your ex-fiancée but didn't give me details about what happened between the two of you, and you don't have to, either, if you'd rather not talk about her," she rushed to assure him.

At some point, he would have told Raina about Charlotte, and he figured now was as good a time as any if it helped give her a better sense of the boy he'd been and the man he'd become. "Charlotte and I were high school sweethearts. She was quiet and demure and naive in a way that made me want to take care of her."

"In other words, a good girl?" she asked.

"Yeah, that's what I believed," he said, unable to deny the truth as he briefly glanced from the road to Raina. "I was so infatuated with her. She was everything I thought I wanted when it came to a wife and my future. I always knew we'd get married someday, but I really wanted to be financially stable and have a decent amount of money in the bank before we did get married so we could afford a house of our own and have a family without struggling to pay our bills."

"Not many young people think like that," Raina commented, sounding impressed. "They usually just jump into marriage, have babies, and live paycheck to paycheck."

"Exactly what I *didn't* want," he stated emphatically. "And working at the auto shop full-time at minimum wage wasn't conducive to supporting a wife and family."

"And taking care of your sister," she added softly, remembering what he'd told her at breakfast yesterday morning.

He nodded in agreement. "Yeah, that, too."

"That's a lot of responsibility for someone so young."

"My sister is the only family I have, and I really thought Charlotte was *the one*, and even though she was upset when I signed up for the military and left for Afghanistan without marrying her, I knew I was doing the right thing. I put an engagement ring on her finger as a promise to marry her. I moved her into my small apartment to take care of it while I was gone, and sent money home for both her and my sister to live on, and put the rest in the bank for the future."

He turned into the parking lot to Raina's complex and brought the car to a stop in a space near her unit. She made no move to leave the vehicle, clearly wanting all the details, and so he glanced her way and gave them to her.

"I kept in touch with Charlotte the best I could during that first tour of duty, but as the months went on, her letters and packages grew further apart, and whenever I did get the chance to call her, she always had the excuse that she was busy working or taking on extra hours, but I could feel the distance growing between us, and I think in my gut I knew something was up, even when she swore everything was fine."

He stretched his arm across the back of her seat, touching her silky hair and running the soft strands between his fingers. "After a little over nine months in the military, I was granted my first leave. I wanted to surprise my sister and Charlotte, so I flew back home, and at six a.m. on a Saturday morning, I let myself into my apartment and went to the bedroom, only to find Charlotte in *my bed* with my best friend, Tommy. They were sleeping, but the way they were naked and wrapped around each other told me clearly just how intimate things were."

She sucked in a breath, her eyes widening in shock. "What did you do?"

His fingers found their way to the nape of her neck, and he absently stroked his thumb along that soft patch of skin. "I was sick to my stomach, and I wanted to scream and yell at the both of them and wreak some havoc and flip some tables, but instead, I remained oddly calm and controlled, thanks to military training, and propped my backside up against the wall and waited for one or both of them to wake up."

"Who was the first?" she asked, her voice low but undeniably curious.

"Charlotte. But she didn't see me right away and started to go down on Tommy to wake him up. Surprisingly, by that time I was more disgusted with the both of them than angry, and just when she had him good and hard and Tommy was about to come, I cleared my throat to let them know they had a visitor." He grinned deviously.

She bit her bottom lip, trying to contain the mirth sparkling in her eyes. "You didn't!"

"Yeah, I did, and Charlotte screeched and nearly bit off his dick when she jerked away from him, and Tommy couldn't get out of that bed fast enough, except the sheet got tangled around his legs, and he fell flat on his face with his bare ass up in the air." Their *oh shit* reaction had been comical, and Logan had to admit that having the upper hand in that moment had been so satisfying and had gone a long way in soothing his bruised ego.

She burst out laughing. "Serves them both right. Did you beat the crap out of your friend?"

"I wanted to. Badly," he admitted. "But I knew it wouldn't change anything, and I didn't need to end up in jail for assault while I was still in the military. Besides, Charlotte was just as much at fault, and I figured they could have one another."

He shook his head, still unable to believe her gall. "What gets me the most is that she didn't even have the decency to tell me about her and Tommy. She was living in my apartment, using the money I sent her to live off of, and shacking up with my best friend while I was trying to make a better future for the two of us. And you want to know the excuse she gave me as to why she was screwing my best friend? *She was fucking lonely*," he said bitterly. "As if me being in a godforsaken war-torn foreign country for nine hellish months wasn't lonely, depressing, and miserable for me every goddamn day."

She touched her hand to his cheek, her gaze glimmering with compassion and understanding. "Charlotte didn't deserve a man like you."

"She did me a favor," he said, meaning it as he rubbed his jaw against her palm, her caring warmth suffusing deep into his bones. "In the long run, I'm not sure I would have been happy with someone so passive and weak and insecure."

The pad of her thumb skimmed across his bottom lip, the beginnings of a naughty grin lifting the corners of her mouth. "No more good girls for you, huh?"

"Nope. I much prefer them bad." He caught her

wrist and sank his teeth into the heel of her hand and heard her breath catch in the shadowy car. "Very, *very* bad," he murmured shamelessly.

His voice had dropped to a husky pitch as heated desire replaced those past memories of Charlotte's deceit that no longer felt like a stab to the heart. Yeah, he'd done the right thing by walking away, because now he'd found a woman who was so perfect for him, in so many ways. And he'd do whatever it took to make sure she gave them a chance beyond his temporary assignment as her bodyguard.

She leaned across the console, her breath warm and damp in his ear as she whispered, "Wanna be bad with me?"

Oh, fuck yeah. His dick swelled, totally on board with that idea, as well. "That depends." He moved his head back so he could look into her eyes, which were already eating him up with all sorts of sinful promises. "Are you going to try and cock block me again?"

She laughed lightly and dropped her hand to stroke the hard length of his erection beneath the fly of his jeans, teasing him with her seductive caress. "If I do, you can spank me."

He grinned. God, he loved this delicious power play between them, that sassy mouth of hers, and her attempt to be in control when he knew, in the end, he was going to be the one to make *her* scream, beg, and melt for him. "I've got something far dirtier and kinkier in mind tonight than spanking."

There was no mistaking the flash of excitement that brightened her eyes. "Then why are we sitting in your car when we could be in my bedroom doing those dirty, kinky things?"

Why, indeed.

This was what they were good at and where he could connect with Raina not only physically but intimately and emotionally, as well. And tonight, by the time he was done with her, he'd make sure that she was marked and claimed and there was no question in her mind that she was completely and utterly his.

DIRTY, KINKY, MESSY, filthy, with a whole lot of improper fucking thrown in for good measure...Raina wanted it all with Logan Cruz.

Desire suffused her entire body as she leaned back against the wall by the closed front door, impatiently waiting while Logan did his normal sweep of her apartment. Within a few minutes, he finished his job and was walking toward her, his stride purposeful, as was the blazing-hot gleam in his eyes that told her she was in for another wild, intense, and pleasurable ride with him tonight.

She pressed her hands to the wall behind her, her

heart beating heavily in anticipation as he closed the distance between them, his toned, muscled body moving with lithe grace—a gorgeous body that was nothing short of a woman's sensual playground. *Her* playground for tonight, she thought, already feeling the deep, clenching need he so effortlessly ignited in her.

"Everything good?" she asked breathlessly.

His green eyes glittered with wicked intent. "Yeah, but it's about to get a whole lot better."

As soon as he reached her, he plunged both of his hands into her loose hair. His fingers gripped the strands tight against her scalp, and he tipped her head back, holding her in place as his head descended. Her lips parted on a soft gasp, and he seized her mouth in a deep, tongue-tangling, scorching kiss that stripped away every thought in her mind except for the lust and hunger vibrating between them.

This was exactly what she needed. Mindless pleasure and a blissful distraction from everything that had happened earlier at his sister's, along with the hurt and disappointment she wanted to forget. Making sure all those vulnerable emotions were locked away, she focused on the here and now and this delicious man who was all hers for the night.

With a soft moan against his lips, she pulled his T-shirt from his jeans and pushed her hands beneath the hem until she touched his firm abdomen. She quickly skimmed her hands higher, dragging the soft cotton with her, and he broke the kiss so she could strip the shirt over his head and toss it aside. Then he was back again, his mouth devouring hers, his hips grinding his confined erection seductively against her pelvis.

Reaching her hands between them, she unbuttoned his jeans, unzipped them, and skimmed her palms into the waistband of his pants and briefs, then around to his backside. She pushed both down off his hips and slid her hands over his firm ass, then lower, until his jeans and underwear were bunched around his thighs and she felt his rigid shaft spring free.

She brought her hands back around and wrapped her fingers around his cock, feeling the solid length of him in her hand for the very first time. He was thick and hard, his flesh like heated velvet over a rod of steel. She squeezed and stroked him in a tight fist, and with a deep growl, Logan pulled his mouth from hers and slowly unraveled his fingers from her hair as his gaze met hers, burning with the need to dominate.

"Get on your knees and suck my cock," he rasped darkly.

His command made her wet and her stomach flutter. She wanted to obey that order, and he obviously *expected* her to, but she planned to exert her own bit of power over him while she still could, because she knew with him, having any kind of upper hand wouldn't last long. "There is nothing I'd love to do more than get on my knees and suck your cock," she said, skimming her tongue across her bottom lip in anticipation. "But I have one condition for you."

He raised a dark, insolent brow, clearly not used to negotiating anything. "And what condition is that?"

She leaned forward and licked a path up to his ear, tasting the salt on his skin. "Flatten both of your palms on the wall and keep them there while I suck you off," she said as she circled the pad of her thumb around the head of his shaft. "If you touch me with your hands in any way to try and dictate how this blow job is going to go, I'll stop, and you can finish the job yourself."

He chuckled, a deep rumble in his chest. "You're so fucking bossy."

"My mouth. My rules." She gave him a sassy grin. "No hands allowed. Think you can manage that?"

"Oh, hell yeah," he drawled, his gaze glimmering much too confidently as he splayed his hands on the wall on either side of her head. "No touching. My hands won't ever leave this spot on the wall."

"I've yet to get my mouth on *you*, and I've got a lot of ground to cover and don't want any distractions," she said, placing a hot, damp kiss on his neck, then lightly biting a patch of skin, making him groan, long and low, and shift restlessly on his feet. "I want to lick you, taste you, and make you burn."

"Already there, sugar," he said huskily.

Determined to enjoy this small amount of control that was hers for a while, she leisurely kissed her way down his neck to his shoulder, then across his wide chest. She grazed her teeth across his nipple and flicked it with her tongue.

On a sharp inhale, Logan's hips jerked reflexively, rocking his erection into the clasp of her hand.

Smiling, she continued her journey downward, loving the way the chiseled muscles of his abdomen flexed and tightened against the hot, open-mouthed press of her lips against his taut flesh. She used her tongue to trace and count each one of his eight-pack abs and followed the tempting, well-defined line of muscle that led from his hip down to his groin until she was finally on her knees in front of him.

She circled the base of his shaft with her fingers and took him between her lips, sucking on just the tip of his cock before leisurely running her hot, slick tongue all the way down the thick length of him, then back up. She swirled her tongue around the swollen head and drew on him like a sweet lollipop, tormenting him a bit, over and over, until his breathing grew labored.

"Stop teasing," he growled in aroused frustration.

"But it's so much fun," she murmured, taking just a few inches of him into her wet, warm mouth. Especially since he couldn't touch her, which gave her all the delicious power of seducing him.

She elicited another suctioning pull on the head, and he swore beneath his breath.

"*Deeper*," he ordered and didn't give her a choice.

His hips pushed forward, slow but steady, and even when she tried to pull back to release his cock from her lips, he kept advancing, until the back of her head pressed against the wall and the tip of his shaft hit the back of her throat. He was buried to the hilt in her mouth, and feeling as though she might choke, she panicked and splayed her hands on his thighs, prepared to push him away.

"Relax your jaw and breathe through your nose, sugar," he commanded gently, giving her time to adjust to the fact that she was now at his mercy. "Let me fuck your mouth."

He was asking, not demanding, and she let her tense body and mouth go slack around his length.

"Good girl," he murmured and started moving, withdrawing slowly until her lips were wrapped around the head of his cock, then thrusting deep again.

He slid in and out of her mouth, groaning and shuddering with pure bliss. He took what he wanted, what he needed, all without breaking her rule about using his hands. She cast a glance up at him and found him watching her, his eyes dark and scorching hot with desire. He was breathing hard, his chest rising and falling as he filled her mouth once more and she eagerly took all of him.

"Jesus, Raina." His hands curled into fists against the wall, as if he had to resist the urge to plow his fingers into her hair. "Watching my cock slide in and out of your mouth, and feeling your throat tighten around the head when you swallow around the tip, is hotter than fuck."

She moaned at his dirty words and realized that, while he might be the one to control the pace, she alone had the ability to push him over the edge. That heady power was all hers, and she embraced it. When his hips pumped forward again, she tasted the salty drops of pre-cum on her tongue and felt the vein running along the underside of his shaft pulse. She sucked him hard on the retreat, grazing him lightly with her teeth all the way back up to the ridge of his crown while raking her fingernails down his muscled thighs.

His eyes rolled back, and a hiss of pleasure left his lips. "I'm so fucking close," he rasped, sounding like a desperate man. "If you don't want this, push me away."

She wanted everything. All of him. Her own arousal thrummed through her, making her ache, and very, very wet. She doubled her efforts to get him off, and it wasn't long before his big body was shuddering, his hips jerking erratically. His abs rippled and his thighs flexed beneath her hands as he shoved deep one last time, lodging himself against the back of her throat. With a hoarse shout, he came, and she swallowed every last bit of the creamy fluid.

He pulled out of her mouth, and she looked up at Logan. His forehead was pressed against the wall, his face was etched with ecstasy, and he was struggling to catch his breath. Pleased with herself, she gradually kissed her way up the length of his body, until she was standing on her own shaky legs in front of him. He lifted his head and opened his eyes, his gaze replete with satisfaction. "*Goddamn*," he breathed, and managed a hot, sexy smile. "That was pretty fucking epic."

She laughed, knowing he'd gotten off on switching their roles, so that he was the one with all the authority. "Who ended up being the bossy one after all?" she accused lightheartedly. "Do you *always* have to be in charge, one way or another?"

"Yeah, pretty much," he drawled huskily. "But I didn't break your rules."

She caressed her hands across his chest and brushed her thumbs over his erect nipples. "I have to stop underestimating you."

"Yes, you do." A much-too-smug look passed across his features. "*Always* expect the unexpected, sugar."

He curved a big hand around the back of her neck, tangled his fingers in her hair, and pulled her close while dipping his head toward hers. He kissed her, deeply and thoroughly, definitely *unexpected* and very much a shock after what she'd just done to him. He obviously didn't care, and the voracious way his mouth ate at hers and the carnal sweep of his tongue tasting *everything* was so freakin' hot she moaned and melted against him. The ache between her thighs turned into a burning need, and she was so tempted to wrap her legs around his waist so she could rub up against him and take her own release.

He finally ended the kiss, a knowing smile on his lips. "I still have big plans for you tonight," he said as he took a step back and let his hands fall to his sides, his entire demeanor shifting to the dominant man she found so hard to resist. "Get in the bedroom and get undressed. Now."

Chapter Eleven

RAINA COULDN'T GET to her bedroom fast enough, and Logan was right behind her when she turned on the bedside lamp. He'd pulled up his pants and zipped them up but left the top button undone, his chest still bare, making him look even more ridiculously gorgeous and sexy than he already was.

"If you make me ask you to get undressed again, it'll be followed up with a few swats of my paddle to your ass," he said, snapping her attention back to him and the specific order he'd given her.

He'd left the spanking paddle he'd used on her the previous evening in her nightstand, along with the rest of her naughty toys, so his threat wasn't an idle one. Wanting to skip any kind of punishment tonight, she pulled off her sandals and began unbuttoning the front of her dress while he went into the adjoining bathroom. When he returned, he was holding a clean towel, and she was down to her underwear.

His gaze raked the length of her like a physical caress, and her nipples tightened into hard peaks, which he noticed. "I suppose you want my panties for your collection?"

He gave her a slow, wicked grin. "Absolutely, sugar."

She pushed them off her hips and down her legs, then tossed him the scrap of satin and lace. He caught them in his free hand and rubbed his thumb over the cotton panel, his eyes darkening and his nostrils flaring, as if he'd just inhaled her scent.

"They're fucking soaked with your juices."

His gruff voice and his unrefined words made her even wetter. "Sucking you off turned me on."

"Then let's do something about that." He arranged the towel across her chaise lounge, then turned back to look at her. "Just in case things get messy," he explained with both heat and amusement in his tone as he motioned to the chair. "Make yourself comfortable."

Sitting down on the elongated chair, she leaned back into the slight incline and stretched her legs over the curved midpoint of the lounge, designed to relieve stress on her lower back and enhance maximum relaxation. She'd always enjoyed reading on this chaise after a long day at work, and it now suddenly reminded her of one of those contoured sex chairs she'd seen online. And judging by the purely sinful way Logan was eyeing her as he approached the foot of the chair, he was thinking and imagining the same thing.

"Spread your legs so I can lie between those gorgeous thighs and see just how wet you are," he said as he knelt on the floor down by her feet.

Realizing how exposed she was about to be, she ignored the surge of heat low her in belly and parted her thighs. As soon as they opened and made room for him in between, he moved his upper body up the sloped end of the chaise and draped her calves over his shoulders so that he was just a few inches away from her pussy. Since she was still sitting up, she could see his face just as clearly, and there was no mistaking the flare of lust burning in his gaze.

He slid his hands along the outsides of her thighs and splayed them on her hipbones, then lightly skimmed his thumbs along the grooves that led down to her sex, teasing her with the promise of a more provocative caress. "I'm dying to fuck you with my tongue, but I want to watch you touch yourself more. Show me what gets you off," he murmured, rubbing the stubble on his jaw against the soft, tender skin of her inner thigh.

A shudder stole through her, and she bit her bottom lip, deciding if he wanted a peep show, she was going to give him one that shattered that control of his. Placing both hands on her breasts, she kneaded them in her palms and plucked at the taut nipples with her fingers, watching as Logan's gaze darkened with hunger as he turned his head and lightly bit her thigh, then soothed the sting with his tongue.

Raina inhaled a sharp breath, feeling that searing, wet lick all the way up to her pussy, which clenched and tingled with the unbearable need to be touched and stroked.

A bad-boy smile curved the corner of his sensual mouth as he looked up at her with heavy-lidded eyes. "You tease me, I'll tease you," he said in a dark, rumbling voice as he blew a hot stream of breath across her damp folds that made her hips buck toward his mouth, which he quickly moved away.

She'd never known a man to be so damn arrogant and charming at the same time, but Logan managed to pull it off with undeniable confidence. Giving him what he wanted, she trailed the fingers of one hand down her belly and between her legs. She lightly traced them along the smooth, waxed outer lips of her pussy and lower, where she was so wet and slick with desire. She spread the moisture over her clit, felt the huff of Logan's hot breath against her skin, and moaned softly.

She closed her eyes and rolled her head back on the chaise, needing so much *more*. "Logan..." she whispered huskily.

"Tell me what you want," he demanded.

She was so empty deep inside... "Your fingers."

He brought his hand around from her hip and grazed his palm up her thigh. "Where?"

"In me," she breathed, and just in case he needed more specific instructions, she gave them to him. "Fuck me with your fingers."

She gasped as he thrust two fingers inside of her, filling her all the way and taking her pleasure to another level as he pumped them in and out of her channel. The tips of his fingers dragged against that sweet spot along the inner walls of her vagina, and with each slow, deep thrust, she worked her clit more quickly, until she was arching her hips into the delicious friction and the heels of her feet dug into Logan's muscled back as she climbed closer and closer to release.

Right at the precipice, he grasped her wrist with his free hand and pulled her fingers away.

"*Noooo*," she protested, unable to believe he'd stop her right on the edge.

"*Mine*," he growled, and she wasn't sure if he meant her or the orgasm, then she no longer cared as he replaced her fingers with an open-mouthed, suctioning kiss on her sensitive clit that shot her straight back into the stratosphere of orgasmic bliss.

She moaned helplessly as he licked her in long, firm, rhythmic strokes and used his tongue in wicked, depraved ways designed solely to make her come. And she did. Explosively. A hoarse cry escaped her as she twisted her fingers in his hair, her entire body shuddering and writhing beneath the onslaught of his mouth and the rich, decadent pleasure coursing through her veins.

It seemed like forever before she floated back down from that delightful cloud of ecstasy. Her body felt limp, her entire being languid. Sighing, she released her hold on Logan's hair as she glanced down at him, still between her thighs. "That was…"

"Fucking epic?" he supplied with a shameless grin as he licked the taste of her from his lips.

She managed to laugh at his presumptuous comeback. "Pretty damn close."

He raised a challenging brow as he moved off the chaise and stood up. "I guess next time I'll have to try harder."

She couldn't even imagine.

Her gaze was drawn to the stiff length of his erection straining against the confines of his jeans, and she smiled invitingly, her body still sprawled on the chair. "Speaking of *harder*, do you want to take care of that hard-on you're sporting?" The release he'd given her had been fantastic, but she loved the feel of him when he was stroking deep inside her.

"Oh, I plan to. That orgasm was all about getting you soft and pliable," he said as he made a little circular motion with his finger. "Turn around and straddle the lounge chair."

Yes, her body was definitely soft and pliable, so very relaxed that she was willing to do whatever he asked. While she turned around and sat astride the chaise, she heard him open the bedside drawer. She cast a curious glance over her shoulder and watched him walk back toward her with her velvet sleep mask in his hand.

"You're going to blindfold me?" she asked.

"Yep." Without even asking her permission, he slipped the mask over her eyes and adjusted the band around her head. "I want all your other senses at peak levels."

She shivered as his voice caressed her ear, her sense of hearing already heightened as she listened to him return to the drawer, rummage through the contents, then return and set some items on the table next to the chair. The sound of his zipper, along with the rustling of fabric, made her picture in her mind him shimmying out of those jeans and kicking them aside, leaving him magnificently naked.

"Rest your hands on the headrest, and arch your back so your ass is pushed back for me," he said as he swept the length of her hair over one shoulder, then smoothed his flattened palm down her curved spine to the flare of her hips and bottom.

"Fucking perfect," he murmured as he straddled the seat right behind her, the thick length of his shaft nestling hot and hard in the crack of her ass.

She felt him shift and reach over to the table, and a moment later, she heard the cap of a bottle open, and the scent of vanilla and coconut permeated the air. She recognized the fragrance as a massage oil that was also a lubricant, and after a few seconds, his slick hands touched down on her shoulders and began to knead the taut muscles there.

She couldn't stop the sensual moan that bubbled out of her. She dropped her head forward and luxuriated in the large hands and skilled fingers working out the last of the day's tension.

"You're very good at this," she murmured as his hands glided around to her breasts and gave them attention, too. Squeezing the mounds and plucking at her stiff nipples.

"I'm good at a lot of things," he said, a smile in his voice.

Oh, yes, he was, she thought, as his adept, slippery fingers trailed down her belly and dipped oh-so-slowly between the folds of her pussy with just enough pressure and friction to reignite a pulsing need between her legs before his touch fell away.

She let out a sound of disappointment, and he chuckled behind her.

"So impatient," he chastised lightly.

She heard him uncap the oil again, but instead of putting it in his hands, she felt it drizzle along her back, making her shiver. His hands rubbed and massaged the oil into her skin, except for a trail of liquid gradually trickling its way down the center of her spine, then in between her spread legs. When he was done kneading her muscles, he brought his hands back up to her neck, then applied a firm pressure with his thumbs and followed that last slick trail of oil down each notch in her vertebrae and lower, until he was pressing firmly against her untried back entrance. She tensed, and he leaned against her back and nuzzled his mouth against the side of her neck.

"I want to fuck you here," he rasped as he pushed his oiled thumb inches inside her. "Will you let me?"

He was *asking*, not demanding, and she swallowed hard as her mind contemplated the intimacy of giving herself over to Logan so completely. No other man had ever pushed her *this* far or even come close to tapping into those dark desires she craved. Then again, she'd never trusted a man to give her what she needed without him making her feel cheap or sleazy for wanting something so forbidden.

But there was something she knew about Logan with certainty. He respected her body, and he respected *her*, and that made all the difference in her decision to allow him to fulfill a fantasy she'd always secretly harbored.

"Yes," she whispered.

He released a gust of breath against her shoulder, as if he'd been holding it as he waited for her answer. "I'm going to make you feel so fucking good," he promised, and she believed him.

Trusted him. With her body and a part of her heart that she knew would take a long time to recover once their affair was over. She pushed those thoughts out of her head, grateful for the velvet mask covering her eyes that concealed deeper emotions she knew would be reflected in her gaze. Without her sight, all she had to do was feel and enjoy what Logan was about to do to her.

"I found this dual vibrator and clit stimulator in your drawer, and I'm very intrigued. You have the best toys," Logan teased as he leaned toward the table next to their chair—probably to grab the object that had fascinated him. "Lift up just a bit so I can put it in you."

Knowing exactly what that particular toy was capable of, her heart raced wildly in her chest as he wrapped an arm around her waist, helping her to stand a few inches. She felt the blunt head of the silicone dildo glide through her folds before Logan pushed the phallic shaft all the way into her body. When he set her back down, it felt as though she was straddling a man's cock—just as he no doubt intended. But it was the soft oral sex simulator nestling against her pussy that already had her pulse fluttering in anticipation, and he'd yet to turn the toy on.

He added more oil to her backside and used his fingers to prep her. She felt him stroke his cock, lubricating himself before he positioned the slick head right against that tight ring of muscle, then gradually pushed into her. She tensed, moaning at the bite of pain as he breached her, the slow burn as he slowly filled her. He pressed his palm against the small of her back, making her arch for him and allowing him deeper access until he was buried to the hilt.

He was much larger and thicker than the plug he'd used on her the night before, and she gasped at the shock of it, at the thrill of him claiming her *there*. Her fingers dug into the headrest of the chaise to keep her grounded when her body wanted to instinctively struggle against the sensation of being so dominated.

He aligned his chest against her back, surrounding her in his heat, his strength. "You feel so damn good.

So tight and hot and mine."

The possessive growl of his voice, his words, and the slow rocking motion of his body that produced shallow, teasing thrusts made her desperate for more. "Logan, I need …"

"I know what you need, sugar," he murmured huskily. "Three times the pleasure."

She sucked in a sharp, startled breath as he turned on the toy and *three times the pleasure* took on a whole new meaning. The shaft inside of her began vibrating against her G-spot, and the soft synthetic mouth positioned over her sex started constricting against her pussy. The suctioning, licking sensation had her trembling, panting, as did the way Logan was now sliding in and out of her ass, each stroke longer, harder, deeper than the one before.

The hand wrapped around her waist locked tighter against her hips so each grinding thrust consumed her with overwhelming pleasure. His own heavy breathing rushed hotly over the skin of her neck, and she managed to push back against him just as he pumped back into her. He swore fiercely and fisted his free hand into her hair, pulling her head back so his mouth grazed her cheek and he was riding her, taking her, and she let him, moving shamelessly against every long surge of his shaft shuttling inside her.

The dual penetration of him and the silicone cock,

combined with the vibrating, fluttering caresses against her clit, was too much, and not enough. Her nerves were stretched taut, her need for release so damn close. "Oh, God, Logan…"

"Come for me, sugar," he commanded, his voice like a direct line to her body, her soul. "I've got you."

A sob escaped her at his promise, and for the first time in her life, she gave herself completely, utterly, to a man's care…physically and emotionally. Closing her eyes, she focused on the shimmering haze of passion beckoning to her, and she moaned as ecstasy rushed in, converging between her legs, then exploding in a torrent of astonishing bliss that flooded her entire body. He held on to her as she screamed and shattered, and caught her in his arms after the free fall before allowing himself his own searing release.

RAINA WAS QUIET and a bit distant the following morning as Logan drove her to Sugar and Spice, just as she'd been last night after one of the most intense sexual encounters of his life and, he was betting, hers as well. A woman didn't let go physically the way that Raina had with him without some kind of trust between them. She'd given him something she'd never given another man, surrendering herself so beautifully to him, and he was well aware of just how intimate her gift had been.

There had been an undeniable emotional shift between them last night, and while he was ready to embrace his growing feelings for her, Raina was obviously putting up barriers to protect herself from potential hurt. He knew his sister's overblown reaction yesterday hadn't helped, either. He wanted to understand those fears, but she wasn't ready to share, and he wasn't going to push. He wasn't going anywhere, and if giving her time to process their changing relationship was what she needed, he was willing to give her the space to do just that, without him pressuring her for promises.

He wanted more with Raina than just this temporary fling they'd established, because what he was starting to feel for her was about more than just sex. Fucking was easy. But what he craved with her was a relationship based on more than just heated lust and fulfilling physical needs.

There were so many qualities about her that he admired, traits that totally meshed with his personality and attracted him to her beyond her gorgeous looks. Her playful humor made him laugh in ways he never had with another woman. He loved her confidence and strength, while at the same time, he wanted to take care of her, even though she was fully capable of taking care of herself. She made him feel deeply protective and possessive, and the thought of not being with her and around her after this job was over felt like a stab to the heart.

Not gonna happen.

He exhaled a breath to force himself to relax as he turned into the driveway leading to the back entrance of Raina's shop, where the employees parked. She was scheduled to open the store at ten, with Aaron coming in at noon, and right now the lot was fairly empty. He pulled into his normal slot, and before he could turn off the ignition, Raina's sharp gasp had him following her line of vision to the gray metal door of her shop, which was covered in bright red, spray-painted derogatory slurs.

Whore. Slut. Cunt. Tramp. Bitch.

She stiffened beside him, her fingers pressed to her lips to hold back the small noise of distress trying to escape, but there was no disguising the look of dismay in her eyes.

"He was here," she said unnecessarily, her voice small and fractured.

Fuck. Fury welled up in him, and he absolutely hated that she'd been subjected to someone's cruel, heartless scheme. Hated more that he couldn't do anything to stop it until they figured out who was responsible for these sadistic mind games.

He picked up his cell phone, and Raina's gaze shot

to his. "What are you doing?"

"I'm calling the police," he said firmly. "They need to take a report of this incident, and we're not going into your store until I'm absolutely certain there's no threat inside." He didn't give a shit that her security system hadn't been set off. He wasn't taking any chances with her safety.

She nodded, then glanced out the passenger window so she wouldn't have to look at the horrible words emblazoned on her door while he dialed 911. After requesting police assistance, he called Dean at the office and told him what had happened to keep him updated, as well.

Less than five minutes later, a police car that had been patrolling the nearby area arrived, and two uniformed cops got out of the vehicle. Only then did Logan get out of his car and allow Raina to do the same. The activity drew the attention of people from the neighboring businesses, and as they whispered about the crude names spray-painted on her back door, Raina wrapped her arms around herself as if she could block out what was happening.

In a monotone voice, she answered one of the officer's questions as he filled out the vandalism report, while the other cop asked some of the people milling around if they'd witnessed any suspicious activity. Nobody had seen or heard anything, leading Logan to believe the perpetrator had done his dirty work in the middle of the night.

When the police officer asked if Raina had experienced any other incidents lately, she told them about the handcuffs and note she'd found on her door a few days ago. The man included that in the report, as well, but there was clearly nothing they could do without any evidence pointing toward any particular person.

Both cops conducted a thorough search of the store, and once it was deemed safe for them to enter, Logan led Raina inside. The report process had taken nearly an hour, and it was past time for the shop to open, so Raina put the register drawer in and opened the front doors, giving Logan no time to talk to her alone and really see how she was doing mentally and emotionally. But her detached actions and tense body language spoke volumes. She was going through the motions, greeting her customers with a smile that didn't reach her eyes, and operating on autopilot when they asked for help in finding a particular item.

Just as the store emptied out and Logan had the chance to talk to Raina, her best friend, Paige, burst through the front doors, her green eyes filled with worry and her auburn hair flowing wildly around her shoulders as she strode purposefully into the boutique. She walked right up to where Raina was standing behind the counter and wrapped her in a tight hug.

"Oh my God, Raina," Paige said softly, compassionately, then stood back to look her over. "I just heard what happened and couldn't get here quick enough. Are you okay?"

Logan stood off to the side, letting the two friends have their moment.

"Thanks for coming, but I'm fine," Raina said with a forced smile. "Really. It was just...words."

But those carefully chosen words had affected her much deeper and more emotionally than she was letting on. They were nasty, crude words that were meant to hurt and humiliate, to mess with a person's head and make them feel worthless and ashamed, and there was no doubt in Logan's mind that Raina was struggling with every single one of those feelings.

"Fucking asshole, whoever he is," Paige said fiercely. "I'm going to rip his balls off and stuff them down his throat as soon as Dean or Logan figures out who the creep is who's harassing you."

That made Raina laugh, but Logan inwardly winced. He wouldn't put it past Paige that, given the chance, she'd emasculate the guy responsible for tormenting Raina. The other woman was feisty and gutsy, and she was the kind of friend who had Raina's back.

"How did you find out about what happened?" Raina asked.

"The grapevine called Jillian," Paige said with a suddenly impish grin. "Dean told her, and she called me immediately. She's in a meeting this morning with a client or she'd be here. She wanted to make sure you were all right, and so did I."

"I really do appreciate it," Raina said, absently rubbing her arms. "I have the best girlfriends."

"Damn straight you do," Paige replied, waggling a finger at her. "We're all here for you, always."

"I know." Raina's voice was soft and a bit choked up. "Thank you."

The front door to the shop opened again, and Sawyer, one of Logan's friends and co-workers at Noble and Associates, walked inside, a can of paint in one hand and a plastic bag from a hardware store in the other. Both women turned around to acknowledge who they thought was a customer, but instead of greeting him, Raina stared at Sawyer in shock, and Paige sucked in a startled breath as her wide-eyed gaze clashed with Sawyer's.

His friend came to an abrupt stop, and the *oh, shit* expression on Sawyer's face, combined with the extreme tension vibrating in the air, made it apparent that there was some kind of connection between Sawyer and Paige, and not necessarily an amicable one.

Logan stepped closer, wanting to dispel the awkward silence that was starting to make *him* feel uncomfortable. "Do you all know one another?"

"Uh, yeah," Sawyer finally said, his voice hoarse as he nodded politely to both women. "Raina. Paige."

Logan frowned as he watched the dynamics play out between the trio. No *nice to see you.* No *how are you doing?* Nothing cordial or friendly, just a wariness that he'd never seen shake Sawyer's confidence before.

After a moment, Raina replied very curtly. "Hi, Sawyer."

Paige said nothing, but now that the initial shock of seeing Sawyer had worn off, there was an unmistakable glimmer of pain in the other woman's eyes. There was history of some sort between her and Sawyer, and when Paige finally glanced away, Raina touched her friend's arm protectively.

Sawyer shifted on his feet, his features etched with silent regrets. He looked as though he wanted to say something more, but instead, he gave his head a small shake and met Logan's gaze. "Dean sent me over with supplies to paint the back door," he said, indicating the items in his hands. "And I need to discuss a few updates about this case with you, as well."

"Yeah, sure." Logan nodded his head toward the rear of the shop, where the storeroom and office were located. "Bring that stuff to the back, and we can talk where it's quiet."

Logan cast a quick glance at Raina, who looked

relieved that he was taking Sawyer away from Paige. He headed toward the back of the boutique with Sawyer following, and heard the two women talking quietly but couldn't make out what they were saying, but it sounded as though Raina was now comforting Paige in a low, hushed voice.

As soon as Logan and Sawyer walked through the doorway separating the main floor from the back rooms and he knew for certain they were out of earshot of the women, he turned to Logan and didn't hesitate to ask, "What the hell was *that* all about?"

"Nothing," Sawyer muttered irritably.

"I'm going to have to call bullshit on that one," Logan replied, only half joking. "There was definitely *something* going on between you and Paige."

Sawyer met his gaze, his jaw clenched tight and his eyes reflecting a darker misery. "I don't want to talk about it."

Logan immediately backed off. Sawyer had only been working for Noble and Associates for a few months, ever since being honorably discharged from the military, but the two of them had become good friends in a short period of time. And right now, Logan respected the other man's need for space and privacy and turned the conversation to business.

"What did you need to talk to me about?" he asked, making sure he still had a clear view of Raina and the customers entering the store.

Sawyer set the can of paint and the bag of items on the floor near the back door, then withdrew his phone from his back pocket and swiped his finger across the screen. "Dean and Mac finally had a chance to take a look at the footage from the security tape from Raina's place on the night that someone left the handcuffs on her door. Unfortunately, it's hard to get a good look at the person, even when Dean tried to zoom in on the guy. He gave me the short clip to show you. Take a look."

After pulling up the video feed on his phone, Sawyer handed it to Logan. The building's camera caught a man in a bulky jacket heading up the stairs to Raina's apartment, the collar flipped up around his neck and a baseball cap pulled low on his forehead to shadow and conceal his face so it was impossible to see his features. He quickly clipped the handcuffs around her doorknob, then turned around and averted his face away from the security camera once again as he made his way back out of the complex.

"Shit," Logan muttered in frustration. "The guy was obviously aware of the security cameras." He handed the phone back to Sawyer. "Send me the video, and I'll have Raina take a look at it to see if the guy looks at all familiar to her."

"Done." Sawyer pressed a few buttons on his

phone to text the clip to Logan before putting the unit back into his pocket.

"The other thing Dean wanted me to tell you is that since the clip doesn't really help to identify the person and Raina thinks the stalker could be the guy from The Players Club, he suggested that you and Raina go back to the club on Thursday, the same day she was there last week, to see if she can single out the man who harassed her so management can at least question him."

Logan scrubbed a hand along his jaw and exhaled a deep breath as he glanced at Raina, who was ringing up a customer's purchase, with Paige standing nearby. He hated to put her through the stressful ordeal of going back to the club for the sole purpose of pointing out the man she suspected was the culprit, but at this point, they didn't have a choice. It was the next logical step in finding out who was terrorizing her.

He looked back at Sawyer and nodded. "I'll talk to her about it tonight."

"I'll get the outside of the door painted back to gray," Sawyer said, picking up his supplies once again. "And if you don't mind, once I'm done, I'll leave the *back* way." He gave Logan a wry grin.

To avoid another awkward confrontation, obviously. "Sure. Thanks, man." Logan slapped him on the back. "I appreciate you coming by and taking care of the door, and I know Raina does, too."

"No problem."

Logan opened the back door to let Sawyer out and made sure it was locked securely behind him.

The rest of the day passed uneventfully. Aaron arrived for his shift at noon, followed by Callie two hours later. Raina helped the customers who browsed the store, a smile always on her face despite the weariness reflecting in her eyes.

Logan would never equate the term fragile with Raina, but after this morning's incident, he could see that vulnerable crack in her normally unshakable composure, the lackluster look in her eyes, and by four o'clock in the afternoon, he decided that he needed to get her out of this environment and take her to a place where she wasn't surrounded by reminders of the person stalking her. Where she felt safe and protected.

And he wasn't giving her a choice in the matter.

Chapter Twelve

WHEN LOGAN ANNOUNCED they were leaving the store for the day, Raina had been too weary and emotionally exhausted to argue as she normally would when a man tried to take charge of any aspect of her life. Knowing that Aaron and Callie had the night shift covered made it easier to go along with Logan's suggestion, and honestly, she was grateful to be away from the store and the reminder of what had happened earlier that morning.

He drove onto the freeway, away from her apartment, and she didn't even ask where he was taking her, because it didn't really matter. Just getting out of the store made her breathe easier, but unfortunately, it didn't make her forget.

After a while of enjoying the comfortable silence, she looked over at Logan and posed the one question she'd been meaning to ask him all day long. "When did

Sawyer start working for Dean?"

"A few months ago," he said, meeting her gaze, his own curious. "It was hard not to notice all the tension between the three of you, and Paige especially, when he walked in this morning. Is there something going on between him and Paige?"

She hesitated for a moment before answering. Logan and Sawyer were co-workers, and possibly friends, so how much did she reveal? "Currently, no," she replied, keeping her response neutral. "But they were dating about a year and a half ago, right before he left to serve his last tour of duty in the Army."

He casually glanced in the rearview mirror, keeping an eye on the cars around him. "So what happened?"

Again, she paused, then wondered why she was trying to be so careful with the truth when Sawyer had caused her best friend a wealth of hurt. So, she told Logan exactly what his friend had done. "Sawyer cheated on Paige with her stepsister."

Logan's head whipped around and he stared at her in disbelief. "Cheated, as in…"

"Slept with, fucked, screwed," she clarified so there was no doubt in his mind what had transpired. "Any of those verbs will do."

He grimaced as he returned his gaze back to the road. "Oh, damn," he said quietly. "I never would have pegged Sawyer for that kind of guy."

"Well, he did, and it was bad. *Really* bad," she said, clearly recalling that awful phone call she'd received from Paige and how devastated her best friend had been because she had fallen in love with Sawyer, had trusted him, and he'd shattered her heart. "And to make things worse, he did it the night of Paige's birthday party. Happy fucking birthday to her, right?"

He winced and shifted in his seat as they exited the freeway. "I'm sorry I asked," he said, only half joking.

Raina didn't say anything more. But the worst part of the situation was that despite Sawyer's involvement with Paige's stepsister, Paige wasn't over Sawyer, even a year and a half after the humiliating incident had occurred. She couldn't bring herself to date, she was insecure about those full curves of hers, and she didn't trust men's motives and interest in her, and that was the part that made Raina the most upset for her friend because Paige deserved a good man in her life.

Raina glanced around at their surroundings and frowned when Logan turned into a familiar upscale neighborhood in La Jolla—where his sister lived. Dread tightened her chest. Was the man trying to totally stress her out? The last thing she wanted or needed today was to make polite small talk with a woman who clearly disapproved of what she did for a living. Especially after those degrading words that had been spray-painted on her store door and were still taunting her in the back of her mind.

"Why are we going to your sister's?" she asked, unable to keep the panic out of her voice.

He reached across the console and squeezed her hand. "We're not going to Emily's," he assured her quickly. "We're going to my house. I live in the same neighborhood, a few blocks away from my sister."

That completely caught her off guard. "You live in this area? Are you independently wealthy?" Because the exclusive custom homes in this part of San Diego did not come cheap, and Logan himself didn't come across as rich and affluent. He didn't wear designer clothes and accessories, and while he drove a midrange sports car, it was an affordable and practical vehicle.

He shrugged, though a smile curved his lips. "I've done okay. I took all that money I'd been saving for Charlotte and me while I was in the military, along with the rest of my monthly paychecks, and made some really good, solid investments while I was in the service. By the time I got out, I had a really nice nest egg." He put both hands back on the wheel and made a right-hand turn down a street, slowing for the children playing on the sidewalks. "I waited until a house in this area went into foreclosure, and when it went to auction, I put in a bid and got it for a steal."

She added *smart businessman* to his many talents.

He waved to one of the mothers standing out in

her yard, a baby on her hip while two other kids tossed a ball back and forth. "I love this neighborhood. It's kid friendly, it's in a reputable school district, and it's a great place to raise a family."

That Logan had already thought that far ahead made Raina's stomach twist with envy, as well as the knowledge that she would never fit into that image he saw for himself and his future. This was the kind of prominent neighborhood where the women stayed home to be housewives and raise their children, and moms joined the PTA and got together for coffee klatches while the kids were in school so they could catch up on neighborhood gossip. Just like in high school, there would be cliques and women who would look down on and judge someone like Raina who owned an adult novelty boutique and didn't conform to their rules and standards.

Yes, it was a nice community with stunning homes, as well as a safe place to raise a family. And while Logan might have moved on from Charlotte, he was clearly still holding on to that image of having a conventional marriage with a woman who would be that perfect, quintessential wife and fit into his ideal of a picturesque life.

And that classical, traditional woman wasn't her. Not by a long shot.

"We're here," he said, pulling Raina out of the reality of her thoughts as he turned into a brick-laid driveway.

His single-story house was located at the end of a cul-de-sac and occupied the biggest corner lot. The home itself was big but not monstrous, and Mediterranean in style, with a stucco exterior, low-pitched tiled roof, and a front yard that was impeccably landscaped and maintained. He drove his car into the garage, pressed a button on a remote to close the rolling door behind them, then turned to Raina with an irresistible smile.

"Come on, I'll give you a tour of the place."

She followed him inside, and as they walked from room to room, she had to admit that the interior was spectacular, with clean white walls and open, airy living spaces with beautiful columns. The ceilings were high, with rustic wood beams, and the decor was simple yet inviting, and he gave credit to his sister, Emily, for her help in that department. He showed her the bedrooms first, all of which had been furnished and decorated, and when they came to the master bedroom and adjoining bath, he proudly showed her the infinity walk-in shower that he'd installed himself during the remodeling process.

As she followed him back out of the bathroom, she couldn't help but notice just how spotless the entire house was, which wasn't normal for most bachelors. "Okay, your place is *way* too clean. Do you have OCD?" she teased.

"No," he said with a laugh. "I'm fairly neat because the military was strict about keeping things orderly, but my housekeeper comes in on Monday and Friday mornings, so the timing was perfect."

He opened a sliding glass door in the master bedroom, which led to a wraparound patio and the backyard. There were palm trees and floral shrubbery, a fire pit with chairs, and a built-in barbeque and outdoor bar for entertaining. Not to mention the big pool out in the middle of the yard, complete with a rock-formation waterfall. They followed the patio around to another glass slider, stepped back inside, and ended up in the kitchen, which was gourmet size, with travertine countertops and custom cabinetry Logan had also done himself with the help of a few of his co-workers.

"Have a seat and I'll open a bottle of wine." He waved a hand toward the wrought iron stools tucked under the counter.

She slid into a chair as Logan retrieved a chilled bottle of wine from the refrigerator and two glasses from the cupboard. "I thought you'd be more of a beer kind of guy."

"I can appreciate a good bottle of wine," he said with a grin as he set the stemware on the counter and poured them each a generous amount. "I like a cold bottle of beer after a hot afternoon of doing yard work, and if I'm going out for the evening, I'll order a high-end Scotch whisky."

She took a drink of the white wine, savoring the crisp, cool taste while Logan went back to the refrigerator and pulled out a container of defrosted chicken breasts and some fresh vegetables and set them on the wooden island in the middle of the kitchen to make them dinner.

"Can I help with the prep work?" she asked.

"Nope," he said as he grabbed a bottle of quick-set marinade and smeared it over the chicken breasts. "You just sit there and relax. I've got dinner covered."

She had to admit that it was nice to let someone else make dinner, to take care of her for a change, and she certainly didn't mind watching this gorgeous man as he moved around the kitchen with purpose. He used a metal grate on top of the stove to grill the chicken while he roasted the asparagus in the oven with garlic and butter. The delicious scents made her stomach growl hungrily.

She finished off her glass of wine, and when Logan walked by, he filled it right back up again with a flirtatious wink. It didn't take long for the wine to make her mellow and relaxed, which was very nice after the day she'd had.

They ate dinner around casual conversation about him and some of his funnier antics in the military that made her laugh. When they were done, Logan insisted on cleaning up the dishes and the kitchen, then took her hand and led her into the living room. He sat down on one end of the plush, comfortable couch, and she sat down beside him, suddenly realizing that he had a serious look on his face as he turned toward her.

"I really hate to bring this up, but I need to talk to you about a few things," he said as he retrieved his phone from his front pocket.

She had no idea what he wanted to discuss, and despite the wine that had soothed her mood, she felt a wariness building up inside of her. "Okay."

He opened a video and met her gaze, seemingly just as reluctant to broach this particular topic with her. "This is a clip from the security camera by your apartment, and it shows the guy putting those handcuffs on your door. Unfortunately, he was wearing a bulky jacket and a ball cap to hide his features, so there's no real good shot of his face. But you need to take a look and tell me if this guy looks at all familiar to you."

She glanced at his phone, hoping that she'd be able to identify the person who was wreaking havoc with her life and her emotions so it would finally be over.

She gave Logan a slight nod, and he pressed play, allowing her to see the video of that night. Just as Logan had told her, the oversized jacket and the way the man hunched his shoulders and purposely averted his face away from the cameras made it impossible to distinguish anything about the guy.

She shook her head in frustration. "I don't recognize him at all."

"He knew about the cameras and made sure they didn't catch his face." Logan set his phone down on the glass coffee table in front of the couch. "Dean made a suggestion about what we should do next, and when I tell you about his idea, I want you to keep an open mind, okay?"

A sense of dread swirled in her belly, and she pulled her legs up under her on the couch, as if she could somehow protect herself from what was coming next. "What's his suggestion?"

Logan stretched an arm across the back of the sofa. She was close enough to touch, and he gently brushed his fingers along the curve of her neck and shoulder. "He wants you and me to go back to The Players Club on Thursday, to see if you can identify the guy who came on strong last week. I don't like making you go back there, but I agree that it's the best way. You'll be safe."

She swallowed hard, not entirely sure how she felt

about that. *Scared?* Maybe. *Nervous?* Definitely. "You'll be with me the whole time?"

"I'll never leave your side," he promised, his voice low and possessive enough to make her shiver. "This is all about going to the club and trying to find the man who wasn't happy about you turning him down, so Dean and the management can talk to him."

She had no doubt that Dean would interrogate the shit out of the guy and intimidate him as well. Going back to the club for the sole purpose of singling out the arrogant man who'd wanted to bound, gag, and flog her was not her idea of a fun evening, but if it meant the end of all this harassment, she was willing to do it. Ultimately, she trusted Dean, and she trusted Logan to keep her safe and protected while they went in search of this guy, and that made all the difference to her decision.

She exhaled a deep breath and nodded before she changed her mind. "Okay. Let's do it."

"I'll let Dean know." He paused for a moment, his fingers continuing their soft, languid caress across her bare skin, as if he were soothing a skittish kitten. "Now I want to discuss what happened this morning at the shop, since we haven't had any time alone today to talk about it."

She glanced away from his searching gaze, afraid he'd see too much vulnerability in her eyes. "What's there to talk about?" she said flippantly, even though the reminder of those slurs brought some ugly memories rushing to the surface.

"*You*, and how you're doing."

"I'm fine," she lied, still not looking at him, her posture way too stiff. "They were just words, Logan." It was the same thing she'd told Paige, but damn if those *words* hadn't made her feel worthless and *ashamed*, which she'd hated the most.

He touched his fingers to her chin and turned her face toward him again, not giving her the chance to hide anything from him. Not her insecurities that she knew reflected in her gaze, not the hurt that still ran bone deep, and not the painful emotions that were trying to break through the protective wall she'd built around her heart so she'd never have to experience that kind of degradation again. Her throat grew tight, and burning tears she hadn't shed in years stung the backs of her eyes. She was *not* going to cry.

"They were harsh, cruel words that have no reflection on you, personally," he said adamantly, his jaw clenched in anger—not at her, she knew, but the situation. "You know that, right?"

She wanted so badly to say *yes*, but the truth was, there was a small part of her that believed those awful slurs—that young eighteen-year-old girl who'd done nothing more than make out with a boy and had been berated and punished and cast out as a tramp and a slut by her own father.

"The night my father found me with my boyfriend, he called me every single one of those names and *meant* them." Her voice cracked, and those stupid tears filled her eyes as her ex-fiancé's words looped through her mind, as well: *Choose me or your business, because I don't want my friends and family to think I'm marrying a whore who gets off on selling porn.*

"I know that's not who and what I am just because I own an adult boutique, but that's how people tend to label me." She blinked, and a tear escaped, which she quickly wiped away. But another one fell just as quickly. "And for the most part, it doesn't bother me, until someone I trust or care about calls me those names." Then it felt personal and real and true. A stigma that was always there, reminding her that she wasn't good enough for anyone to love.

"C'mere," Logan said, his voice rough with emotion as he reached for her and pulled her onto his lap.

She went willingly, curling into the warmth and strength of his body, needing to feel safe and protected, which Logan did so effortlessly. She wrapped her arms around his neck and buried her face against his throat as an unwanted and painful sob unraveled out of her, then another.

"Aww, baby," he said, pulling her closer and holding her like nobody ever had before, as if she mattered to him, and that caused another convulsive catch of her breath. "I've got you. Just let it all out," he whispered as his hands stroked along her back, comforting her. "You're always so strong and independent and brave. Just let me take care of you for a little while, okay?"

As if he'd given her the permission she'd needed, the dam broke, and there was no holding back the torrent of emotion that came with it. Years of suppressing her pain and heartache all came to a head and poured out of her. It was an ugly cry—loud and inelegant and gut-wrenching, and she didn't even care because it felt so cathartic to finally let it all out.

Her sobbing eventually subsided and turned into those spasms that came after a long crying jag, leaving her spent, exhausted, and utterly drained. She closed her eyes as he stroked his fingers through her hair, calming her and lulling her into a deep, heavy sleep.

Chapter Thirteen

RAINA WOKE UP the next morning alone in Logan's big king-sized bed. She rolled to her back and pried her puffy eyes open, trying to remember how she'd gotten there. Bits and pieces came back to her—the way Logan had carried her to bed after she'd fallen asleep on him in the living room and how she'd been so tired that she hadn't protested when he'd gently pulled her clothes off her limp body, leaving her in just her panties, then stripped off his own shirt and jeans and slid beneath the covers until he was spooned against her backside. Then he'd tucked a strong arm around her waist to hold her close, cocooning her in the warmth and the familiar male scent of his body. Feeling safe and secure in his arms, she'd fallen right back into a deep, dreamless sleep.

It was the first time in days that she'd crashed

through the entire night, without abruptly waking up because she'd thought she'd heard something in her apartment, with her heart hammering in her throat and images of some deranged stalker attacking her.

Unfortunately, there *was* some crazy person terrorizing her, and until that ordeal was over, those nightmares would probably continue to haunt her.

She stretched the kinks from her body and glanced around the room for a clock. She found a digital one on the nightstand, the red letters glowing 9:23 a.m. Normally she'd be in a panic for sleeping in so late, but the last thing that Aaron had told her when she'd left the store yesterday afternoon was that he would open the shop in the morning so she didn't have to rush in, and she could arrive later and take the closing shift. She was grateful for the switch, because she still needed to head back to her apartment for a clean change of clothes.

Time to get moving. She rolled out of bed, and since she was still in just her underwear, she grabbed the T-shirt that Logan had worn the day before and had tossed onto the floor last night and pulled it over her head so she wasn't walking around half-naked. A pair of socks and his jeans were also in a heap on the floor, and she couldn't help but smile knowing that, yeah, he was a normal guy who didn't pick up his clothes until he absolutely had to—or someone else did.

Heading into the adjoining bathroom, she emptied her bladder, then went to wash her hands when she saw a new, packaged toothbrush sitting on the counter for her to use. A thoughtful gesture he probably extended to all the women who happened to stay the night. The stab of jealousy she experienced at that thought was unexpected but there nonetheless. She hated the mental image of other women in Logan's house and his bed.

Shoving those too-possessive thoughts aside when Logan wasn't hers to claim, she brushed her teeth, then glanced in the mirror, cringing at the dreadful-looking woman staring back at her. She looked a wreck. Her hair was a disheveled mess, her makeup and mascara smeared around her eyes from her crying episode.

Embarrassment coursed through her. She wasn't in the habit of feeling sorry for herself and indulging in a pity party, but last night, everything had come to a head. Feeling so vulnerable and alone, she'd succumbed to a moment of weakness. But now it was time to put her big-girl panties back on and deal with the situation without falling apart again.

Exhaling a deep breath, she washed her face, ran a brush through her hair, and followed the savory scent of bacon and coffee out to the kitchen. She entered the bright and open space and smiled to herself when she found Logan standing at the stove, removing strips of crispy bacon from a pan and putting them on a paper towel covering a plate, while scrambling some eggs in another frying pan. He wasn't yet aware of her presence, and she was content to lean against the far counter and just watch him for a few quiet moments.

He was wearing a gray T-shirt that stretched across his broad, muscled shoulders and tucked into a pair of dark jeans that did great things for his ass. His hair was damp from a shower, a light stubble covered his jaw, and an arousing trickle of heat curled through her when she thought of how seductive that shadowed beard felt scratching against her neck, her breasts, her thighs...

A soft, needy sound rose up out of her throat before she could stop it, and Logan turned around, a ridiculously sexy smile lifting his mouth when he saw her standing there.

"Hey, beautiful," he said and strolled toward her, making her heart race with each step that closed the distance between them. "I was just about to wake you up. Breakfast is ready."

She flushed, knowing she looked far from beautiful, considering she'd just looked in a mirror.

As if it were perfectly normal for her to be in his kitchen, as soon as he reached her, he slid an arm around her waist to bring her body flush to his and slid his other hand along the side of her neck, using his thumb to tip up her face as his mouth lowered to hers. The kiss was slow and hot and deep, making her soften and melt against him as he slid his hand lower and found his way beneath the hem of the T-shirt she was wearing.

His palm cupped her ass, giving it a possessive squeeze as he rubbed the thick length of his erection against her mound. She moaned as desire heated her blood, and she was beginning to think, *and hope*, that she was going to have *him* for breakfast.

Much too soon, he ended the kiss. "You taste good," he murmured huskily as he ran his tongue along her teeth and nipped at her bottom lip before lifting his head to stare down at her. "Minty and sweet."

"Yeah, thanks for the new toothbrush you set out for me. You supply them for all your overnight guests?" She meant to be light and teasing, but damn if a bit of the green-eyed monster didn't slip through.

He smirked at her, clearly enjoying her little flare of jealousy. "No, you're special."

She rolled her eyes, trying once again for humor. "I bet you tell that to all the girls who sleep over."

She tried to step away from him, but he kept his arm firmly around her waist, his stunningly clear green eyes very serious and direct. "You're the first and *only* woman to ever sleep in my bed. I don't bring random women here. That's what The Players Club was for."

Was. Past tense. As if he didn't intend to go back anytime soon and she was the reason why. As if he didn't want or need any other woman now that he'd had her.

Pain squeezed her heart, which told her just how fast she was falling for this man. She swallowed hard, knowing he might feel that way about her now, while they were in the throes of their sexual, off-the-charts hot affair, but she knew from experience that his interest wouldn't last, that when the lust and attraction faded and he really thought of his future and what he wanted, she was the furthest thing from his ideal woman.

And that part hurt most of all, which was why she was determined to end their fling just as soon as she was safe again and didn't need a daily bodyguard.

"Just for the record," he said, finally releasing her and giving her the room she needed to breathe, "I buy more than one toothbrush at a time, so that was my extra one."

"Well, thank you." She managed a smile. "I appreciate it."

He walked back to the stove and reached for two plates from the nearby cupboard. "Why don't you make a cup of coffee while I dish up our breakfast."

Welcoming the distraction, she went to the coffee maker and poured herself a cup, then mixed in her cream and sugar. Logan carried their plates back to the bar area, where they'd eaten dinner the night before, and she joined him there.

After a few bites of the fluffy, buttery eggs, Logan glanced at her. "Can you take today off from the shop? We could go to the beach for the afternoon," he suggested.

She knew what he was doing. He was trying to give her a day to unwind and relax after yesterday's incident at the store, and while that sounded like a fantastic idea and a wonderful mental escape, she also knew spending an entire day in Logan's company, just the two of them, was not a smart thing for her emotionally.

She shook her head as she took a drink of her coffee. "I really should go into work today."

He lifted a dark brow, silently countering that statement.

"Okay, I really *need* to go into work today," she corrected as she bit into a crispy piece of bacon. "I have a bunch of things I should have finished yesterday but couldn't think straight enough to get the paperwork done. And I refuse to let this person, whoever he is, scare me away from my own store."

"Okay, work it is," he said, not pushing the issue.

They finished breakfast, and while Logan cleaned up the kitchen, Raina changed into the clothes she'd worn the day before for the ride back to her apartment. Once they arrived at her place, she took a shower, washed and dried her hair, and put on a light amount of makeup.

Logan had her at the store before twelve thirty in the afternoon, and from the moment they walked in, Raina was a whirlwind of busy. Between helping customers, restocking the shelves, assisting Callie in packaging online orders, and doing inventory so she could place an order for various products they were low on for both the store and Internet sales, she was constantly on her feet and had no time to even get to the paperwork still awaiting her in the office.

Raina was grateful that there were no other incidents, and it was a normal afternoon at the boutique. The only conflict all day was when Jared arrived to pick up the boxes and packages and Logan watched the other man while he loaded up his truck, refusing to leave him alone with her. Jared glared at Logan and made the comment that he didn't need a babysitter to do his job, and made no attempt at hiding his irritation at the situation.

The tension between the two men was tangible, like two boys fighting over the same toy, and Raina

knew she was the reason, which was ridiculous because she had absolutely no interest in Jared. And she
was certain he wasn't responsible for the two incidents
so far. He was just a nice guy and had never shown her
any aggressive tendencies.

By six in the evening, with Callie and Aaron having
been at the store since ten that morning, she sent them
both home. With Logan in the shop, and only two
more hours left to go on a Tuesday night, one of their
quietest evenings of the week, she wanted to give her
two employees an early night off.

At eight, Raina locked the front doors and started
closing up the store, realizing she needed at least an
hour in her office to cash out the day's receipts, pay a
few outstanding invoices, and place an order for
inventory since she was getting low on items from her
increasing website sales. Except her stomach twisted
with hunger pangs, and she had a splitting headache
because she realized that she'd skipped eating any
lunch or dinner.

She sat behind her desk, rubbing at her throbbing
temples and feeling a bit light-headed when Logan
strolled in.

His expression immediately reflected concern.
"Hey, are you okay?"

"Actually, I'm starving." Being the healthy guy that
Logan was, he'd brought two protein shakes as meal

replacements and had already drunk them. She should have brought something substantial from home, as well. "And the granola bar in my desk drawer just isn't going to cut it."

"Want to go and get something to eat?"

She shook her head, realizing her hands were shaking, probably from low blood sugar and needing protein. "I really don't want to leave. I've got to get this stuff done tonight before I go." The receipts, invoices, and inventory order on her desk really couldn't be put off another day. "Would you mind running down to the corner deli and picking me up a chicken sandwich?"

He braced his hands on his hips, a slight frown creasing his brows. "I don't like leaving you alone."

"It'll take you maybe fifteen, twenty minutes max, and I'm locked up tight here in the store," she reasoned. "I'll be fine. You have a key card, and I promise not to answer anyone who might knock on the door."

Still, he hesitated, his reluctance palpable.

Her belly gnawed hungrily again, this time with a slight wave of nausea. "*Please?* My head is killing me, and I feel like I'm going to pass out if I don't get something substantial in my stomach."

That he seemed to understand, and he exhaled a deep breath. "Put your cell phone on the desk where you can grab it if you need to call me for anything."

She did as he asked, setting her phone nearby. "Thank you."

He nodded. "I'll be right back."

She heard him leave out the back door, as well as the lock clicking into place after him. She signed on to her computer, then picked up an invoice, doing her best to concentrate on getting the bills paid online so she could move on to placing her inventory order. The sooner her paperwork was done, the sooner she could go home.

Five minutes after Logan left, the back door opened again with a buzz, then shut again, then...silence. Curious as to why Logan would have returned so soon, she stood up, then rounded her desk and walked toward the office door.

"Logan? Did you forget something?" As soon as she stepped out into the hallway, she came to an abrupt stop as her gaze collided with Jared's. She stared at him in confusion for a split second, which quickly gave way to unease since it was after hours and he was dressed in jeans and a T-shirt, instead of his courier uniform. She also realized that since she hadn't used the final exit pass code on the door, his key card was still active.

He looked at her much too insolently, and a shiver stole through her at the contempt etched across his features. Pushing away the niggle of fear attempting to claw its way to the surface, she squared her shoulders and tried to remain calm so she could assess him and the situation.

"What are you doing here, Jared?" she asked, her voice surprisingly strong and confident, despite the increasingly sick feeling in her stomach that had nothing to do with food and everything to do with her instincts suddenly screaming at her that she'd been wrong, and Jared *was* the one stalking her.

He stood there, his entire body taut and controlled in a way that chilled her. "I've been waiting for *days* for your bodyguard to leave you alone so I could talk to you without him hovering around or interrogating me."

The thought of Jared spying on her, watching her from afar, and following her made Raina's skin start to crawl. "That's Logan's job."

"Well, he's not here now, is he?" he said, clearly relishing that fact.

"He'll be back soon," she blurted out, desperation in her voice.

He shrugged, the gesture detached and uncaring. "I'll be done with you by then, and he can have whatever's left over."

Jared smirked, and she realized that in his current and clearly unbalanced mental state, he believed himself untouchable. A dangerous prospect for her. He could do a lot of horrible things in the fifteen minutes that Logan was gone, and the only thing she could think of was to keep Jared talking.

"Why are you doing this?" she asked, keeping her voice even and unthreatening. "I thought we were friends."

"*I never wanted to be fucking friends,*" he screamed, his expression distorting with a rage that made Raina's heart hammer hard and fast in her chest with fright and panic.

He stabbed his fingers through his hair and inhaled a deep breath, giving the perception that he was suddenly back in control of his anger. He wasn't. She'd seen and had been the recipient of these kinds of violent outbursts in her father—an explosive flare of temper one second and seemingly rational speech the next. But the calm never lasted long, and she knew just how brutal and vicious this encounter could get.

She swallowed hard, trying not to let her growing anxiety and terror overwhelm her.

"You've made me very, very upset, Raina," he said and slowly started toward her. For every step he took forward, she took one back. "I tried to be nice. I asked you out for drinks and dinner and coffee, and what excuse did you give me? That you were too busy with the store and not in the frame of mind to date anyone, yet here you are, fucking that asshole and acting like a whore."

She flinched at the word and the hatred dripping from his voice. *Keep him talking.* "You put the handcuffs on my door and spray-painted those words?"

"The handcuffs were a gift I thought we could use together. I mean, take a look around your store, Raina. You clearly like it hard and rough and kinky, and I could have given you that." He took another deceptively casual step toward her. "I was waiting so patiently for you to come around, to realize that you and I belong together, and I don't appreciate Logan taking what is mine," he said, the spite in his voice spewing out like venom.

"I'm not *yours*," she said, the words slipping out before she could stop them. The last thing she needed to do was agitate him further.

"Not anymore you're not." His gaze raked down the length of her in disgust. "Now you're nothing more than a filthy, dirty slut, and I'm going to treat you like the fucking tramp you are."

He quickened his steps, and in a panic, she spun around, desperate to get to the open storeroom so she could dart inside and lock him out. Just as she reached the doorjamb, he caught her hair and pulled hard, jerking her head back and throwing her off balance. Before she could regain her equilibrium, he shoved her down to the tiled floor. She hit the ground on her hands and knees. The jarring impact sucked the breath right out of her and made her head spin.

She tried to scramble back to her feet but didn't move quickly enough. He pushed her again from behind, flattening her body to the floor, then roughly flipped her over and straddled her thighs. She lashed out with the only weapon she had—her hands and nails. She went for his face and eyes and managed to put a couple of deep scratches across his cheek before he caught her wrists and yanked her hands away.

A spine-tingling madness burned in his gaze. "Goddamn bitch!"

He manacled both her wrists in one hand, his grip so strong it felt as though he could easily snap her bones. She was utterly helpless. She couldn't move her arms without crying out in agony. It felt as though he were going to fracture her hands, and she clenched her teeth against the sharp pain while tears of frustration filled her eyes.

He reached into the front pocket of his jeans and pulled out a pair of silver handcuffs—just like the ones he'd left on her door. He snapped one around her wrist, then jerked her hands over her head and looped the chain around the solid steel leg of one of the shelves in the storeroom before securing her other hand, rendering her completely defenseless. He sat back on her thighs and touched his fingers to the blood trickling down his face where she'd gouged him. Fury filled his expression as he rubbed the red substance between his fingers, a cruel smile forming on his lips.

"See, I knew you liked it rough," he said callously. "And that's exactly what you're going to get."

He ripped open the front of her blouse, scattering the buttons across the floor. Her chest heaved in real terror at what was about to happen. She tried to buck him off, but he had her hips pinned beneath his weight, and judging by the lust darkening his eyes, he seemed to like her struggles. He moved down a little farther, shoved her skirt up to her waist, and tore her panties off in one fierce tug.

She cried out in anger, and when he started to unzip his pants, she knew she had one last chance to try and reason with him.

"You really don't want to do this, Jared," she implored softly, attempting to appeal to some kind of sympathetic and rational emotion in him. "Not by force and not without my consent. You're hurting me, and it's *wrong*."

A flicker of hesitation glinted in his eyes but was quickly snuffed out by anger. "Shut the fuck up, bitch!" He slapped her so hard across the cheek with the back of his hand that her ears buzzed and she saw double. "You deserve it like this," he yelled bitterly.

He forced her legs wide apart, and despite the pounding in her head, her blurred sight, and her shackled wrists, she thrashed her lower body, refusing to make any of this easy on him. His weight beared down on her, and she squeezed her eyes shut, her entire body stiffening against the assault to come. But instead of being violated, she felt his chest lift from hers as he jerked back with a grunt.

Startled and confused, she opened her eyes and saw Jared in front of her, still kneeling between her legs as he frantically clutched at the muscled arm wrapped around his throat. Logan stood behind him. *Thank God*, she thought in a rush of relief. Jared's face turned red, his eyes bugged out, and awful, gurgling sounds rose from his throat as he struggled to breathe...and then suddenly his entire body went limp.

Logan dragged him off of her and threw him to the floor. A sob of gratitude escaped her, but when Jared didn't move, horror replaced that brief reprieve. "Oh, my God, Logan. Did you *kill* him?"

A muscle in his jaw flexed, and his gaze flashed with a barely concealed violence. "I should have strangled the fucker, but I only choked him out. He'll be unconscious for about a minute, so I need to get him restrained quickly, before he comes to." He stepped over Jared's lifeless form to one of the inventory shelves and pushed aside an array of toys in his search for something he could use.

"There's bondage tape on the second shelf," she told him. "You can bind his wrists and ankles with it."

Logan found the item and none-too-gently secured Jared's hands and legs before opening a new package of handcuffs to retrieve the universal key inside. He knelt by her side and freed her. She sat up, and he took one look at the reddened marks on her wrists, then at the welt she knew was forming on her cheek, and a new wave of rage transformed his features.

"*Fuck*," he said furiously, which was so at odds with the tender way he touched his fingers to her injury. "Are you okay?"

"Yes, thanks to you. You have impeccable timing," she said with a forced smile, then winced at the pain that gesture inflicted to the side of her face. "He slapped me, but that's the worst of it."

"Thank God that's all he did." He wrapped his fingers around the back of her neck and pressed his forehead to hers, their mouths inches apart. "When I walked in the back door and heard Jared's voice, I was so afraid that I was too late, and I'd never be able to forgive myself if he'd—"

Hearing the anguish in his voice, she pressed her fingers to his lips, not wanting him to speak the words. "He didn't." And that was all that mattered.

A groan from behind Logan ended their conversation. He switched his attention to Jared, who was starting to regain consciousness.

Logan stood and helped Raina up, too. "Go into your office and wait there," he said, pulling the sides of her blouse back together so she was covered decently again. "I'm going to call the police, and you don't need to be in here with this prick when he wakes back up. *I'll* deal with him."

She nodded in agreement and did as he asked, grateful that the whole ordeal was finally over and she could get back to a normal life. Which also meant the end to her and Logan. Because despite everything wonderful they'd shared, she understood what he refused to believe. That the novelty of being with her would wear off quickly, and most importantly, she didn't fit into that traditional white-picket-fence family he still so clearly wanted and envisioned for himself.

Chapter Fourteen

AN HOUR AND a half later, Logan was finally driving Raina home. The police had arrived within ten minutes after he'd called 911, and Logan had also called Dean to let him know what had happened. Raina agreed to press charges against Jared, and the other man was put under arrest and taken to jail. Then came the multitude of questions and statements that seemed to go on forever when Logan could see just how exhausted and weary Raina was. At least he'd been able to coerce her into eating half of the chicken sandwich he'd gotten for her, even though she'd insisted that she had no appetite after the attack.

When he arrived at her place, he parked the car and cut the engine, then opened the driver's-side door to get out, but she caught his arm before he could exit. He glanced back at her. Since leaving the store, she'd been quiet, her body language stiff and withdrawn, and he absolutely hated those walls she was already erecting between them.

"You don't need to walk me to my door," she said quietly.

"Yes, I do," he said firmly.

She released a breath and finally looked at him, resignation in her gaze. "Your job is done, Logan. I'm not your responsibility anymore."

Was she fucking kidding him? Apparently not, and he tried very hard to keep his irritation over her sudden casual brush-off in check. She'd just gone through a traumatic event and obviously wasn't thinking straight. She couldn't be, given everything that had happened the past week, and especially tonight.

He gave her a tight smile. "I'm not the kind of guy who dumps a woman off at the curb under *any* circumstance, so humor me, okay?"

She said nothing more and thankfully didn't argue further when he escorted her up to her apartment. When they reached her unit, he took the key from her hand and unlocked the door, holding it open so she could go inside before him and disengage the security system. She walked into the kitchen, set her purse on the counter, and faced him with a whole lot of distance separating them.

She tugged the sides of the sweater she'd put on back at the store to cover up her torn blouse, wrapping it around her like a shield. Her chin lifted a fraction, her headstrong personality making an appearance, which was completely at odds with the bruise already discoloring her pale cheek.

"Thank you, for everything," she said, her tone frustratingly pleasant and bland. "But you don't need to stay."

"You're still shaken up, Raina." He could see that she was barely holding things together, trying to be so capable and strong, but the truth was, she looked pale and fragile and on the verge of an emotional meltdown, and he wasn't letting that happen without him being there to give her the comfort she needed. "I'm not leaving until I'm absolutely sure you're okay."

"I'm fine," she insisted, then shook her head, the weariness in her gaze returning. "I'm going to take a shower."

He watched her walk away and toward her bedroom, her shutout clear and painful. He scrubbed a hand along his jaw and knew he had two choices...leave her on her own and let her isolate herself and her emotions, or force her to face those trust issues of hers and tear away every reason she had to doubt his intentions and his growing feelings for her.

His choice was a no-brainer. Raina was his, and he wasn't giving her up without a fight.

Determination fueled his steps into her bedroom,

and he followed the trail of her clothing on the floor into the adjoining bathroom. She was already in the shower, her naked silhouette visible through the frosted glass, and he didn't hesitate to strip off all his own garments, then opened the door to join her.

She was standing still under the spray, letting it beat down on her back and over her shoulders. Her arms were crossed around her waist, and in that unguarded moment, her beautiful blue eyes were huge pools reflecting all the pain she'd tried to hide from him out in the kitchen. She looked so desolate his heart ached, and he stepped inside the glass enclosure and came to a stop in front of her. The tips of his toes touched hers, and she stared up at him, the longing in her eyes unmistakable, even if she couldn't voice that too-vulnerable emotion out loud.

She didn't have to say a word. He'd give her everything she needed. A safe haven. Security. Stability. And yeah, even love, he thought, knowing without a doubt he was already heading in that direction with her.

"I'm not leaving you alone tonight," he said huskily, wanting to make sure he made that very clear.

This time, she didn't argue.

Very gently, he pulled her arms from around her middle, then brought one of her wrists to his lips for a tender kiss where her skin was still chafed and sore from Jared's manhandling, then repeated the process on the other. He stared deeply into her eyes. "Let me take care of you." *Always*, he wanted to add but kept that to himself for now.

She moaned softly, as if struggling with the urge to give herself over to him so completely. Emotionally. Mentally. Physically.

He touched his fingers to her damp cheek, and she closed her eyes and gingerly rubbed her face against his palm. "Let me in, Raina," he whispered. *Trust me not to hurt you.*

Her wet, spiky lashes fluttered back open, a combination of heat and desire swirling in the depths of her gaze. "Logan…" she breathed, a sweet, sensual hitch in her voice.

"I'm right here, sugar," he murmured as he skimmed his thumb along her bottom lip. Whatever happened tonight, it was up to her to make the first move. But once she did, all bets were off, and he was going to make certain she knew that she belonged to him. Her heart, her body, and her soul. He'd leave no part of her untouched. Unclaimed.

Tentatively, she pressed her hands to his chest and dragged her palms down his tight abdomen, her mouth lifting up to his. "I need you," she said against his lips, the words anguished. "*Please.*"

With a groan, he buried his fingers in her wet hair and crushed his mouth to hers, kissing her deeply, passionately, as he backed her up against the glass wall and pinned her there with his slick, wet body. As if he'd flipped a switch inside of her, she turned just as aggressive, pushing her hand between them and wrapping it around his hard cock, stroking his thick length as if this had suddenly become a battle of dominance she intended to win.

He'd played this game with her before and knew she was angling to be on top, so to speak, so she could be the one in control and keep her emotions under wraps. So she could keep this encounter all about pleasure, without letting messy feelings take over.

Not gonna happen tonight, because when he had Raina beneath him, he was going to make her feel *everything* that was changing between them. There would be no hiding from her fears and no denying what she meant to him.

He tore his mouth from hers, shut off the shower, and in a move so quick it startled Raina, he picked her up in his arms and carried her to the bed without drying her off. He set her down on the comforter, and before she had the chance to sit back up, he moved over her, using his knee to push her legs wide apart so he could settle his hips in between her soft thighs. The tip of his pulsing cock glided through her slit, her slick moisture lubricating the sensitive, swollen head.

She pressed her hands against his shoulders, trying

to tumble him off her. "I want to be on top."

"No." He didn't budge, *wouldn't* budge. Bracing his forearms on either side of her head so that he completely surrounded her, he slowly pushed his dick along her soft, wet folds once again. "Do I need a condom?" he asked gruffly, dying to feel her bare, without anything between them, but only if that was what she wanted, too. The Players Club required regular health screenings; he was clean, and he was religious about using protection, but she made him crave skin on skin.

She bit her bottom lip as she curled her legs tight around the backs of his thighs, which tipped her hips up and positioned his cock perfectly at her entrance. "No, I'm on the pill," she rasped, rocking against him. "I want to feel you inside of me."

Permission granted, he buried himself to the hilt in one long, solid thrust, groaning as the hot, tight walls of her vagina gripped him and caressed the length of his shaft like a silken fist. She felt incredible, so sleek and smooth as he slowly, gradually pumped in and out of her. Again and again, until she was squirming restlessly beneath him and doing her best to try and speed up the pace of his measured strokes.

One of her hands twisted in his hair, giving her the leverage to arch her back so she could rub her clit against him every time he sank into her, while her other hand grabbed his ass and desperately tried to make him move faster. He was bigger and stronger, and no way was he going to let her dictate anything about this encounter.

Untangling her fingers from his hair, he grabbed the palm she had on his ass and pinned both hands right above her head. Careful not to hurt her wrists, he threaded their fingers together so she was completely at his mercy.

She glared at him, even as she panted for more. "Fuck me harder," she pleaded.

She wanted a wild and mindless coupling, the complete opposite of what he was going to give her.

He dipped his head, brushing his lips across hers as he filled her once more, then withdrew so languidly it was pure torture for both of them—especially when her greedy body clasped around the swollen, sensitive head of his cock and tried to suck him back inside. The sharp arousal in his belly threatened his own restraint.

"I'm going to fuck you slow and deep," he promised as he licked his tongue across her bottom lip. "I'm going to make you unravel from the inside out and come so hard you're going to scream." He pushed back into her, watching her eyes glaze over with heated lust. "And I'm going to watch your gorgeous face when it happens."

He kept up the maddeningly erotic pace, now deliberately grinding against that bundle of nerves with every slow thrust inside of her. She gasped, her fingers tightening around his as Logan recognized the signs of her impending orgasm. Her head tipped back, her lips parted on a soft, sensual moan, and her stunning blue eyes dilated with desire. A beautiful flush of ecstasy suffused her complexion, and when her lashes fluttered closed as her sweet body began contracting around his cock, he issued a direct command.

"Look at me, Raina," he growled fiercely.

She did, hiding nothing from him in that moment as she cried out his name and gave herself over to her searing release, her gaze locked on his. Her uninhibited surrender and the exquisite sensation of her inner walls milking him triggered his own mounting orgasm, and he quickened his thrusts. His gut tightened into a knot of pleasure so intense that when it finally exploded through him, he came so fucking hard he didn't think he'd ever be the same again.

Once he was able to move, he rolled off her and pulled her up against his side so that her head was on his shoulder and one of her legs draped over his thigh. He pulled the other side of the comforter around them, and she snuggled up to him willingly. Most importantly, she didn't ask him to leave—which was a damn good thing because he wasn't going anywhere anytime soon.

✧　✧　✧

THE RINGING OF a cell phone at six thirty the following morning pulled Raina out of a deep sleep. When Logan untangled their limbs so he could reach across his side of the bed to grab his phone, the cool air that replaced the warmth of his body became a stark reminder that after this morning, he'd be gone. The thought caused her heart to ache, which told her just how far and fast she'd fallen for Logan Cruz.

He squinted to read the caller ID, then swore beneath his breath before answering. "Hey, Mac," he said, his voice still gravelly from being abruptly woken up. "What's going on?"

Mac. Dean's partner and Logan's boss. Considering the early hour, Raina figured it was an important call. Logan sat up on the edge of the mattress as he listened to Mac on the other end of the line, and she got out of bed so she could put some clothes on. Yeah, she needed that barrier between them, because she knew being naked around Logan would distract her from what she had to do this morning—say goodbye.

"*Today?*" Logan asked, his voice more than a little grumpy as he watched her cross the room to her dresser, then put on a pair of sweat pants and a T-shirt. "What time?"

Sufficiently covered, she turned back around and caught Logan frowning at her, an annoyed look on his face, which she assumed was a result of whatever he had to do today, which interfered with his personal plans. She went to the bathroom, brushed her teeth, and continued to listen to the one-sided conversation.

"Yeah, yeah, of course I'll be there," Logan said, his tone resigned.

Needing a boost of caffeine, Raina headed down the hall to the kitchen just as Logan said, "Fine. Just email me the ticket information and itinerary, and I'll be sure I make the flight."

He was going out of town. Which was probably for the best. Forced time apart would make their separation easier to deal with and give Logan time to realize that she was *not* his forever woman, despite all the emotions she'd felt between them last night.

Swallowing back the lump in her throat, she made a pot of coffee, then leaned against the counter, waiting for Logan to join her. Minutes later, he walked into the kitchen, and the man just didn't play fair at all. He'd put his jeans back on and zipped them up but hadn't bothered to button them, and that tantalizing glimpse of his firm, muscled abdomen made an arousing surge of heat curl through her. He hadn't put on his shirt, either, which left his gorgeous, chiseled chest on display. His hair was tousled, a seductive stubble lined his jaw, and his dark green eyes reminded her of how he'd commanded her to *look at him* when she'd climaxed.

That moment had been so incredibly intimate, as if she'd given him a direct, unprotected glimpse into her heart and soul. He'd stripped her bare—not just physically but in the deepest, most emotional way possible.

The corner of his mouth tipped up in a lazy good-morning smile, and her pulse skipped a treacherous beat. He was so damn hot, so insanely sexy, that it took real effort for her to not jump him one last time here in her kitchen. She purposefully glanced away and reached up into the cupboard for a mug. Just one, because she didn't want to linger with him over a cozy cup of coffee, and besides, he obviously had some-where he needed to be.

"I take it work beckons?" she asked, her tone de-ceptively casual.

"Yeah," he said, not sounding at all happy about that fact. "I was hoping to have this last day off, but the firm is short-handed right now. They need a team to fly to Chicago for a few days to handle security detail for a client attending a political summit."

She poured coffee into her cup and glanced over her shoulder at him, giving him an understanding smile. "Important stuff."

He braced his hands on his hips, his gaze never wavering from hers. "You're just as important."

She swallowed back the swell of emotion that rose in her throat at his words and turned around to face him again. "Logan...please don't make this any more difficult than it already is."

He tipped his head, his expression patient, as if he'd anticipated this argument with her. "Don't make *what* any more difficult?"

A flicker of anger surged through her, that he was forcing her to make this uglier than it needed to be. "You. And me." She cut to the heart of the matter. "I don't belong in your life. Trust me, I'm doing you a big favor by ending things now." She was also saving herself from another devastating heartbreak.

His gaze narrowed as he processed her words. "How can you know that?"

"Because I've been through this before!" she said, her frustration getting the best of her.

He blinked at her in surprise. And now that that revelation was out, she knew he wouldn't leave without an explanation, that she'd need to dredge up the past in order to make Logan understand and believe this was for the best.

"I've been with a man who said he was crazy about me," she said, letting it all spill out before she changed her mind or Logan could interrupt her. "He even wanted to marry me. He was a successful real estate developer, we got engaged, and then one day, out of the blue, a month before the wedding, Derek issued me an ultimatum. I had to choose between him and my business, because he didn't want people to think he was marrying a whore who sold porn. And he certainly didn't want the mother of his children dealing with vibrators or bondage equipment."

"Are you fucking kidding me?" Logan growled in disbelief.

Raina wished she was joking, but the truth still had the ability to feel like a sharp knife twisting in her heart. "You see, his family was embarrassed, no, *mortified*, by the fact that I sold sex toys for a living, and his colleagues had made some nasty and crude comments about me and my business, and Derek couldn't handle it. I refused to give him that much control and power over my life and my business, and I walked away. But the few men I've dated since then have had the same mind-set. I was good enough to fuck in private, but what I did for a living was a dirty little secret they didn't want anyone to know about." And that cycle of being judged and condemned and ostracized had made it evident to her that she was better off alone than going through that pain and disappointment again and again.

Logan was standing only a few feet away, his hands fisted at his sides, and she could feel the anger vibrating off him. "Your ex, and those men, are assholes, and you thankfully dodged a bullet with that pansy-assed developer. I don't give a shit what you do for a living."

"But your sister does," she said quietly, knowing how important Emily, his own family, was to him. "You were there at the dinner table on Sunday. You saw her reaction. She was horrified. I've learned the hard way that what a family thinks of me eventually matters. A lot."

He swore out loud, his jaw clenched. "My sister will get over it."

She wrapped her arms around her waist and shook her head, knowing that was unlikely. "It doesn't matter, Logan." She lifted her chin, trying to be firm and not fall apart. She could do that later, when he was gone. "I'm making the choice for you, for both of us, before things get any deeper between us."

"Too late, sugar." He walked toward where she was leaning against the counter and braced a hand on either side of her. "I'm already falling for you—"

Her heart slammed against her chest, and she pressed her fingers against his lips to stop him from talking, from saying the kind of words that would completely destroy her. "Logan, *no.*"

He gently grabbed her wrist and pulled her hand away. "*Yes*," he said, the emotion in his green eyes unmistakable. "I can *feel* it, and it's like *nothing* I've ever felt for another woman."

The pain inside her grew. "You loved Charlotte."

"I was a boy, a teenager when we started dating," he said, his gaze holding hers. "I loved Charlotte, but I know now that I wasn't ever *in* love with her. If I had been, it would have killed me to walk away from her, even after what she did to me. Instead, I was *grateful*."

"And in the long run, you'll be equally grateful that you didn't stay with me," she refuted. "I'm not the kind of traditional woman you want in your life. The kind of woman you *deserve* to have in your life."

Logan took a moment to inhale and exhale a deep breath after that comment, gathering his thoughts before he spoke. He knew this conversation with Raina wasn't going to be easy, and she was doing everything in her power to push him away because she believed it was the best thing for *him*. But to hear and know that she didn't think she was worthy of him, that she truly believed she wasn't the kind of woman he deserved to have in his life, made him furious at every man who'd ever made her feel less than amazing and worthy of love.

Worst of all, he knew her insecurities and fears weren't unfounded. They were based in reality, in the truth of other people's actions toward her. Starting with her own father and trickling down from there. Well, he was going to be the man who was going to end that cycle of pain, no matter how long it took him to convince her that he wasn't going anywhere.

He let go of her hand and placed his own back on the counter beside her, making sure there was no easy escape for Raina while he put all his emotional cards out on the table.

"Whenever I look at you, I know you're the one," he said, meaning every word. "From the first moment I saw you dancing up in that gold cage in The Players Club, I *knew*. And now, whenever I touch you or kiss you or slide deep inside of your body, I know that you were meant to be mine."

Her eyes shone with disbelief, and she shook her head in denial. "That was lust."

"Part of it, yes, but not all of it," he said, leaning in a bit closer. "That night at the club, you ran, and I chased you, and I've never, *ever* chased after another woman before. I never felt that kind of loss as I did that night when you drove away, thinking I'd never see you again."

He saw the glimmer of tears in her eyes, a shimmer of hope, which she valiantly tried to blink away.

"Throw me any argument you want, sugar, and I'm still not letting you go." She looked away from him, which he wasn't going to allow. He reached a hand up and slid his fingers along her jaw and used his thumb to tip her head back up until her gaze met his again. "Because what I do know is that you want me, too, but you're too scared to trust me. I get that, and I'm willing to be patient and wait until you catch up to me and realize that I'm always going to be here for you."

More doubts swam in her beautiful blue eyes. "You can't make those kinds of promises."

"Yes, I can," he said confidently. "And best of all, I *keep* my promises."

She sucked in a breath, clearly so afraid to believe.

"Whatever those doubts and fears are, I'm going to spend as long as it takes to disprove every single one. You're worth fighting for, Raina Beck. You're beautiful and smart and independent. You make me laugh and feel things I thought were dead long ago. Without a doubt, you are my future, my forever. Believe it, because it's true."

Her entire body shuddered. "You should go. You have a plane to catch."

"Yes, I do," he agreed, knowing she needed time and space to process everything and hopefully realize what he already knew. "I'm leaving because I have to, not because I want to. If I had the choice, I'd take you back to bed and keep you there until you believed every single word I've said to you. Until you accepted that you and I belong together."

He let his hand drop from her face and took a step back, which was one of the hardest things he'd ever had to do. "I'm going to go, but I'm coming back, because you and I aren't done. Not even close."

Chapter Fifteen

GIRLS' NIGHT OUT, otherwise known as Cocktails and Cocks, was usually one of Raina's favorite evenings to spend with her girlfriends. Tonight, more than ever, she needed that girl time and the distraction. Stephanie, tonight's hostess, had made fresh pear martinis, and each of the other women had brought their favorite appetizers to share. Men, sex, and general gossip were always on the agenda. And usually, lots of laughter.

Between her and Paige's more somber mood, courtesy of *men*, the latter part of the night's festivities was sorely lacking. Jillian, Stephanie, Kendall, and Summer were trying to liven up the atmosphere with entertaining stories of clients they'd had during the week at their shops. And while Stephanie's tale about a gay couple who wanted to commission her to decorate an Arabian Nights themed bedroom for them had been funny and amusing, Raina's mind kept drifting, her thoughts consumed with everything that had transpired between her and Logan over the past week since meeting him at The Players Club.

She felt as though it had been much longer than that.

It had been two days since Logan had walked out of her apartment, and she'd spent every moment since thinking about everything he'd said to her. The pain of watching him leave had felt as though she'd cut her own heart out with a serrated blade, it hurt so bad, not to mention the constant wondering if she'd done the right thing by ending *them*. Now, she wasn't so sure.

While he'd been gone, he'd sent her random texts, as if to remind her of all the promises he'd made that morning before he'd left for Chicago. *I miss you. I want you, always. You own me. You're mine.* And then today, at the store, a sleek pink box with a big ribbon on it had arrived for her, along with a note from Logan: *To replace all the ones I've taken and all the ones I plan to add to my collection.*

The message had been confusing until she'd opened the box, peeled away the layer of pink em-bossed tissue, and discovered two dozen pairs of panties folded inside in an array of color, and a few with prints. There was pretty lace and satin and silk. Fun and cute pairs with sexy sayings on them. Others

301

with bows or other embellishments and appliqués. Delicate, elegant G-strings with rhinestones and pearls. And even a few naughty crotch-less ones.

His gift had made her laugh. Then the tears she'd been holding back for two days had finally burst through the emotional levee she'd erected when he'd walked out her door, and out came all the fears and insecurities she'd been carrying with her for so many years. She'd been a hot mess by the time the crying had subsided, but one question kept slipping into her mind and demanded an answer.

When had a man fought as hard for her as Logan was doing?

Never.

That realization forced her to accept that Logan *was* different. Had been from the start. He'd barged his way into her life, held on, and he hadn't let her go. He'd been there through every moment of terror her stalker had inflicted and not only because he was being paid. Somehow she knew Logan would have protected her regardless of his job. At every turn, he'd proven himself to be beyond any man in her past and any she might have dreamed of for her future. And he hadn't let his sister's negative feelings drive him away, either.

Why had it taken her so long to believe in him?

"I'm going to get a glass of water," Paige said quietly, bringing Raina's attention back to the present.

"Does anyone want anything?"

A round of "no thank you" and "I'm good" came from the other women.

"I'll come with you," Raina said, needing a break from the gossip, and followed Paige into the kitchen. Despite her own problems with Logan, Raina was concerned about her friend, who hadn't been the same since her run-in with Sawyer at the shop a few days ago.

Paige retrieved a glass from the cupboard, then poured herself a cold glass of filtered water from the sink's tap. She leaned back against the counter and took a sip, the look in her eyes troubled.

"Hey, you okay?" Raina asked as she settled in beside her.

Paige shrugged. "I honestly don't know how I am," she said, staring into the glass of clear liquid.

Raina waited a few moments before broaching the sensitive topic of her past. "Are you still thinking about Sawyer?"

Paige's lips pursed, and she turned her gaze to Raina, a combination of pain and anger swirling in the depths of her green eyes. "How can I hate him so much after what he did to me but still *want* him?" she asked, sounding horrified at that prospect. "When I saw him walk into Sugar and Spice, I was just so taken off guard. I didn't know he was back in town, and all those awful, gut-wrenching memories came rushing back. But beneath all that hurt, I still felt that same pull of desire toward him. How wrong and sick is that?" She laughed dryly and shook her head.

"You fell hard for him," Raina said sympathetically. "And you haven't dated since he left a year and a half ago. And he was the last guy that you were wildly attracted to, so I'm sure that's part of your reaction to seeing him again, as well."

"Fuck Sawyer for being so hot and sexy and knowing his way around a woman's body like an experienced gigolo," Paige said, a bit of humor slipping through her melancholy. "I need to get over him already."

Raina grinned at her friend's audacious comment. "Yes, you do. There are other hot and sexy guys out there who are more than capable of being good in bed."

Paige lifted her chin with a bit of determination. "Yes, there are. Maybe I just need to find a guy to get totally freaky with, so I can forget about Sawyer."

Raina laughed. "Sounds like a great plan."

Paige grew serious again. "What about you and Logan? Are you going to give the guy a chance?"

Her friend knew most of what had happened between her and Logan, as well as all the reasons Raina had issues trusting men. And even Paige had been insisting that Logan was one of the few good guys out there, and Raina would be crazy to let him go.

"I haven't spoken to him since he left, but I've doing a lot of thinking about the things he told me before he had to go to Chicago." Being alone, especially at night, with only the thoughts in her head to occupy all the quiet time, had allowed her to think about her relationship with Logan with her heart, instead of the fears that had ruled her life for so long.

"And?" Paige prompted curiously.

"For years I believed that I wasn't good enough for any man to want me beyond a physical fling, and it was so much easier to indulge in temporary affairs, instead of being hurt again," Raina said softly. "But with Logan, everything is different. And with him gone, I feel like I've lost the best thing to ever happen to me, and I've never felt that way before. Ever. I feel…so empty inside, and it hurts so much, but this time I know it doesn't have to be that way."

Logan's heartfelt words floated through her mind, *You're worth fighting for, Raina Beck. Without a doubt, you are my future, my forever. Believe it, because it's true.*

Paige lifted a brow. "Sounds like maybe someone is, or has, fallen in love."

Raina's heart beat faster at the truth of her friend's words, and she didn't even bother trying to deny it. Instead, she let the wonderful but scary feeling settle in, to give herself time to embrace everything the emotion meant to her future. Happiness. Contentment. And belonging to someone who'd made it very clear that he wanted her in his life. That he was willing to fight for her, despite every reason she'd given him not to.

Logan wasn't asking her to give up anything, and he'd never made demands or tried to change anything about who she was. He'd been nothing but supportive of her business—hell, he'd even sold products to customers in her store, she thought with a private grin. She'd never felt so cared for and protected, so desired and secure. He made her want all those things she'd never thought she'd ever have in her life, and most of all, he gave her every reason to believe he'd give her anything and everything she'd dreamed of.

When she was with Logan, she was so incredibly happy, and dammit, she *deserved* that kind of joy in her life.

"You look so serious," Paige said, tipping her head to the side as Raina met her gaze. "What are you thinking?"

Raina smiled, the first real one in days. "I'm thinking I'm ready to let go of my fears and ready to let Logan in."

✧   ✧   ✧

THE BRIEF, SPONTANEOUS texts from Logan continued throughout Saturday while Raina was working at Sugar and Spice, and she was grateful that none of his short messages required any kind of reply from her. The next time she said anything to him, she needed it to be in person, face-to-face. She knew taking that first step toward Logan was going to be the most difficult—she was both excited and nervous about her decision—and he needed to see and know how much he meant to her.

While Aaron and another part-time worker covered the floor, Raina spent time in her office making out the schedule for the next two weeks and inputting payroll into the computer. A quick knock on her open door made her glance up to find Aaron's big, muscular frame standing at the entrance.

"Raina, there's a customer out front by the register who is asking to see you," he said, hooking his thumb in that direction.

"Okay," she said, giving him a smile. "Let them know I'll be right there."

"You got it." He nodded, then headed back out to the main floor.

Raina shut down her computer and locked her office before making her way up to the front register. It wasn't uncommon for customers to ask for her specifically, but her steps faltered and her stomach twisted with unease when she saw who was waiting for her.

Logan's sister, Emily. And she looked about as uncomfortable as a nun in a brothel. Her arms were crossed over her chest, her wide eyes were checking out the different sections of the boutique, and she shifted anxiously on her feet. She'd only made it as far as the front counter, as if there were an invisible line she refused to cross into the actual store.

Raina exhaled a deep breath, feeling a bit nervous herself as she approached the antsy woman. "Hi, Emily," she said politely. "What can I do for you?"

"Hi, Raina," she said with what looked like an I'm-trying-to-be-brave smile. "I…umm, could we go somewhere and talk? There's a coffee place a few doors down…"

She couldn't even begin to imagine what they had to discuss, unless… "Did Logan send you?" It was the only thing that made sense, even though he'd promised her he wouldn't interfere.

"What?" Those guileless eyes widened again as Raina's question sank in, and Emily quickly shook her head in horror. "No! He doesn't even know I'm here."

Raina believed her, and she was relieved. The woman was a hot mess, and now that Raina knew that Logan hadn't prompted his sister to come here, she was curious to know what was on Emily's mind.

"Sure, we can talk," Raina said and smiled, trying to put Emily at ease. "Give me a minute to get my purse and let my manager know where I'll be."

Raina quickly did those two things, then met back up with Emily, who'd dared to venture a few more feet into the store and was trying to *casually* check out the front display of women's small, discreet vibrators.

"I'm ready to go," Raina said from behind her and almost laughed as Emily jumped, then spun around, her face flushing as if she'd just been caught with her hand in the cookie jar.

Emily rushed out the door, and Raina followed her. The walk to the coffee shop was a quiet one, and it wasn't until they were settled at a table outside and away from the other customers, with their drinks delivered, that Emily looked across the table at Raina and spoke.

"I owe you an apology for the way I acted last Sunday," she said, her tone laced with genuine regret. "I completely overacted, and I'm so sorry that I treated you so badly, because I really do like you."

"Thank you." Raina truly didn't know what else to say. She definitely appreciated the apology, but she wasn't sure where that left the two of them or if Emily could really accept what Raina did for a living.

Emily glanced at her iced vanilla latte, her fingers wiping away the condensation gathering on the plastic cup. "After you and Logan left on Sunday, Pete and I had an argument," she said quietly and met Raina's gaze again. "He was upset with me because I acted like such...a prude, and I know I embarrassed you, too."

Raina took a drink of her iced tea and remained quiet. Again, she was at a loss for words, but apparently Emily needed to get this all out, so she was more than willing to listen.

"Anyway, Pete decided he wanted to make a point since I was being so uptight about the whole sex toy thing, and on Tuesday morning, he stopped by your store and picked up a few items."

Tuesday was the day that she'd arrived at the boutique in the early afternoon, obviously missing Pete's visit. But Raina was definitely intrigued by Emily's story and where it was headed.

"That night, when Hannah was asleep for the night and I was changing into my nightgown, Pete came into the our room with a black-handled bag and dumped the contents onto our bed, and boy was I taken aback at what he'd bought." Emily pressed her hands to her flushed face, as if remembering that exact moment.

Raina bit the inside of her cheek, absolutely dying to know what her husband had purchased.

Emily leaned across the table, her voice dropping to just above a whisper. "He bought some fuzzy handcuffs and a vibrator and this warming massage oil that tasted like cherries and a sexy lace teddy. He said I shouldn't judge other people unless I've tried it…and so we did."

Go Pete, Raina thought, delighted by the man's creativity, as well as the fact that she clearly had an ally.

"Raina…" Emily shook her head, her expression awed despite the blush sweeping across her cheeks. "I swear, it was the best sex we ever had. I can't help but wonder what I've been missing out on all these years."

Raina laughed. She couldn't help it. Emily was so bewildered, in a good way, as if she'd just discovered the secret to amazing sex. "I'm glad the two of you had fun. That's really what it's about. Having fun with your partner. Enjoying yourself and doing what feels good."

"It felt really, *really* good," Emily admitted and laughed, too. Then she reached across the table and clasped Raina's hand, her expression serious again. "I'm so very sorry that I judged you and made you feel so uncomfortable. I love my brother so much. I want him to be happy, and I can tell that he's crazy about you. The last thing I want is to have my stupid, narrow-minded actions on Sunday come between any of us."

Raina squeezed Emily's hand right back, feeling as though a huge weight had lifted off her chest. She'd decided she wanted things to work with Logan, even knowing his sister had disapproved of her business. But having Emily's blessing now was unexpected but wonderful, and she had Pete to thank for changing his wife's way of thinking.

"We're good, Emily," Raina said, and meant it.

Relief softened Emily's features, and then she bit her lower lip, suddenly looking adorably shy. "I was thinking…maybe you could help me pick out a few things at your store that I can surprise Pete with tonight?"

Raina grinned. "Oh, absolutely."

Chapter Sixteen

AFTER NEARLY FIVE days in Chicago, Logan was back in San Diego, driving home with his stomach in absolute knots. He hadn't spoken to Raina on the phone since he'd left, and the only text she'd answered was the one he'd sent earlier during his layover in Phoenix.

He'd texted: *My flight gets in at six tonight. I want to see you.*

And she'd responded: *I'm sorry. I won't be home.*

That was it. No other comment. No explanation. Nothing. He couldn't help but wonder if it was really over between the two of them, if she was going to shut him out in a way he wouldn't be able to break through. He refused to think of that possibility, refused to believe that the time apart had enabled her to carve him out of her life so easily.

He was tempted to head over to her apartment and

wait there until she returned, but she'd made it clear with her text that she didn't want to see him, and tonight, he'd respect her need for more space.

But it was fucking hard to do when he was the kind of guy who went after what he wanted, no matter what obstacles stood in his way. And despite his take-charge personality, the thing that scared him the most was the knowledge that he couldn't force Raina to be his. She had to come to him on her terms. With her heart open and willing, and trusting that he'd never, ever hurt her.

Frustration squeezed his chest, and he gripped the steering wheel tighter as he turned down his street. Then his heart slammed into his throat when he caught sight of a familiar vehicle parked out by the curb of his house. He turned his Camaro into the driveway, and when he saw Raina sitting on one of the steps leading up to his front porch, he didn't bother pulling the car into the garage.

Hope clashed with a surprising anxiety as he got out, grabbed his duffle, then swung the bag over his shoulder as he headed toward Raina. Considering her earlier text, he had no idea why she was here and prayed to God it wasn't to truly end their relationship.

As he neared, she stood up, her hands smoothing down the flowing material of her gauzy skirt, seemingly just as nervous to see him. She looked so beautiful his heart ached, and she looked so damn perfect standing in front of his house, exactly where she belonged. Her hands twisted together in front of her, and her blue eyes shone with a trepidation that felt like a sucker punch to his stomach.

With a casualness he didn't feel, he stopped a few feet from her. "I thought you had plans tonight."

She swallowed hard, and a tentative smile lifted the corner of her mouth. "I do. Hopefully with you."

He had no idea what that meant, and he wasn't about to assume anything when there was so much tension between them. "Come on in."

He walked past her—so damn hard when he wanted to pull her into his arms and never let her go—and unlocked the front door. He let Raina enter first, then followed her into the living room. He dropped his bag on the floor and turned around to face her, bracing himself for the worst.

"So, I've had a lot of time to think since you've been gone," she said, her voice wavering ever-so-slightly as she dampened her bottom lip with her tongue. "I've been alone for so long, doing everything on my own, and the last thing I was looking for or wanted in my life was a man. And then you happened."

He arched a brow. "I can't tell if that's a good thing or a bad thing."

"It's a very good thing. It just took me a bit longer than you to realize that I want you in my life. That I *need* you in my life, Logan Cruz," she said, her voice gaining strength and confidence. "I'm so tired of being scared and lonely, so wrapped up in my past and fears, and the thought of losing you frightens me even more. You make me believe that you're my future, my forever," she said, repeating the words he'd said to her their last morning together.

He took a step closer to her, his body shuddering with relief. "I am your future, your forever," he said gruffly.

A glimmer of tears sparkled in her eyes as she took her own step toward him, closing the distance between them. "I deserve you."

"Damn right you do," he said and finally pulled her into his arms, holding her tight against his chest, certain she could hear the wild beating of his heart. "Don't you *ever* doubt that again."

"I won't." She wrapped her arms around his waist, holding him just as securely, her face buried against his throat. "Most importantly, I trust you with my heart."

He groaned, her words humbling him, leaving no doubt what this incredible woman meant to him. Threading his fingers through her hair, he gently pulled her head back so that she was looking up at him, their eyes locked with all the emotion flowing between them. "I love you, Raina Beck."

She smiled, even as a happy tear rolled down her cheek. "I love you, too." She touched her fingertips to his jaw, her gaze filled with wonder and awe. "I've never had a man fight for me like you have."

"Sugar, you're worth fighting for," he drawled huskily as he wiped away the moisture on her cheek with his thumb. "I'd slay dragons for you if I had to."

That made her laugh, the sound so incredibly sweet to his ears and one he wanted to hear for the rest of his life.

She released a heartfelt sigh and slid her hand around to the nape of his neck. "It's not easy letting a man take care of me, but I'm willing to try and get used to it."

"I protect what's mine," he said, more fiercely than he'd intended. "Always."

"I want to sleep in your arms at night and wake up curled next to you every single morning," she said, her tone taking a sensual turn. "Is that going to be okay?"

He exhaled a deep breath. "I wouldn't have it any other way. You belong *here*, with me." Remembering the gift he'd bought for her in Chicago, he let her go for a moment. "I have something for you."

He unzipped his duffle bag and retrieved a small square box in a distinctive blue color. The present was monogrammed with the name of a high-end jeweler and wrapped with a white bow.

Her eyes grew wide as he gave her the gift. "What is this?"

"It's for you," he said with a smile, even as nerves tightened in his belly. "To remind you that you're mine forever. Open it."

She looked like a delighted child as she tugged on the bow and unraveled it, leading him to believe that spontaneous gifts were a rare thing for her. It was something he intended to change.

She lifted the lid and gasped, her jaw dropping open. "Logan, this is too much."

No, it hadn't been cheap, but she was worth every penny he'd spent on the platinum and diamond bracelet. "Do you know what that symbol is?" he asked of the design that looked like a figure eight, which was encrusted with glittering diamonds.

She nodded, still stunned by the gift. "It's the sign of infinity."

"Which is exactly how long I will love you." Taking the bracelet from the box, he secured it around her wrist, then looked into her eyes again. "And when you're ready, I'm going to put a ring on your finger and make you my wife."

Another surge of tears filled her eyes, and she bit on her bottom lip to hold back the well of emotion.

"That's a good thing, sugar," he said, hoping he

wasn't moving way too fast for her.

"I know," she whispered, her throat tight. "I just feel like the luckiest girl in the world right now."

She wrapped her arms around his neck and kissed him, slow and deep. Their tongues tangled. She tasted like heaven, and her sweet, feminine scent engulfed him. His pulse sped up, and his thickening cock desperately needed to be deep inside of her.

He lifted his mouth from hers and stared down at her flushed face. "Goddamn, I missed you," he growled, then swooped her up into his arms and carried her to his bedroom, his intentions clear.

He gently tossed her onto his bed, and she landed with a soft squeak of surprise. Before he could join her and strip her naked, she put up a hand to hold him off.

"Wait," she said breathlessly. "I have a gift for you, too."

Standing by the side of the bed, he tipped his head curiously. "Yeah?"

She nodded, a seductive smile curving her lips as she slowly, teasingly pulled up her skirt. He watched the material move up over her knees and slide along her sleek thighs, his dick getting harder and harder beneath the fly of his jeans with each inch of skin she exposed. And then, pretty red lace panties came into view, and if that wasn't enough to make his blood run molten in his veins, she spread her gorgeous legs, revealing the opening in the crotch that framed her smooth, glistening pussy.

His mouth went dry and lust slammed into him like a freight train. "Holy shit, Raina," he rasped, his gaze never leaving her soft, pink flesh.

Her eyes danced with delight at his reaction. "I wanted to make sure I thanked you properly for my other present," she said of the box of underwear he'd sent to her.

Grabbing her ankles, he dragged her to the edge of the mattress, closer to where he stood. "You look so sweet and so damn hot in those panties," he said and feathered his fingers along her wet folds, his touch teasing her. "I can't decide what I want to do more. Eat you or fuck you."

She gasped as his thumb stroked across her swollen, sensitive clit, her darkening gaze taunting him. "How about both?"

He grinned wickedly. "I like the way you think."

He didn't hesitate to go down on her, his mouth ravenous and his tongue ruthless in his quest to make her scream, which didn't take long. He licked and sucked, again and again, and her fingers gripped his hair, her back arching as she cried out in pleasure. Beyond wild for her, he reared back, tore open the front of his jeans, and released his aching cock. He lifted her legs, draping them over his arms so he could keep them wide apart and watch as his shaft sank deep inside of her body.

The sight of his dick surrounded by sexy red lace sent a burst of heat slicing through him and caused his cock to pulse against the tight walls enveloping him. It was one of the most erotic things he'd ever seen. "I think this is my favorite pair of panties," he said huskily.

She laughed, then groaned as he released her legs and moved completely over her, his face inches above hers as he thrust hard and deep inside her. He wrapped the long strands of her silky hair around his fist and tipped her head back, loving the feel of her pinned beneath him, completely and utterly his.

He looked into her passion-glazed eyes, unable to deny the possessive impulse rushing through him. "You're mine, Raina," he rasped, needing her to believe it. Feel it. Accept it.

"Yes," she breathed, her own body quickening around his.

"*Say it*," he demanded, gritting his teeth in his attempt to stave off his own release until she gave him what he wanted. What he needed.

She met his gaze, the emotion playing across her features the most beautiful thing in the world. "I'm yours, Logan."

That's all he needed to hear to let go, to lose himself in the only woman who'd ever consumed his heart, his body, his soul.

Epilogue

THE BELL ON the door tinkled as Raina walked into Couture Corsets, the small boutique in Old Town where Paige designed and sold custom-made corsets for clients.

"It's just me," Raina called out, knowing her friend was in the back of the shop, where all the beautiful creations happened, and she didn't want Paige to have to leave a project she might be working on when Raina could just head back there herself.

The front area of the boutique was decorated to look like an elegant and romantic boudoir, with a sitting area arranged with velvet-covered vintage settees. Gorgeous corsets hung in Victorian armoires for customers to peruse, and a few decorative dress forms displayed some of Paige's higher-end creations. A hand-painted wooden divider separated the retail floor from a private dressing area, where clients could try on the different pieces of lingerie in front of a three-way mirror.

Raina walked past the curtain of glittering crystals hanging in the doorway that separated the retail floor from Paige's work room and found her friend hand sewing small seed pearls to an exquisite white satin corset she was making for a client's wedding night.

"Wow, that looks stunning," Raina said, so incredibly impressed with her friend's ability to create such works of art.

Paige glanced over her shoulder and grinned. "Thanks. Once I add the crystal and lace embellishments along the bodice, this bride is going to knock her groom's pants off when he sees her in this corset."

Raina laughed. "Not a bad way to start off a marriage."

"What? By getting lucky?" Paige asked humorously as she set her needle and thread down on a nearby worktable.

"And being totally turned on by your new wife."

"Speaking of getting turned on," Paige said with a smirk. "You're glowing and smiling all the time, so things with Logan must be good, yes?"

"Really good," Raina admitted, unable to help the fluttering of her heart that accompanied thoughts of the man who'd changed her life in so many ways. Being in love was the best feeling ever. "And I do have to say, it's nice having sex on a regular basis," she teased.

Paige sent her a mock glare. "Yeah, I wouldn't know, so stop bragging."

Her friend's lack of a sex life was why Raina had come by. It was time for Paige to get her sexy on and end her year-and-a-half dry spell. Hopefully, a night of no-holds-barred sex with a hot guy would make her feel desired and boost her confidence so she could finally let her past, and Sawyer, go. It had worked for Raina.

"I have something for you," Raina said and handed Paige an envelope with the word *Welcome* embossed in black across the front.

Paige's eyes widened as she looked at the envelope. "Oh my God, is this an invitation to your wedding? I can't believe you didn't tell me…" Her words and excitement trailed off as she pulled out the card inside and read the message granting her a night at The Players Club.

"Oh, wow," Paige finally said, glancing back at Raina. "I thought—"

"If I was getting married, you'd know about it before I sent out invitations because you'd be my maid-of-honor," Raina interrupted with a laugh. "Besides, I'm not even engaged yet." And as much as Logan was ready to put a ring on her finger, she just wanted to enjoy and savor every step of her relationship with him.

"This invitation is for you," Raina went on. "The Players Club is a place where you can get down and dirty and freaky with a stranger, indulge in a fantasy, or try a particular kink that has piqued your interest."

Unmistakable interest passed across Paige's features. "I have to say, that sounds very tempting."

"There is one thing you need to know." Raina didn't want Paige to be blindsided in any way. "Logan told me that Sawyer is a member of The Players Club. Which, in my opinion, could work to your advantage if he's there the night you decide to go."

Paige frowned. "How so?"

"*If* he's there, think of it as a bit of revenge. Flirt with other guys and enjoy yourself. Show Sawyer exactly what he's been missing and what is no longer his. Men are such jealous, possessive creatures, and it'll drive him nuts to see you with another man."

The corners of Paige's mouth curled into a smile as she thought about Raina's suggestion. Then a daring and bold determination brightened her eyes. "I'm totally down for that."

Find out what happens between Paige and Sawyer in
PLAYING WITH PLEASURE

If you enjoyed Raina and Logan's story, please
consider leaving an honest review for
PLAYING WITH TEMPTATION
at your e-tailer. It only takes a moment and is very
helpful in spreading the word to other readers.
Thank you!

Read on for a sneak peek of what happens between Paige and Sawyer!

PLAYING WITH PLEASURE

Paige Moore has a fulfilling business designing couture corsets for her high profile clientele, but her love life is sorely lacking. Being burned in the worst way possible by Sawyer Burrows has left her guarded and wary when it comes to men and their motives. When her best friend presents her with an invitation to The Players Club, she embraces the chance to enjoy a hot night with a stranger, and finally put her past heart-break, and Sawyer, behind her.

Sawyer knows he devastated Paige with his careless actions a year and a half ago, and he's lived every day since with those regrets. Now, seeing Paige at The

Players Club, he knows this is his chance to make amends and prove that there is still something between them worth pursuing. If sensual pleasure is what Paige is looking for, then he intends to be the man to spend the night seducing every part of her.

Paige's surrender is Sawyer's ultimate goal, but once her desires are sated, will she give them the second chance they deserve?

Chapter One

THE BELL ON the door to Couture Corsets tinkled, announcing that a customer had just walked into Paige Moore's small boutique in Old Town San Diego where she designed and sold custom-made corsets.

"It's just me," she heard her good friend, Raina Beck, call out.

Knowing Raina would just head to the back area of the shop where Paige did all her designing and creations, she continued hand sewing small seed pearls to an exquisite white satin corset she was making for a client's wedding night.

A moment later, Raina walked past the curtain of glittering crystals hanging in the doorway that separated the retail floor from the work room. "Wow, that looks stunning," she said of the one of a kind bridal corset, her voice laced with awe.

Paige glanced over her shoulder and grinned.

"Thanks. Once I add the crystal and lace embellishments along the bodice, this bride is going to knock her groom's pants off when he sees her in this corset."

Raina laughed. "Not a bad way to start off a marriage."

"What? By getting lucky?" Paige asked humorously as she set her needle and thread down on a nearby work table.

"And being totally turned on by your new wife."

"Speaking of getting turned on," Paige said with a smirk as she eyed her very cheerful friend. "You're glowing and smiling all the time, so things with Logan must be good, yes?"

"Really good," Raina admitted, her face flushing with happiness. "And I do have to say, it's nice having sex on a regular basis," she teased.

Paige sent her a mock glare. "Yeah, I wouldn't know so stop bragging," she grumbled, even though she was genuinely thrilled that Raina had found a man who absolutely adored her. "What brings you by?"

"I have something for you," Raina said, and handed her an envelope with the word *Welcome* embossed in black across the front.

Paige's eyes widened as she looked at the envelope. "Oh my God, is this an invitation to your wedding? I can't believe you didn't tell me..." Her words and excitement trailed off as she pulled out the card inside and read the message granting her a night at The Players Club, a very exclusive, members-only sex club.

"Oh, wow," she breathed in surprise, and glanced back at Raina. "I thought—"

"If I was getting married, you'd know about it before I sent out invitations because you'd be my maid-of-honor," Raina interrupted with a laugh. "Besides, I'm not even engaged yet. This invitation is for you," Raina went on with a grin. "The Players Club is a place where you can get down and dirty and freaky with a stranger, indulge in a fantasy or try a particular kink that has piqued your interest."

"I have to say, that sounds very tempting."

Oh, yes, Paige was definitely intrigued. It had been a year and a half since she'd been with a man. A year and a half since the morning Sawyer Burrows had shattered her heart with his betrayal. And the thought of indulging in a night of hot sex with an anonymous guy was incredibly appealing. She needed to do *something* to finally shake Sawyer from her mind and thoughts, and let the painful past go so she could move on with her life.

Easier said than done, but an evening at The Players Club was a good start to putting an end to her dry spell.

"There is one thing you need to know." Raina suddenly looked uncertain. "Logan told me that

Sawyer is a member of The Players Club. Which, in my opinion, could work to your advantage if he's there the night you decide to go."

Paige frowned, not sure how she felt about running into a man she swore she hated, yet still had the ability to affect her on a physical level. Yeah, that part drove her absolutely crazy, but she was curious what Raina meant. "How so?"

"*If* he's there, think of it as a bit of revenge." Raina's eyes danced with mischief. "Flirt with other guys and enjoy yourself. Show Sawyer exactly what he's been missing, and what is no longer his. Men are such jealous, possessive creatures, and it'll drive him nuts to see you with another man."

The corner of Paige's mouth curled into a smile as she thought about her friend's suggestion. It had been too long since she'd felt desired and sexy. Combine the added bonus of possibly showing Sawyer that she was over him by letting him see her enjoy another man's attention, and it really was a win-win situation.

Her decision made, she met Raina's gaze and lifted her chin in determination. "I'm totally down for that."

Chapter Two

One week later…

THE LOUNGE AREA to The Players Club was incredibly lush and elegant, but much more relaxed than Paige would have anticipated, which helped to calm the butterflies fluttering in her belly. The glass of wine she'd ordered from the bartender— part of the club's two drink max rule—also helped to soothe the nervous energy coursing through her.

She'd never been to a sex club before, and from the moment she'd walked into the huge mansion she'd known she was definitely out of her element. Especially since she was probably the only one there who'd yet to pop her sex club cherry, she thought in amusement. But so far, everyone had been friendly and welcoming, and she had to admit that she felt very comfortable and no pressure from the few men who'd already approached her with definite interest in their eyes.

Which was also a nice little boost to her confidence.

Then again, it didn't hurt that she was wearing a custom fitted corset that cinched in her waist, plumped up her full breasts, and gave her Kardashian curves. She'd paired the purple and black embroidered corset with a black leather mini-skirt and four inch heels that Raina had assured her did amazing things for her legs. Paige had always been a little on the plus-size, and it was hard not to compare herself to the other gorgeous, slender women in the room with the kind of centerfold figures that most men preferred.

Sawyer included.

She groaned to herself as the unwanted thought popped into her head, but that painful truth was difficult for her to forget, considering Sawyer had slept with Paige's Barbie look-alike step-sister, Ashley, *while* he'd been dating Paige. The memory still had the ability to make her feel as though someone had punched her in the stomach, as did her step-sister's words after Paige had caught them together.

Paige, you can't expect a hot, gorgeous guy like Sawyer to be content and satisfied with someone as big and fat as you. Men like him want a woman who is slender and beautiful, who doesn't have a belly and chubby thighs. He told me he just felt sorry for you...

That flashback was enough to bring all of her insecurities to the surface and make her question what the heck she was doing in a place like The Players Club. She certainly couldn't compete with the other attractive, seductive women in the lounge, and in a moment of panic, she abruptly turned around to leave—and bumped full force into a solid male chest that stopped her short, nearly sloshing her wine onto the both of them. A pair of strong hands caught her by the arms to steady her.

"Oh, my God," she gasped, her cheeks flushing in embarrassment as she looked up into a very handsome face. "I'm so sorry. I should have looked where I was going."

"No worries." He smiled and very slowly released his hold on her, his head tipping to the side in undeniable interest. "I enjoyed running into you," he teased. "My name is Dane."

He seemed friendly, and knowing it would be rude to continue her mad dash to the exit without a reply, she exhaled a deep breath and returned his smile. "It's nice to meet you. I'm Paige."

He pushed his hands into the front pockets of his slacks, obviously in no hurry to move on as he studied her face. "You're new here, aren't you?"

The flush on her cheeks escalated to a slow heat, that he'd so easily pegged her for a newbie. "Is it that obvious?"

He laughed, the sound warm and easy-going. "Actually, I have a thing for red heads," he said, and lifted a hand to follow the end of a soft wavy strand that curled against the upper swell of her breast. "You caught my eye the moment you walked into the lounge. If you'd been here before, I would have remembered you."

The desire in his eyes as he glanced from her cleavage, to her mouth, and back to gaze, should have elicited some kind of physical reaction from her, but unfortunately, didn't. "I'm a first timer," she admitted.

He dropped his hand back down to his side, displaying all signs of a true gentleman, which she appreciated. "Then I insist on giving you a personal tour of the place," he said amicably. "Just as soon as I get myself a drink. Would you like a refill on your wine?"

She shook her head, wanting to be sure she kept a clear head. "No, I'm fine. Thank you."

"Then I'll be right back."

Paige watched him walk away and toward the bar. Unfortunately, she felt no spark and she sighed. She really wished otherwise, because not only was the man good looking, but he was a genuinely a nice guy. But she'd told herself before arriving that if she was going to be with anyone tonight, there had to be some kind of chemistry and a mutual attraction. Straight out lust would even be better. Regardless, she planned to leave the club afterward without any kind of personal attachments to complicate matters.

Maybe, while she and Dane were perusing the club things would change and she'd find him more sexually attractive, she thought as she took another sip of her wine.

While she waited for him to return, she glanced around the lounge. New men and women had arrived and were talking and mingling, while others had paired up and were sitting together in one of the intimate, den-like areas across the room, which Paige just noticed. Her curious gaze swept along each of the secluded spots and the couples within, some of which had opted to release the sheer drapes tied off on either side of the alcove for more privacy.

And that's when she saw him—*Sawyer*—casually sitting on one of those velvet couches while a gorgeous and perfectly built woman was draped across his lap with her arms around his neck. One of his hands was on her hip, the other rested on her thigh, and the long haired brunette was smiling at Sawyer in a way that was familiar and seductive as she leaned in close and said something in his ear.

Shock riveted Paige's feet to the floor as she watched his full lips move as he issued some kind of response. Paige's mind screamed at her to *look away* before he caught her, but instead her traitorous gaze lifted from his mouth to his eyes. She sucked in a sharp breath as her gaze collided with his, and even from across the room she could feel his intense, heated stare, focused on *her* like a laser.

An unexpected—and definitely unwanted—surge of desire poured through her, and a traitorous ache settled between her thighs. She desperately tried to ignore both, reminding herself despite the fact that Sawyer still had the ability to make her body come alive with just a look, there was no forgiving him for what he'd done to her. Pretending as though seeing him there at the club had absolutely no affect on her at all was one of the most difficult things she'd ever had to do, but she forced herself to remain indifferent and glanced away just as Dane arrived back by her side with his drink in hand.

"Ready for your tour?" he asked, and offered her his arm in a very charming fashion.

Grateful for something to hold on to so her weak knees wouldn't buckle, she slipped her hand through the crook of his arm and gave Dane a smile. "I'm looking forward to it."

For the next half hour, he escorted her through the mansion, which kept her mind distracted with all the various activities the club had to offer—themed fantasy boudoirs, viewing rooms, open playrooms, and the dark and very intense dungeon. In the lower level, a Mardi Gras themed party was in full swing, complete with beads being awarded for naked breasts while other couples openly kissed and groped and fucked.

They ended up back at the lobby area, standing in front of the split staircase that led to two separate wings of the house where the public and private rooms were located. Another stairway led down below to the dungeon with all its Medieval-like furniture and contraptions that were way out of her first-timer league.

Dane turned to face her, his gaze clearly expressing his interest in her. "I'm heading down to the dungeon, which is my personal preference here at the club," he said, holding her hand in his. "Care to join me?"

"I don't think I'm ready for all that." Paige wouldn't have pegged him for a man who enjoyed those mock torture devices, but hey, she wasn't one to judge. And considering there was still no chemistry or any kind of sexual tension on her end, she decided it was time to part ways.

"I'm going to walk through the viewing rooms upstairs and get a better feel for what interests me," she told him.

"Good girl," he said, clearly respecting her decision, despite the flicker of disappointment in his gaze. "Never do anything that makes you feel uncomfortable or that's out of your comfort zone. That said, if you change your mind and want to play in the dungeon, I'd enjoy being your partner for the night."

She didn't see that happening. "It was nice meeting you, Dane."

He strolled downstairs, and Paige climbed the winding staircase to the second level, wondering if she was going to be able to find a man tonight worth ending her year and a half sexual drought.

✧   ✧   ✧

WHAT THE FUCK was *she* doing here?

It was the first thought that leapt into Sawyer's mind the moment he caught sight of Paige in The Players Club lounge. There was no mistaking the rich shade of her wavy auburn hair he used to love wrapping around his hands, or the soft curves of her body she tried to conceal beneath the corset she wore. Both had been embedded in his brain for the past year and a half, slipping into his dreams at night and taunting him with the way those curves felt beneath the stroke of his hands, and how sweet her breasts tasted in his mouth.

Shock didn't even come close to describing the emotion that tightened his chest, or the way every muscle in his body tensed when her vivid green eyes met and held his from across the room.

He'd seen her briefly a few weeks ago at Raina

Beck's shop—their very first encounter since he'd left for his fifteen month, and final tour, in Iraq. It had also been the first time he'd seen Paige since that awful morning after waking up in her step-sister's bed, naked, disoriented, and his head pounding like a mother-fucker.

Yeah, that was another less pleasant memory firmly seated in his brain, as was the absolute horror of realizing that he'd slept with Ashley—the evidence of fucking her indisputable. There was no forgetting how she'd cuddled up to him, her hand on his dick to try and persuade him into a morning quickie, but he hadn't been able to get out of her bed fast enough. She'd pouted unhappily, like the spoiled, rich girl she was, while he'd pulled on his pants, shoved his feet into his shoes, and grabbed his shirt before racing out of her room and down the grand spiral staircase in the opulent mansion where Paige lived with her step-sister and step-mother.

He had no fucking idea how he'd ended up in Ashley's room, his only thought at the time was that he'd had too much to drink the night before at Paige's birthday party and had done the unthinkable—and how the fuck was he going to explain this to Paige? Just as he'd reached the entryway, his stomach roiling, Paige walked out of the adjoining living room. She froze in place when she saw him, her gaze traveling from his disheveled, half-naked state, to her step-sister, Ashley, who had chased after him in nothing but a robe that was sheer enough to see that she had nothing on beneath.

He'd been caught in the act, and the devastation that played across Paige's features in that moment had destroyed him, as well. He'd crossed the marbled foyer to talk to her, very aware of Ashley watching the whole scenario play out from where she was standing at the top of the stairs.

He stopped in front of Paige, the bright pain in her eyes equivalent to a knife twisting in his heart. He wanted so badly to touch her, to reassure her, but how could he explain something that he didn't even understand himself?

"Paige..." His voice was like gravel, and he whispered the only thing he could. "I'm so sorry."

She'd slapped him hard across the cheek, trying so valiantly to keep the tears shimmering in her eyes in check. "You're a fucking asshole." Lifting her chin in an attempt to salvage her pride, she turned around and walked away.

Utterly defeated and wracked with guilt, he headed back toward the front door, not sure how he was going to repair the damage he'd done. When he glanced up at Ashley, the smug smile on her face made his gut churn. The goddamn bitch was actually *pleased* that she'd just shattered her sister's happiness, and he'd had the sickening feeling that he'd fallen into some kind of trap of Ashley's making.

Even after leaving the house that morning, he'd tried to text and call Paige, until she'd blocked his phone number, making it very clear that they were over. And because he had no excuse for what he'd done, he'd respected her decision. Five days after that, he'd been deployed to Iraq, and he'd spent the next fifteen months immersed in guilt as he replayed that morning over and over in his mind.

He'd probably never know the real truth of how he'd ended up in Ashley's bed, but he definitely had his suspicions.

"You seem distracted tonight," the woman sitting on his lap said into Sawyer's ear, bringing his thoughts back to the present. "What's going on with you?"

Jenny was someone he occasionally hooked up with at The Players Club. Neither of them were looking for a commitment, so their arrangement worked well. She liked being tied up and restrained and enjoyed a bit of pain with her pleasure, which matched perfectly with Sawyer's own need to dominate and be in control. That was a part of himself he'd hid from Paige when they'd dated, because he'd wanted to be sure they had a solid relationship, as well as trust between them, before he introduced her to his penchant for ropes and the sting of a crop on her flesh.

It had taken him weeks to coax Paige into being confident about her body and sensuality, to make her believe that she was sexy and desirable exactly the way she was. In fact, that night on her birthday, he'd planned to show her just how good it felt to let him be completely in control of her pleasure... only to have her sister obliterate everything between them.

Still ensnared by Paige's gaze, he absently replied to Jenny's question without looking away. "I've just got a lot on my mind."

She trailed her fingers from around his neck and down the front of his shirt. "Maybe I can give you something else to think about," she murmured huskily, her insinuation clear.

Paige was the first to break eye contact with him, appearing completely unaffected by his presence, which only served to irritate the shit out of him since his insides were tangled up in a knot when he thought about the reasons *she* was here at the club. Dane, a regular at the mansion who enjoyed his encounters with women more on the hard core side of things, walked up to Paige, offered his arm, and escorted her out of the lounge.

Jealousy shot through Sawyer like a hot spear, along with something darker and more possessive he couldn't subdue, no matter how hard he tried. He still wanted Paige, in every way imaginable, and the thought of another man touching her brought out the beast in him, as well as triggered the need to be the one to master her body and mind.

And that's when he decided that if any man was going to introduce Paige to any sort of forbidden limits, it was going to be *him*.

Jenny nuzzled her lips against his neck, reminding Sawyer that he still had a very willing female sitting on his lap. One he suddenly had no interest in at all.

He tipped her face up to his and very gently said, "I'm really sorry, Jenny, but there's something personal I have to take care of tonight."

Her smile was tinged with disappointment, but he knew she understood. They weren't exclusive in any way, and there were plenty of other men in the room who'd enjoy what Jenny had to offer. She slid off his lap and looked into his eyes.

"I hope she's worth it," she said softly.

Paige was. Always had been, and always would be.

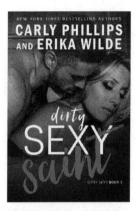

DIRTY SEXY SERIES
By Carly Phillips and Erika Wilde
RELEASE DATE: January 19, 2016

New York Times bestselling authors Carly Phillips and Erika Wilde bring you a dirty, sexy, smoking hot SERIES featuring three bad boy brothers bonded by shocking secrets and their damaged past. Sinful, addicting, and unapologetically alpha, these men are every woman's erotic daydream … And your ultimate dirty fantasy.

Are you ready to get Dirty Sexy with a Saint?

Clay Kincaid knows he's more a sinner than a saint. Especially when it comes to women. With a rough and damaged past that has left him jaded, he doesn't do committed relationships. But he does like sex—the hotter and harder, the better. He likes it fast and filthy, which is why he refuses to even touch someone as sweet and guileless as Samantha Jamieson. Until he discovers that she likes it just as down and dirty as he does. Let the sinning begin . . .

Other Books in The Players Club Series

Book 1: Playing with Temptation (Raina and Logan)
Book 2: Playing with Pleasure (Paige and Sawyer)
Book 3: Playing with Seduction (Kendall and Jase)
More Players Club Stories Coming Soon!

Other Books by Erika Wilde

The Marriage Diaries Series

THE AWAKENING (The Marriage Diaries, Volume 1)
THE SEDUCTION (The Marriage Diaries, Volume 2)
THE TAKING (The Marriage Diaries, Volume 3)
THE TEMPTATION (The Marriage Diaries, Volume 4)
THE INVITATION (The Marriage Diaries, Volume 5)
THE CAPTURE (The Marriage Diaries, Volume 6)

To learn more about The Marriage Diaries and interact
with the series and characters, please like my Erika
Wilde Author Facebook Fan Page at:
www.facebook.com/erikawildeauthor

About the Author

To learn more about Erika Wilde and her upcoming releases, you can visit her at the following places on the web:

Website:
www.erikawilde.com

Facebook:
www.facebook.com/erikawildeauthor

Twitter:
www.twitter.com/erikawilde1

Goodreads:
www.goodreads.com/erikawildeauthor

50343608R10197

Made in the USA
Middletown, DE
24 June 2019